I0741107

DARK
SURVIVOR

DARK SURVIVOR

THE QALDRETH WARRIORS #2

Tiny, a blind doctor, desperately wants normalcy and a chance to make a difference despite her disability. Yet, she's turned aside at every job application. In a twist of traumatic events, she lands a position on an ice hauler as the resident medic.

But everything isn't as it seems. When a crewmate unexpectedly dies, she realizes that her 'safe' world holds a den of vipers, but blind and trapped, what can she do?

Nenn's a Qaldreth male who pays the ultimate price to train with the Ivoyans. Chosen to accompany an Ivoyan servant on a quest to find who was behind the death of the Senate, he's hopeful for the chance to climb cliffs, explore space, and try this face-latching humans are fond of.

When he meets a purple-haired female named Tiny, her blindness intrigues him as does her need for independence. The Ivoyans can heal her eyes without augmentation, but she'll have to return with him to Ivoy.

Something he admits he yearns for.

Except, exposing her to the Ivoyans might make her a target for experimentation, discrimination, or revenge—possibly all three.

He must choose what he's willing to sacrifice: his tribe's honor, Tiny's life, or a chance at finding a love mate.

Unless he can convince the Qaldreth Command Council *and* Tiny that she's perfect for him. Without starting a rebellion.

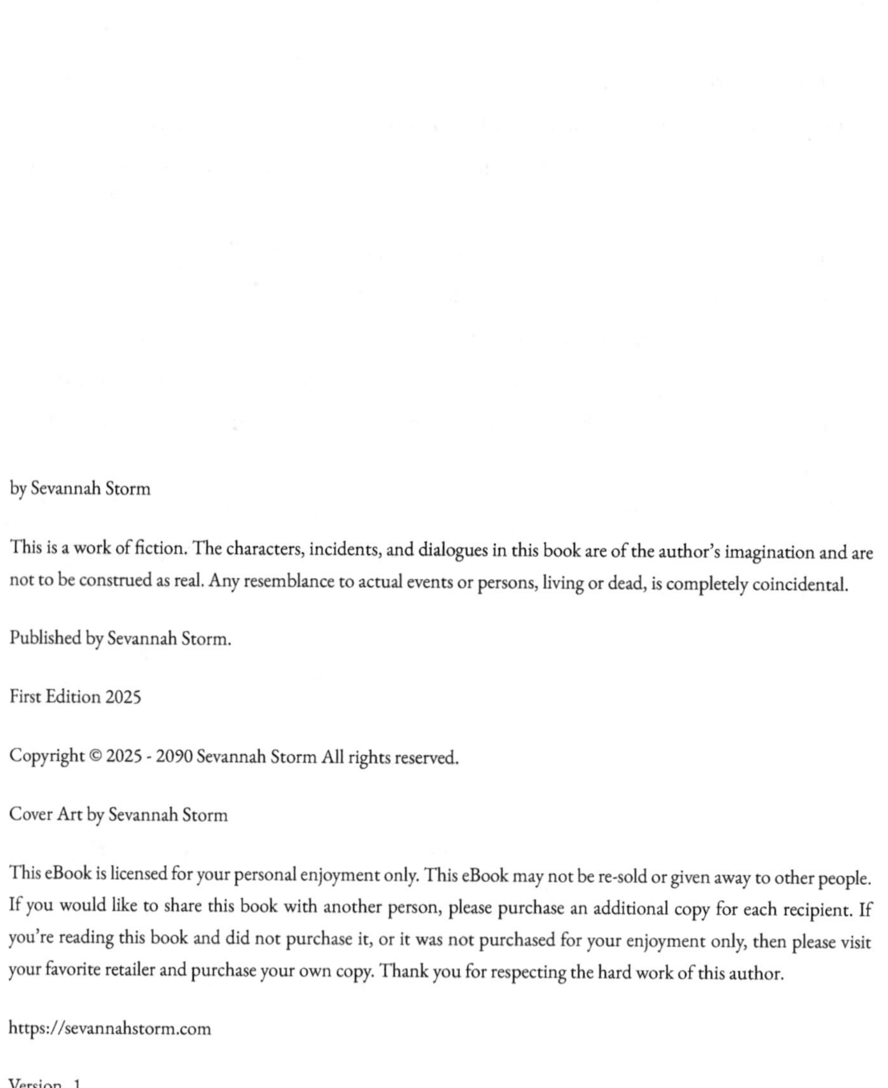

by Sevannah Storm

This is a work of fiction. The characters, incidents, and dialogues in this book are of the author's imagination and are not to be construed as real. Any resemblance to actual events or persons, living or dead, is completely coincidental.

Published by Sevannah Storm.

First Edition 2025

Cover Art by Sevannah Storm

https://sevannahstorm.com

Version_1

ALSO BY SEVANNAH STORM

The Blood of Legends Series

The Huntress

The Healer

*

The Gifting Series

Soul Forged

Fate Forged

Sun Forged

War Forged

Star Forged

Shadow Forged

Earth Forged

Lust Forged

Fire Forged

*

The Qaldreth Warriors

Sol Survivor

*

The Space Hunter Chronicles

The Shikari

The Justisaar

*

Plump Playwright Series

Plump Jane

Seducing Amelia

Loving Finley

Keeping Tessa

Kissing Navy

*

Standalones

Xiaxan Fox

Ire of Silver

The Crucible of the Eternal

The Lady and the Assassin

Inkoded

*

COMING SOON

Time Forged

Hope Forged

GLOSSARY OR PRONUNCIATIONS

Places or Planets

Aguura – agg-oo-rah

Amikar – ahh-mee-car – cliffs just below the med-tech spire.

Certorth – sir-torrth – mother city of Ivoy

Ivoy – eye-voy

Ki'irinzi – key-rinze-zee

Nadaar – nay-daar

Qaldreth – kal-dreath

Creatures

Garak – gah-ruck

Hudu – hoodoo

Itaya – itt-tigh-yah – yellow creatures – attach to the outside of ships and feed off sol.

Kurrula – coo-roo-lah – winged creatures (the meat is eaten raw)

Vibuy – vee-bye – black lizard

Calpli – cull-plee – orange lizard that skims across lava rivers.

Vasquva – vass-coo-vah

Zalziki – massive stork-like bird on Ivoy.

Terminology

Audinna – or-dee-nah – a variegated-yellow mushroom that grows inches above bubbling lava.

Carne – car-nay – Carne Corporation

Cucooya – coo-coo-yah – a bulbous tree – a mixture between cactus and baobab. Has beautiful white flowers.

Darasaho – darr-uss-ah-hoe – brother (Awayar only)

Girda – gur-dah – a stone used to sharpen blades.

Gevatia – geh-var-tee-ah – beloved

Hadie – hah-dee – heart

Hirihadie – hee-ree-hah-dee – sweetheart

Mhi' hadie – mee-hah-dee – my heart

Jakar – jah-kar – priest

Koq – cock

Mhi' vatia – mee-var-tee-ah – my love

Teyor – tay-orr – card game based on warring colors.

Uhann – oo-han – The Rite of Uhann

Vatia sahaar – var-tee-ah sah-haar – love mates

Velorx – hoverbike

Venai – venn-igh – stones that glow.

Military Rankings

Udap – oo-dapp – Commander

Arrak – ah-ruck – Protector

Sava – sar-vah – Security

Karu – kah-roo – Trainee/Cadet

Maed – mah-eed - Med-tech

Taed – tah-eed – Tech

Ot – ott – General

Zi – zee – Traveler

Lo – low – Teacher

Uz – ooz – Servant

Names

Qaldreth

[tribal name] + [first name] + [rank]

    Bavu – bah-voo

    Caah – car

    Cainus – cay-niss

    Drafe – dray-fe

    Gusin – goo-sin

    Igar – eye-gar

    Juunn – june

    Kael – kale

    Kish – kish

    Larya – lah-ree-yah

    Nenn – nen

    Saha – sah-hah

    Srim – s-rim

    Tiyl – tail

    Umda – oom-dah

    Ulvus – ull-viss

    Vaen – vah-en

Ivoyan

[last name] + [first name] + [rank]

    Luharp Vadril – loo-harp vah-drill

    Fumart Dau – foo-mart dow

    Vizen Aehort – vizz-enn ay-ort

Human

Ande – andie
Dieter – dee-ter
Leah – lee-ah
Nikko – nick-oh
Themba – tem-bah

Religion

Qaldreth

Kreta – kree-tah – evil (she)
Osnir – oz-sneer – good (he)

Tribes

Awayar – ah-vigh-yar – live in or around water – coloring is: white hair (like a polar bear)/gray skin/white eyes
Borven – bore-ven – live in and around canyons – coloring is: brown hair/gray skin/gold eyes
Giniiri – gin-ee-ree – live around volcanoes – coloring is: red-orange hair/gray skin/red eyes
Jeerlud – jeer-lood – live in the jungle – coloring is: brown hair/gray skin/green eyes
Meorri – me-orr-ree – live in the desert – coloring is: black hair/gray skin/amber eyes
Riermus – rear-miss – live in the mountains – coloring is: gold hair/gray skin/black eyes
Zuphayr – zoo-fah-yer – live high in the clouds (snow/mountains) – coloring is: white hair/gray skin/dark blue eyes.

Foods

Meorri Tribe

Tulsig made from 'meal' – a heather-like plant and salt.

Garak – soft, dark meat, a little sweet.

Giniiri Tribe

Audinna - yellow fungi

Onis - black moss (tastes like licorice)

Russnar - purple medicinal herb

Usturo - red root

Vibuy – black lizards

Calpli – orange lizards (skims across the lava surface)

Banaari – direwolf-wildcat hybrid

Tiaez – mosquito/dragonfly

Riermus Tribe

Barks/tubular roots

Zuphayr Tribe

Kurrula – bird

Os-ayy (insects)

Jeerlud Tribe

Anbru – un-broo – (mango-pawpaw fruit juice)

Borven Tribe

Patsil - cyan-colored moss

Raslu - white algae

Cave creatures

Awayar Tribe

Malugu - eels are bad)

Alpara coral

CHAPTER ONE

Year: 2213
Planet of Qaldreth
Giniiri Tribe
Erasril Volcano

THE LAVA RIVER, AS constant as the suns, radiated heat, bringing tears to Nenn's eyes. This was his land, his home, where molten rivers converged and their shelter was made of the rock it left behind. Still, this close to it was hazardous.

He flashed a grin at his friend standing beside him. Fully grown, they shouldn't be playing games, but the pocks this morning were perfect. Dark crusts like scabs flowed at jumpable distances, the challenge too much to resist.

"Ready, Tugo," he asked, then leaped onto the first pock.

It wobbled beneath his weight, but before it could tilt, he threw himself at the next. One by one, he crossed the river to Always Island, their name for the eye-shaped strip of land that divided the volcano's constant flows. 'Old Erasril had a runny nose,' they used to say as children.

Tugo hopped from pock to pock, some dipping under his bulk. The second he moved onto the next one, the rock would flick into place, splashing up a little lava. The colors were mesmerizing in bright reds and oranges. They knew to avoid anything blue or white; still, if Tugo's mate found out that he was here…

"See, not so hard," he said, landing beside Nenn, his breathing ragged.

"It has been a while, my friend." Nenn settled on the cliff's edge overlooking the lava waterfalls tumbling into a pool below. Along the 'shore,' his people, the tribe of Giniiri, gathered cooling rocks, scoops of lava, and scrapings of onis. He shuddered, not liking the flavor of the black moss.

Movement caught his gaze. Orange-red lizards skimmed across the river's surface, catching tiny insects riding the heatwaves. The symbiotes in his blood whispered of a time when food had been scarce and the insects the only nourishment they could find. He followed the flittering of the tiaez, its transparent wings seeming to carry insufficient sustenance for an adult Qaldreth. How had they harvested enough to feed the tribe? Images flashed in his mind, the memories of his past fathers' lives.

He drew in a deep breath, wondering what his symbiotes would share of his life with future generations of Qaldreths. What slumped his shoulders was the impending rite of Uhann, where the chosen representative would be granted an opportunity to have his name revered for all time.

An Ivoyan aldermen would take the chosen off-world to a star not visible in their night's sky. Tugo thought him mad to long for this, but his big friend had a vatia sahaar, a soul mate. Nenn had only his aging father, who was on the verge of waddling into the waterfall below, as expected of anyone too old to serve. His father's mind had wandered off after their mother went missing in the forests around the Ki'irinzi Mountains. None had seen or heard from her since.

It was true that the menewberries nearest to the mirror pools were the juiciest, which explained why his mother had ventured farther than was deemed safe. The symbiotes shared nothing but her life experiences. Her death was flashes of a blurred shadow. Many nights, the elders would poke at it like it was a mystery they needed to unravel. Ideas were thrown out though all knew, nothing had been found: not a shoe, a lock of her hair, or the hem of her dress.

The male his father once was had long gone, leaving behind a husk devoid of emotion. Still, Nenn clung to the male who'd taught him how to pock leap and to scavenge for the best medicinal plants and herbs the healers needed.

"There is value in service, my son," his father had said.

Nenn clasped the hilt of his harvesting knife sheathed to his belt. The blade had been passed down from father to son from as far back as the symbiotes remembered. Carved into the banaari tooth forming the handle was the petal of a russmar, the rarest and most potent plant on Erasril. Many a male had lost a limb or his life gathering the purple mushroom living in the deepest crevices of the volcano. Descending and hacking at the base destroyed its usefulness. Each cluster had to be massaged, then plucked, leaving the roots to encourage more growth.

Which brought him back to the problem at hand. The rite of Uhann was soon, and he had yet to earn a nomination. No tribesman had been injured to warrant the need for russmar, a sure way to garner favor. And he had zero cooking skills, his farming lacked enthusiasm, his stone carving broke too many slabs, and he couldn't fight to save his life. Defending the tribe from baraanis would most likely get him killed.

"Your thoughts are heavy, Nenn," Tugo said, nudging him with a shoulder. "Looks like Panior will be seeing the stars. Perhaps at the next rite?"

Why did it have to be Panior? As the most beloved, handsome, sought-after male in the tribe, everything seemed to come easy to that male. Nenn shut his eyes to the reality of his situation. Tugo meant well, but another year doing nothing except watching his father slip away? No, Nenn needed to leave before his last memory was the cleansing of his father's soul in the fires of Erasril.

It would be abandonment, but he didn't have the strength to 'lose' yet another parent. If he was gone, he could imagine all was well. That his father had made a full recovery and would be hearty by the time Nenn returned.

It was childish of him, but the crushing grip around his hearts wouldn't ease. Some days, he could barely draw in breaths. Not that he could hide his inner turmoil from a Giniirian, not with the symbiotes revealing all secrets.

Osnir, help me. He raised his gaze to the sky, wishing he could escape this burden.

"Come, it is time." Tugo slapped his tree-trunk thighs and rose. The size of an ancient banaari, his friend served the tribe well. Anything that needed moving, pushing, squashing, or building, then Tugo was the male to call. He would be nominated without hesitation if he wanted to serve the Ivoyans.

But he'd fallen for the beautiful Kimgi when they were no taller than their fathers' knees.

"You are right." Nenn forced a smile. "I suspect your *gevatia* is ravenous."

Tugo chuckled. "She would be with a child on the way."

The pocks were farther apart than was wise to traverse. They had only this route to return to the main mountain, but to risk it... Again, Nenn went first, hopping across as fast as he could. The last pock sank, spilling lava over its edge. He lunged for the bank, landing with a grunt on the hard rock. Rolling over, he gaped at the pock when it crumbled, the lava consuming the chunks.

Fear slid down his neck, over his shoulders, and sparked his hearts into a gallop. Tugo was already halfway across with no way of turning back.

In the distance, the wailing call of a banaari made things worse. He whipped his gaze to the volcano's peak and peered at the shadow forming. *No, no, this cannot be happening.*

"Tugo, my dear friend, now is the time to move your ass." Nenn scrambled to his feet and urged him to rush.

Sure, he could kill a banaari with his bare hands but not Nenn. All he had on him was his harvesting knife. A spear, an ax—anything larger and longer would've been better.

Tugo reached the next pock before peeking at the mountaintop where two banaari now stood.

"Foq, Tugo, please hurry." Nenn withdrew his knife and faced the approaching beasts.

Their large brown bodies, great big heads, two eyes on either side, and long, pointy ears were fearsome but more so were their razor-like fangs in three concentric rows and a lolling tongue eager for a taste of his innards.

A scream snapped his gaze to Tugo, who'd leaped the greater distance and failed to clear it, dipping his foot into the lava. His boot was on fire, parts of it glowing and melting off. Nenn yanked his waterskin off his belt and doused the flames, then used Tugo's waterskin for added measure.

The leather had melted into the charred or bubbling skin. Tugo whimpered even as the whining rumble of the banaari drew nearer. Nenn swung his focus between his friend lying on the hard rock to the approaching death in the form of teeth.

"Foq," he muttered, then knelt beside Tugo to hoist him over his shoulder. "We have to make a run for it."

"Leave me." Tugo shoved Nenn back. "Let me die."

"Do not be a fool. Kimgi needs you." Again, Nenn grabbed Tugo's arm to tuck his head under it, attempting to lift his bulky friend over a shoulder.

Everything pinged in protest, from the muscles in his back, up his neck, and along his thighs, to the popping of his knees. He staggered under the weight and staggered two paces before twisting to glance at the banaari. They inched closer; he was sure of it.

"I am going to run. Tell me if they charge at us." Without waiting for Tugo's response, he bolted, sprinting down the path they'd trudged up hours ago. He bellowed warnings as he did, letting anyone nearby know of the danger. Hot air across his back made him believe the banaari were near enough for their breaths to bathe him in fetid heat.

Still, Tugo said nothing other than to whimper with every step Nenn managed.

"What is the meaning of this?" Elder Lama demanded, halting them in their tracks.

"No time to talk," Tugo said from between clenched teeth.

"Two banaari behind us." Nenn flicked his head as if he could indicate which direction with a heavy male across his shoulder. He skirted Lama and continued.

Lama squeaked and hurried after them, urging Nenn to run faster.

Tugo yelled when the banaari lunged at Lama.

Nenn's knees threatened to buckle, but he persevered. Sweat dripped off his chin, his arm cramped around the backs of Tugo's thighs, and his smoldering foot bounced in Nenn's peripherals. *Foq.* Of all the things that could've happened, this wasn't one he'd anticipated. Guilt sliced through him, churning his stomach. He sucked in great gulps of air to calm the nausea.

He'd have to find russmar and pray it would heal Tugo. Thankfully, Panior would travel off-world, leaving Nenn to carry Tugo's burdens until he was well enough.

"Duviz," Lama hollered, panic in the warble of his voice.

A giant of a male, Tugo's father, leaped into the path at the base of the mountain. His eyes widened. He lowered his spear while roaring a battle cry that always made Nenn's insides vibrate. He'd never been able to fathom if his reaction was from fear or awe. Perhaps a mixture of the two?

Behind him, more males appeared, their weapons ready.

Nenn wished he could watch the scene play out, but he was unable to bear Tugo's weight for much longer. As soon as he broke through the line of warriors forming, he fell to his knees and rolled Tugo off him. Sprawling beside his friend, he stared at the sky, trying to breathe through the pain throbbing in every inch of his body.

Females gathered to tend to him, but he waved them to Tugo, whispering where he was injured. Someone brought Nenn water, their features a blur. When his hearts calmed, he sat up.

"What happened?" Elder Qon demanded, kneeling beside Tugo.

"His foot dipped into the river." Nenn crawled to his feet.

"That is not what the symbiotes shared," someone called out.

The voice was familiar, but Nenn didn't have the time to find out who'd spoken. He had to harvest the fungi before night descended.

"Take care of him, Elder Qon. I will find a fresh cluster of russmar."

"That is madness, young Nenn. The suns will set within an hour. It will take you that long to reach the crevice." Elder Qon pointed to Tugo. "We might not even need it."

Nenn glanced at Tugo whose face was pale, his eyes squeezed shut. White lines formed around his mouth where he pinched his lips. A study of his injury told its own story.

"I go," Nenn said.

The first five steps locked his knees, then he pushed on, hobbling to the vast cavern below the lava pool. Two warriors were on guard, their gazes vigilant. Nenn didn't pause to identify them, not having the time to peer through their iron helmets. Sheets of stone lined the side, ready for export. He slipped in through the broad archway. Along the winding ramp, he sprinted, desperate to reach his home two levels below Tugo's, to not waste a second.

He burst inside, startling a yelp from his father asleep on his pallet.

"What is it?" he asked, sitting up. For once, his red eyes weren't glazed over.

"I need...russmar. Tugo could lose a—" Nenn swallowed, yanking a coiled rope off a hook and looping it over his shoulder.

"You know where to go." Father stumbled toward Nenn only to grab the empty pouch that sat beside the water barrel and shove it into Nenn's hand. "Be prepared for anything," he rasped before wrapping his arms around Nenn, his strength gone.

Nenn gathered his father close, wishing he could pour his life force into him and grant him a few more years. He ushered him to his bed and settled him. "You taught me well," he said, offering a a weak smile. "Rest. I will not be long."

He stepped back and waited a few precious moments for his father to drift off. After tucking a blanket over his sleeping form, Nenn sprinted out of his home, up the ramp, and into the suns' fading light, veering right toward the rarely used paths up to the crevices.

Certain death lay ahead going that way. Young males used to believe mapping the widths and depths would garner them a nomination. After so many lives lost, the elders had forbidden to attempt it. He marched on, the rippling volcanic rock rolling out before him. Qon was right to point out the suns setting, but Nenn knew the way, having gone with his father many times.

When the path disappeared, he carried on, aiming for a boulder that looked like a fossilized tree with its top half missing. Ahead, dark, jagged scars came into view, scouring the mountain's side. The one he needed was hidden in the valley of a ripple, wide enough for a male to slip through. A breeze cooled the sweat on his temple. He rolled his shoulders, trying to ease the constant throb of abused muscles. None of his discomfort mattered, not when time did.

He paused beside a row of boulders and specifically near the one that looked like a distorted nipple, narrowing at the top. Tying a knot on the rope gave him a moment to focus his breathing, to gather his thoughts.

"Do not enter the mouth when worry is on your mind," his father had warned.

Nenn hooked the rope on the nipple, then wrapped it around his wrist before peering into the darkness. Far into the distance, a glimmer of orange implied magma awaited him should he fall. He couldn't let that thought control his actions. With a shake of his head, he fitted the pouch across his chest, the opening in the front for easy access. He turned, his back to the gap, then with his heels on the edge, he released the rope and repelled down.

The rope skidded through his grip, sending him plummeting. With a cry, he tightened his hand. Fire blazed along the skin of his palms. He jerked to a halt, the rope whiplashing then bouncing him until it stilled. A gust of heat flicked his hair back and made his eyes water. The stench of sulfur hung thick in the air.

Below his dangling feet gaped the Habqus Abyss.

He set his heels flat on the rock wall and scanned the area, searching for a glimmer of purple. Osnir must have abandoned him because he spotted nothing. With a grunt, he twisted to peer below, hoping something would guide him. To the far left, where a dribble of lava leaked down the rock, he caught the palest glow of lilac. He could be wrong, but he had to try. Already the sky above had darkened. Soon, only the magma below would light his way.

He dropped, caught himself, and sparked a hiss at the sting of rope against chaffed skin. The farther he sank, the brighter the bioluminescence, and the confirmation flooded his chest with warmth. There was a chance he could reach it in time.

A nudge on the rope not his doing had him glance up. White eyes peered at him. A banaari.

Fear seized his throat. He was alone and unarmed for the most part. Salvation from someone else wasn't a possibility.

No, do not think about it. Focus on the russmar. His symbiotes spewed warnings: the rope could snap, the banaari would attack the moment he returned to the surface, or the russmar could shrivel up if he wasn't gentle enough.

He willed them to quieten as he lowered himself, keeping his feet firm. Inch by inch, he descended, the heat from the lava trickle almost too much to bear. With a deep inhale, he swung himself over it, then slipped down until he was at eye level with a crack. Rows of yellow audinna sheltered the delicate purple russmar in full bloom.

He grinned. Perhaps Osnir was with him.

When he reached his hand into the narrow opening, something lunged at him. On instinct, he pushed himself away, slamming his back against the opposite wall. Two eyes peered at him while a gray tongue flicked out from a black body.

He laughed, relief pooling in his belly. Indeed, he was blessed. For this night, he might be able to entice his father to eat with fresh vibuy meat.

Whipping out his knife, he lunged across and thrust out, killing the lizard in an instant. A curse slipped from his lips at the ruined clusters of russmar around it. With a sigh, he skirted to the right and stroked the nearest plant, massaging it like he would a sore thumb. One by one, he worked along the ledge, gathering what russmar he could. When he had to blink to see better, he glanced up and scowled. The suns had set.

He sheathed his knife, grabbed the vibuy, then shoved it into the stuffed pouch. White eyes gleamed at him while he climbed, the wailing rumble of banaari growing louder even as a cool breeze bathed his face.

When he was a foot from the surface, the banaari shoved its snout closer, its teeth inches from his hands. He hesitated, then whipped out his knife, slashing across to either injure the beast or scare it off. All he needed was a moment to find his feet on solid ground.

With a huff at the lost meal, he took out the vibuy and tossed it through the crack. It landed with a thud on the opposite side of the path. When the banaari leaped over the crevice, he hurled himself up and out, his gaze on the banaari tearing into the lizard.

He untied the rope and gathered it into a loop, not daring to blink lest the beast decided it was still hungry. Then, with the rope over his shoulder, he inched backward. The beast watched him between bites, its eyes glowing with intent. The crunch of lizard bones between its teeth made him wince. When he stumbled and caught himself with his hand on the rock, he didn't glance away.

Once far enough, he swiveled on a heel and exploded into a run. The banaari wailed. The thomp-thomp of its massive paws chased him down the mountain. He leaped over boulders, skirted the fossilized tree, all while aiming for the flickering torches that marked the cave's entrance. He bellowed warnings, his voice hoarse.

The two guards rushed forward, spears drawn.

Nenn skidded to a halt and faced the banaari, his harvesting knife in hand.

"Another, Nenn?" Laec demanded, his red eyes glowing.

His brother, Juirr, harumphed. "You have been busy."

"How fares Tugo?" Nenn asked, not taking his gaze off the banaari hovering on the outskirts of the torch light.

"Not well. The damage is too much for his symbiotes to heal him. It is good you left for the russmar." Laec nudged him. "Go! We can take care of one beast."

Nenn hesitated then sheathed his knife. "My thanks. I assume he is with Kimgi?"

"Indeed," Juirr said, then flicked his head as if to say 'hurry.'

Nenn did, sprinting into the cave, taking great leaps over the narrow steps and into the bowels of the volcano. Warmth poured off the hewn walls. Steam rose from pools a few used to bathe in. He spared it all a token glance. Along various tunnels, he loped, wincing whenever he trod funny or jarred his legs. His poor body had endured much this day. Exhaustion hounded him, dogging his feet. When he rested, his body would recover.

At the fourth torch, he veered left until he reached the seventh door carved into the stone. He yanked on the chimes made of precious stones, strips of discarded metal, and molded balls of volcanic rock. The clang reverberated through him after the silence of the past hour.

The door, made of a thin sheet of stone, slid away to reveal Kimgi's pale face. "Nenn?" A smile twitched her mouth.

"I have them." He looped off the pouch and shoved it at her.

She took it, her fingers trembling. "Come." She shifted aside and gestured for him to enter.

Elder Qon kneeled beside Tugo, bathing his foot in water. Tugo chomped on a strip of leather, sweat trickling over his cheeks.

"Nenn?" Elder Qon raised a hopeful gaze. "Did you find any?"

"I did," he said.

Kimgi hurried forward, the pouch in a death grip.

"Good." Elder Qon broke off a petal, pulled out the leather strip, and shoved the russmar into Tugo's mouth. "We wait a moment for the numbness to take effect. I need boiling water, Kimgi, to make a paste."

She darted around their home. A bed carved into a wall housed Tugo's bulk with ease. Alcoves acted as shelves for food and garments. And a fire burned in the hearth, fueled by the gases leaking through cracks in the mountain.

Elder Qon worked in silence, mashing all the petals into a paste before applying it to Tugo's foot.

"Nenn," he crooned. "Where have you been?" A giggle escaped him, and he slumped, his gaze on the ceiling where tiny embedded venai stones merged to offer a warm light, shining like the stars in the sky. "What happened? One moment, we were pock-leaping and the next, I am home with my *gevatia*. And why is my tongue furry?"

Nenn forced a grin when he was far from lighthearted. "Banaari hunted Elder Lama down the mountain. I have never seen him run so fast." No, he hadn't caught a glimpse of the 'agile' Elder Lama, but the imagery was amusing. "You missed it all, my friend."

Tugo mumbled as sleep claimed him.

"Find Dumis, and tell him, there is hope," Elder Qon whispered, rising to squeeze Nenn's arm. "You did well, young Nenn."

"But they believe you caused it." Kimgi clasped her hands before her, sadness in the gaze resting upon her mate. "The symbiotes refuse to reveal what led to this until your return. The tribe gather in the hall below."

Nenn gaped, his mind reeling. "Why would I harm—"

"You risking the abyss in an attempt to be heroic...and nominated," Elder Qon said. "Go. Allow the symbiotes to reveal the truth."

Chapter Two

Tiny glanced at the wall clock while Riaan was mid-thrust. He had her pinned to a shelf in the storeroom—the only place in the store without sec cams. She'd thought a quickie would be just the thing to take the edge off her uneasiness. In a little less than an hour, she had to be at her parents' for dinner.

He grunted, his arms gripping her too hard. She studied his expressions, and despite his handsomeness, she felt nothing... No impending orgasm, no frisson of excitement, more like she was checking a box. Promiscuous during med school? Check.

She had too many of those.

Earn a scholarship? Check.

Get a part-time job at a convenience store for extra tokens? Check.

At least it allowed her to study, but it also meant she survived on minimal sleep. Par for the course.

Realizing time was slipping past her with no signs of Riaan finishing, she dug her nails into his back and fake-groaned. She tightened her legs around his hips while writhing as if God himself had blessed her with an almighty orgasm.

"Oh, Riaan," she mumbled, adding a breathlessness to her voice. A finality settled on her. They were done. She couldn't muster enthusiasm for a relationship that was purely for convenience.

At last, he gasped, his hips stilling.

A sense of uncleanliness washed over her. The urge to bathe caught hold of her mind and wouldn't release her. She scowled. Now she'd have to head home first. As soon as he stepped back, she lowered her legs and straightened her clothing.

He smirked. "That was fun."

"Sure," she said, swinging the door open wide.

In about twelve minutes, Kenny would arrive for his shift. Riaan had to be gone by then. One glance showed him nowhere near ready. She tucked in his limp dick, condom and all, and carefully zipped him shut. A quick brush of her fingers over his T-shirt had him looking halfway descent. Maybe his chiseled chest had swayed her?

She snorted at that bit of nonsense. Any man would do in her quest to 'find herself,' or so she told her friends. But deep down, her recklessness had to do with her parents. She grimaced. Another glance at the clock confirmed Kenny's arrival was imminent, and yet Riaan lingered.

"What's wrong with you?" he asked, at last catching on to her less-than-happy mood.

"I'm having dinner with my family."

He frowned. "Oh, I'm sorry, Tiny." He tried to pull her into a hug, but she slapped his hands away.

"As in now, Riaan. Please..." She nudged her chin at the automatic doors. "I still need to hand over to Kenny."

"Fine, but I'll text you later." He kissed her temple and left.

His disappearing shoulders brought her a flicker of joy. She clung to that and hurried to capture the stock counts. Everything was token-based with the printing of cash having dwindled after the Great Water Shortage, so she didn't need to account for payments. However, pickpockets still existed. Her stock numbers had to align with sold products, and any discrepancy came out of her wages. She couldn't afford to lose a single token.

And of course, Kenny was late.

She glared at Kenny as she swept past him, not daring to say a word unless she wanted to spew curses. Her day hadn't gone well, having received not-so-favorable feedback on her last assignment. The scholarship's continuity depended on her results.

She hurried to the bus stop for the autobus that drove past every fifteen minutes. When her ass touched down on the seat, she texted her mom using the device embedded in her palm.

Gonna be late.

No reply was forthcoming. She released a slow breath. As a little girl, she'd learned not to expect common decencies from her distracted parents. Knowing this didn't stop her from hoping this time would be different. She rolled her lips then pinched them, letting the pain squeezing her chest ease.

She took a sol-bath as soon as she got home, grateful for the warmth of the beam as it scanned her body and made her squeaky clean. Pity it couldn't remove the Riaan-shaped smudge off her soul. Because Mom didn't respond, Tiny took the time to dress in black tailored trousers, a crisp, white blouse, and her ankle boots in pseudo-leather. She fluffed her hair and was out the door, this time calling for a taxi.

With her palm pressed to her ear, she said, "Need a taxi to downtown Old Lake City."

"Ten minutes," the AI droned.

She waited on the pick-up point marked with a yellow dot outside her dorm. With her gaze down, she didn't need to converse with anyone—her mood was that dismal. Her thoughts circled on how to improve her grades with the time she had available and what would be the best approach, and laughingly considered seducing the older professional. That, at least, got a snort out of her. Dinner would be free except for the emotional trauma. Although, she'd scoff noodles if it meant not having to spend any time with her parents. That was a lie. Her dad...

She sighed. *I love them.* She did. Dad more so.

The taxi ride was too short. She raised her gaze up the apartment block, one of many mass housing spires piercing the sky and sucking up the sunlight with their sol-paneled exteriors. After taking a moment to square her shoulders, she strolled into the lobby. Every step was like trudging through hip-height mud. At last, she knocked on the door of her old home. Half of her hoped that no one would answer.

Dad ended her silly hope, yanking her into the apartment and his crushing hug. "How's my girl?" He shoved her back to study her. "You look good, Tiny. Dark shadows under your eyes, but that's to be expected." He sidled closer. "Your mother's made meatloaf. Jamie's on some sort of health kick."

"Real meat?" she asked, arching a brow before peering into the open-plan living area levels above the city below.

Dad's grimace said it all, as did the burnt-organic aroma hanging in the air. "Something to drink?"

"She knows where everything is. She's not a visiting dignitary," Mom said, glaring at Dad. "Come, Tiny, help me set the table...since you're late without notifying me."

Tiny stiffened, tempted to swivel on her heel, and leave. Her glance caught her brother lazing on the couch, a gaming controller in hand. Beside him was a beer.

"Now," Mom snapped, thrusting a plate at her.

When Tiny grabbed it, she hissed. It was still hot from the sol-powered dishwasher. With singed fingertips, she almost threw the stainless-steel plates onto the table. Mom trailed her, nudging them into position as if they hadn't been burned in the fires of the sun.

"Cutlery," she said.

Tiny wasn't an idiot and used the oven mitts to set out the knives and forks, all while glowering at her useless brother.

Younger than her, he was her parents' baby. In their eyes, he never did anything wrong, required more compassion, and deserved a bigger allowance. They even dismissed his delinquent behavior as that of a young man lost in a world of temptation.

She tossed aside the mitts and accepted the glass of cold fruit juice Dad offered her. He took his place at the head of the table when Mom placed the brown lump at the center. It didn't look appetizing.

She sat to the right of Dad, Tiny to his left, with a place beside Mom for Jamie.

"Honey, it's dinner time," Mom sang.

"Five minutes, Mom," he growled, jerking and punching his console.

"All right, sweetheart," she said.

Tiny widened her eyes at Dad, but he just shrugged. Reaching for the 'meatloaf' got her hand smacked. She snatched it back, curling her fingers into fists.

"We're waiting?" she asked.

Mom pursed her lips while draping the napkin across her lap. "If you'd been here on time—"

"We'd still wait, Mom." Tiny winced at the whine in her voice. When Mom said nothing, Tiny eyed the impending gastric experiment she was about to suffer through. "So, how has work been?" She glanced at Dad.

"Oh, the usual," he said, nudging his knife to the side and back with a fingertip. "Might be up for a promotion."

"That's wonderful, Dad. You work so hard," she said, flashing him a smile. He'd been a factory foreman for as long as she'd been alive. Perhaps they'd realized he was worthy of becoming the manager. They could use the additional tokens, too.

When she met her mother's gaze, she stayed quiet. Manners demanded she ask the same of her mom, but she couldn't bring herself to speak.

Jamie leaped to his feet, screamed at the wall-mounted screen, then threw the controller onto the floor. It clattered across the metallic flooring.

"Jamie," Dad said, using a tone that brooked no argument.

Jamie slid into the chair next to Mom, bringing his beer with him. "Sorry, Dad." He looped an arm around Mom and kissed her cheek. "This looks amazing, Mom."

She beamed. "Vegetarian, you said."

"I did." He rubbed his belly, shifting his T-shirt and revealing a few needle marks.

Tiny scowled. *He's using again.* His arms were clear, and like an idiot, he thought he could hide his addiction. She studied her parents. *Do they know?*

Mom dished up on Dad's plate first, then for Jamie, herself, and Tiny... In that order. Tiny's portion was the smallest but, under the circumstances, something to be grateful for.

"How's school?" Dad asked as he'd been doing since she'd started at kindergarten.

"Good." Because she'd earned the scholarship and self-funded her lifestyle, they knew nothing and had no say about her grades or daily life. And once she graduated and headed off to residency, she never needed to see them again.

Tears stung her eyes. She'd miss her dad. Guilt twinged with guilt at abandoning him, forcing him to deal with Jamie's downward spiraling alone. But she couldn't live Dad's life for him.

"What are you up to these days, Jamie?" she asked, taking a tiny bite of the mashed brown clumps on her plate. The flavor of scorched cauliflower coated her tongue. She sipped her juice while staring at her brother, expectant.

"He's considering a local art school," Mom said, grinning.

"Oh?" Tiny forced a smile. "I didn't know you could draw."

He dropped his fork on his half-eaten meatloaf and jumped to his feet. "Let me get my portfolio."

She almost mouthed 'portfolio' but managed to rein in her wayward lips.

He returned carrying a sketchpad with actual paper. When he shoved it at her, he waited, his expression showing his eagerness for her feedback. She took a moment to savor the smoothness of the paper, swiping her thumb back and forth. Then with a deep breath, she focused on his sketches. She sniffed, picking up a hint of sweed—distilled seaweed.

They were done with ink. Thank the Lord. Charcoal cost a fortune.

Her gaze followed the vibrant strokes. The images were recognizable, from faces to metal trees, still life to landscapes. Potential was there. "Jamie... Wow. I didn't know." He could make it a career if he was serious. If he pursued this. If it wasn't yet another phase.

He puffed out his chest and cradled his sketchbook. "Mom and Dad think I stand a good chance of being accepted." He sank into his seat and placed the book on the table beside him. "Not all of us are smart enough to become doctors."

She gritted her teeth. Every meal with her family resorted to this: that she dared dream of doing something meaningful with her life. She'd been twelve when she revealed her dream to a favorite teacher. Which had, in turn, reached her parents. Dad had praised her. Mom had scoffed, solidifying Tiny's determination to succeed.

"This meatloaf's amazing, Mom," Jamie crooned.

Dad's was half-eaten; Tiny hadn't had more than two mouthfuls. Mom, too.

Tiny drained her juice and rose. "Thank you for dinner."

"You just got here," Dad said, disappointment in his eyes.

"Sorry, Dad, studies come first." With a kiss to his temple, she bolted for the door before anyone could say anything more.

"I'll walk you down," Jamie said, close on her heels.

She sighed, waited for the door to shut, then faced him. "How much?"

He leaned against the wall, folding his arms and crossing his legs at the ankles. "About a hundred should do it."

She laughed. "Forget it. What I have I need."

"Come on, Sis, for me." He cupped her shoulders, giving them a squeeze while flashing his most charming smile. It had stopped working on her a decade ago.

"I wasted tokens on a taxi to get here, so no, no, no." She stomped off. "Find some other way to fund your addictions or grow up and get a job."

He didn't follow her, for once not nagging her all the way down to the lobby and pleading while she waited for another taxi until she finally shut the vehicle's door on his pouting. She sagged against the seat, twitched her toes in her too-tight boots, and gazed ahead. Only a windscreen with a smooth dash filled her vision while the autodrive shot along the roads to her dorm.

Alone, at last, she planned the rest of her evening. Some much-needed confectionery would be a good start.

Chapter Three

Whispers rippled over those gathered in the great hall. That didn't bode well. Nenn gritted his teeth, ignored those calling his name, and focused on Elder Qon's request. He needed to find Dumis. Spotting the male beside the central bonfire, he pushed through to reach him. The older male stared into the flickering flames, his shoulders bowed.

He must have sensed Nenn's presence, whipping his head up. "How bad is it?"

"He will heal," Nenn said.

Dumis's smile went from tentative to broad. He yanked Nenn into a crushing hug. 'Thank you." He glanced at those watching. "Do not pay them any heed. You have never harmed anyone or anything for personal gain."

"I find the symbiotes' silence on this matter alarming," Nenn said, poking his soul.

Dumis frowned. "They have reason."

Nenn's shoulders jerked when a shiver slithered down his neck. "What is it?"

Dumis glanced at someone behind Nenn. "Elder Lama?"

The elder's face softened. "Nenn, your father—"

"No," he gasped, staggering back as if he could run from the news. "Why?" he wailed. "Why now?"

Dumis gripped Nenn's arm. "He—"

Images blasted through Nenn, dropping him to his knees. The sheer agony of the lava consuming his father's flesh and melting his bones lasted a minute, no more, but it was enough.

"Stop," he cried out.

He'd caught a fleeting taste of the pain when Tugo's foot had dipped into the river. In the chaos afterward, the symbiotes hadn't focused on it. But a soul cleansing was to be experienced by all, to honor the person who'd outlived their usefulness. And yet, when it happened, Nenn's symbiotes hadn't shared it. Saving it all for now.

Tears poured free even as his hearts ceased to beat, now lumps of grief weighing down his body until he could barely keep his head up. Someone lifted him, set him on a bench, then shoved a mug of nulci into his hand.

The hot wine, made from berries and herbs, hit his stomach like a kick to the head. Hours ago, he'd lamented the state of his life. Now, he had an injured friend, survived two banaari sightings, and lost his father. He slammed the mug on the table and dipped his face between his knees to suck in deep breaths.

"He left you this…" Elder Lama looped father's amulet over Nenn's head.

It thumped against his chest. The warm and faceted rock, almost transparent with a hint of a yellow flame at its core, had been a gift from his mother when they'd first courted.

"And a nomination," Dumis whispered.

Fresh tears stung Nenn's eyes. "Family does not count."

"Yes, they do, for a soul cleanser." A suspicious sheen coated Elder Lama's red eyes.

Nenn shook his head. "I wanted to leave, but not like this. Never—" He broke off to pin his chin to his chest. "Never like this," he rasped, grief so crushing, he dared not move.

His wounds and sore muscles—the symbiotes had begun to heal. But this agony, as if every muscle had torn and sheets of stone pinned him to the spot, was beyond his capacity to bear.

"You have my nomination," Elder Qon called, slicing through the crowd of blurred faces.

"And mine." Kimgi smiled, crossing to loop her arm through Dumis's.

"Then you shall have mine," Tugo's father said.

Nenn didn't speak; his ability to care had abandoned him. He was spared from any response when Dumis shoved a refilled mug into his hand with a whispered command to drink. He did so, emptying it and relishing the familiar burn when it exploded heat in his core and numbed his mind and heart. Tomorrow…he would mourn.

A beat began like the steady thump of a great oobara's heart. More drums joined in. A bonfire's flames flickered, reaching toward the cave's ceiling. His symbiotes bombarded him with images, memories peppered with his mother's delicate face, with his own through the years until he'd reached malehood. And it all was coated with a love so precious.

Tears slipped free, dripping onto his tunic. Dumis dragged him to the fire and forced him to join arms with Panior to form a circle around the bonfire. In unison, they danced, the beat pulsing within him while the wine clouded his vision. Many hugged him, whispering their sorrow and sharing their admiration for his father while the symbiotes served as witnesses.

When the heat merged his tears with his sweat and made breathing difficult, he swiveled on his heel and left, staggering by rote to his home. The door was ajar, needing minimal effort to slide aside. His father had lost the strength to close it.

He stood on the threshold and gazed at the carved walls made smooth over the generations that had come before him. Like Kimgi and Tugo's home, a ledge with thick furs served as his bed. Shelves above a dead fireplace held pots, mugs, garments, and weapons. Benches were carved on either side of one corner for sitting and eating. And a tall pot housed fresh water he had to fetch every morning from the underground river.

Silence, darkness, loneliness poured into him. Gone was the warm welcome of his mother. Lost was the steadfast existence of his father. And he'd wanted to believe his father lived while Nenn traversed the stars. He sprawled on top of the furs and stared at the venai stones painstakingly embedded in grooved slots. The symbiotes replayed scenes from his day, showing Tugo hesitating, teetering, then leaping when he shouldn't have. They revealed Nenn's desperation to save his friend, from carrying his heavy ass to descending into Habqus Abyss.

All was revealed.

And none of it mattered.

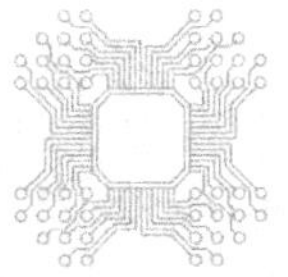

DAYS BLURRED. DUMIS BROUGHT Nenn food he didn't eat. Elder Qon checked on the injuries Nenn's symbiotes were attending to and shared the progress of Tugo's healing. Elder Lama informed Nenn he'd be traveling with the Ivoyans. When all this happened, what time or which day, he couldn't say.

He rolled onto his side only to ease an ache in his back or to drink a ladle of water.

With his father's soul cleansing, he'd hoped the symbiotes would reveal the true nature of his mother's death. They hadn't. And perhaps they didn't know. He'd grown up understanding that what he did would be revealed to all; everyone guarded everyone, so to speak. Whenever he and Tugo got into trouble, the tribe had so severely chastised them on their way home that Father hadn't bothered to discipline them.

In a way, he had many fathers. He sat up, the realization soothing a tiny portion of his grief. He had family even though they weren't related by blood. He gazed at his home, at the stillness of it, at how things sat where his father had left them and, in some cases, where his mother had... Her dust-covered garment on the top shelf had remained untouched since her disappearance.

Pain crushed his chest so tight that he struggled to breathe.

He bolted, shoving the sheet out of the way to sprint up the carved steps. Many greeted him, but he didn't stop. He needed the sky above him, a warm breeze on his face, the solidity of volcanic rock beneath his feet.

The suns were setting.

Heat traveled through his toes. He grimaced at his bare feet.

"Nenn," Juirr said by way of greeting. "You cannot meet the Ivoyans like that."

Nenn jerked back. "When—"

"This evening, when the moons touch the horizon, or so Elder Lama says." Laec elbowed his brother. "I shall guard. Escort Nenn to the pools."

Juirr nodded and tossed his spear at Laec who caught it from the air. With his arm thrown across Nenn's shoulders, Juirr led him into the cave.

"But—" Nenn gazed at the sky with longing.

"You have our Giniiri honor to uphold," Juirr was saying.

As much as Nenn had wanted a chance to travel off-world, losing his father had tainted his dreams. A season from now, yes, he'd embrace the chance to serve the Ivoyans. Now, not so much. It seemed...pointless.

Had he left with the Ivoyans last season, if he'd never come home, his father would have lived forever. Until he stepped onto Qaldreth. He slumped. There'd be no way to avoid grieving. He was foolish to try. A change in scenery might be what he needed.

"Bathe, dress, and eat." Juirr shoved him toward the farthest pool, steam rising off the bubbling water. Alongside it sat a bar of soap and a stack of clean garments not his.

"And these?" Nenn asked, but Juirr had abandoned him.

He shrugged, stripped off garments that stank worse than a dead vibuy, then tested the water's temperature with his big toe. It was too much to bear, even for a Giniiri used to heat. He hissed, then winced when he sank onto the carved ledge.

With the Ivoyan alderman's arrival imminent, Nenn couldn't waste hours. Laec and Juirr had been right to urge him to prepare himself. Should he pack? And if so, what? He had no idea what would be needed. He clutched the amulet around his neck. This, of course, he would take with him.

"I came to wish you Osnir's blessings," Panior said, squatting beside the pool.

The male was too perfect by any standard. His garments were clean and well-stitched. His orange-red hair, indicative of a Giniiri, looked combed. He was inches taller than Nenn, had prowess with sword, spear, and bow, and had outrun them all since they were young.

"May He bless you also," Nenn said, as per their custom. "I must confess, I did not anticipate this...chance."

Panior grinned. Even faced with disappointment at having to wait another solar cycle to leave this world, he behaved with honor. When all Nenn could hope for was to not bring shame upon their tribe.

"There is method to His blessings. I trust this will go well for you, Nenn." He glanced over his shoulder at the hall. "My time will come. For now, I serve here."

When he rose to leave, Nenn said, "Wait, do I pack anything?"

Panior chuckled. "Not that I heard of. Go as you are. Anything you need, they provide for." He gripped his dagger sheathed to his belt. "I would take this though. A weapon is always useful."

"My thanks," Nenn said, for he had no such blade, and grabbed the bar of soap.

"Do not tarry. Three roast banaari await, care of this season's chosen." Panior strode off, his shoulders back, his stride buoyant.

As Nenn soaped and rinsed, the warmed fragrance of oldarr bark and black moss surrounding him, he decided to emulate Panior in his future actions. Well, as best he could. He climbed out of the pool and dried himself with a woven cloth someone set out for him. By the smell, he'd say Kimgi.

The leggings were brown banaari leather and soft, clinging to his damp legs when he wiggled into them. On a normal day, he'd run his fingers through his hair and be done with it. Today, from his temple to the base of his spine, he dragged a comb through his hair, shivering when the tines scraped his scalp. The cream-colored tunic was well-made, the stitches almost invisible. Who'd gifted him with these? His boots were his own, though, made to fit his feet when he attained adulthood.

He weaved around the other pools, crossed the main path, and strode into the gathered crowd. The sweet aroma of banaari filled the air. He far preferred the saltiness of vibuy, but as feasts went, this one was appreciated.

"Sancnuss," someone yelled, waving a stone mug of nulci in the air.

His tribe cheered, chanting his name.

Dumis slapped Nenn across the back. "I am not certain their excitement is to see you leave or in thanks for the venison."

Nenn laughed. "Both?"

"You and Tugo have always been the troublemakers, the ones we could trust to get up to mischief." Elder Lama offered a tooth-gapped smile. "Never a dull moment and the instigators of many fireside stories."

"I shall miss you," Tugo called from where he sat on a bench, Kimgi hovering nearby.

"You are well?" Nenn gasped, shifting his gaze between Kimgi and Elder Qon.

"I am...better." Tugo grimaced. "Thanks to you, I will not lose my foot." He gestured to those closest. "I can confirm it was my foolishness that led to this."

"We know," Elder Lama said. "The symbiotes revealed all."

"Take this." Dumis shoved a blade at Nenn. "Your harvesting knife will not be needed, but this dagger will serve you better."

Nenn blinked at the intricately carved tooth as the hilt and the shimmering steel of the blade. "I cannot." He glanced at Tugo. "This is yours, my friend."

"I want you to have it, and my father agrees." Tugo staggered to his feet, his face paling, sweat beading his temple. "You are like a brother to me, Nenn. Please, take the ceremonial dagger, and think of us when you are among the stars."

"It would be rude of you to not accept," Kimgi said, slipping under Tugo's arm to usher him onto the bench.

Dumis caught Nenn's hand and placed the dagger on his palm. "Come. Eat."

Laec exploded into their midst. "The Ivoyans have arrived." He ushered Nenn aside with a grip on his shoulder. "It is custom for you to meet them alone."

Nenn jerked back. "I did not know that."

"Only the chosen learn of this," Elder Lama whispered. "Leave. Quietly. For to stroll out surrounded by revelry is not the Giniiri way."

Nenn swept a gaze across his family. "My thanks to all of you."

"Return well and with honor," Dumis said, clasping Nenn's forearm.

"I will." He inched backward, spun on his heel, and marched up the path toward the cave's entrance.

At the same time, Elder Lama addressed the tribe, drawing their attention.

Each step took courage, the cheers and singing fading as Nenn faced his future. Juirr said nothing when Nenn passed him. Guided by the yellow moon, he veered left along the path he'd descended with Tugo over his shoulder. His thighs burned from the steady pace he set.

In the center of the caldera, with pockets of lava bubbling at its edges, sat a sky vessel. It shone black and orange, reflecting the rock beneath it and the volcano around it. Its door slid open without making a sound. An Ivoyan glided out. His orange body rivaled that of the freshest lava, glowing in the soft light spilling from within his vessel. In dark blue leggings and a tunic that formed one garment, he approached Nenn on bare four-toed feet as if the hot rock didn't bother him. He was taller than Tugo and Panior, his head bulbous. A strip of transparent material covered the top half of his face, strange lights and symbols flickering across it. Only two nostrils, a thin mouth, and a pointy chin were visible.

"Nenn aac Giniiri," he said, the words clipped. "Do you accept this task offered to your tribe?"

"I do." Nenn drew closer.

"The Ivoyan Senate accept your servitude." He swept out a long arm, indicating to Nenn to climb into the vessel.

He did, crossing as fast as he could, in case the Ivoyan changed his mind. With one glance at his beloved Erasril, Nenn bid his home farewell.

CHAPTER FOUR

Year: 2215
Two Years Later
Earth
Old Lake City
Mainframe, a Nightclub.

TINY RAN HER HAND over her waist to her hip in the blurred reflection of the bathroom mirror. She giggled, her thoughts swirling, buzzing. Her hearing thumped in sync with the beat pounding through the walls.

She was one shot away from throwing up or passing out. With a stumble to the basin, she splashed water onto her face. The cool shock granted her a moment of clarity before the fuzziness returned. Instinct whispered that she should call it a night. Tomorrow was her graduation. As it was, she'd be suffering from a hangover when she accepted her medical degree.

Leaving, though, was another story altogether.

Squaring her shoulders, she gave herself a final glance; her jeans hugged curves that hadn't been there when she'd first started her studies. Same for the pink T-shirt showcasing her fuller breasts. Too many midnight study sessions with takeouts or cupcakes. The downward spiral of her changed appearance—and not for the better—would trap her in the bathroom.

She swallowed past the cocktail-flavored bile pooling at the back of her throat and yanked open the door. The music lambasted her traumatized ears.

"About time," Shelly said, wrapping her arm through Tiny's.

"One last dance, Shell, then I must go." Tiny used a firm tone, hoping to convey her determination.

"Aw." Shelly pouted. Dark smears of smudged mascara gave her an unintentional smoky look, and her lipstick had faded, leaving behind pink lips.

"Don't give me that look, babe." Tiny pressed her cheek to Shelly's sweaty upper arm. "I'm tired, and my feet are killing me."

"Fair enough." Shelly dragged Tiny onto the dance floor, shoving people aside to do so.

The lights were overwhelming: too many colors flickering everywhere. The crush of people sucked the air from the room; the stench of unwashed bodies, stale perfume, spilled drinks, and vomit assaulted her nose. And even as the music vibrated up the heels of her stunning, new boots, the rhythm didn't compel her to dance.

Still, she pushed through the need to leave, forced a smile, and managed to do a few hip swings.

"Don't look now, but you're being stalked, girl," Shelly screamed into Tiny's ear.

The compulsion to look grabbed her. She wasn't in the mood to be groped by whoever thought she was a quick fuck. Still, curiosity won out, and she peeked, scanning the general area Shelly had gestured at. Against one wall leaned a man. Not a student, if she judged his tailored pants and crisp, white button-up. His dark hair flopped over his brow on one side, and his brooding stare rested on her.

On another night, she might have been flattered. But she'd spent what free time she had on her back, as expected of a young woman 'discovering herself.'

"Oh, and Riaan's here, too." Shelly wiggled her eyebrows.

That was Tiny's cue. Running into her ex-fling was beyond her capacity to deal with. Not now or ever, for that matter. "I'm out, babe. See you tomorrow."

Shelly waved then latched onto a random woman shimmying past.

Tiny bolted before her dearest friend changed her mind and chased after her. The balls of her feet burned at the abuse she'd put them through. Thoughts of her dorm room filled her with longing. A sol-bath, her bed, sleep, and in that order.

She strode out of the club with barely a wobble. Night air bathed her, making her shiver. She veered around couples and smaller groups loitering near the entrance to reach the pick-up point marked with a yellow dot on the walkway. A streetlight shone down, illuminating her in a pool of white.

Tapping her palm, she dialed for a taxi, then pressed her hand to her ear, her wrist closest to her mouth. As soon as the call was answered, she said, "Hi, yes, I need a ride from Mainframe, please."

"Five minutes," the AI intoned.

She shut her eyes, taking slow breaths when sleep teased the edges of her mind. Fifteen more minutes, and she'd be home.

"Leaving so soon?" a man asked, snapping her eyes open.

She swiveled, gaped, then shut her mouth.

Mr. Brooding-Stare stood beside her.

She shifted, her instincts warning her that he was trouble. Danger poured off his broad shoulders, despite his casual stance with his hands shoved into the pockets of his pants. In the light, they were a dark silver color and looked expensive.

"Yes. It's been a long night," she said, forming fists so she wouldn't be tempted to flick her hair out of her face.

"I see. It's unsafe for a woman to be alone this late. Waiting for someone to fetch you?"

She stiffened at his subtle dig for information. This man wasn't to be trusted.

"My ride's on its way." She flashed a tight smile. "Thank you for keeping me company while I wait."

He jerked back, raised his head, and studied the passing autodrive vehicles. "If you were my sister, I would guard you better."

She winced. Jamie was a far cry from the world's best brother. She hadn't seen him for months, and he only contacted her when he needed tokens.

"Not all brothers love their sisters," she said, then dipped her gaze to her boots.

"That is especially true for you," the man said when an autodrive pulled up before them.

She blinked at him. "Do I know you?"

He laughed and opened the door for her. "No."

When she climbed in, she expected him to bid her goodnight.

Instead, he bent to meet her gaze. "But Jamie does."

In he slid, pinning her to the seat.

She squeaked and struggled, but he kept her in place with his strength alone. Nor did the autodrive pay her any heed. In the calmest voice, he gave it a new address, one far across the city.

She gaped at him, unable to form words. As drunk as she was, she couldn't grasp what he wanted from her or how she'd landed in this situation. Nor could she anticipate the injection-gun he pressed to her neck. A blast of liquid-cold bit into her.

"What are you doing?" she gasped, cupping her neck.

"Making sure you're complacent." He shifted back, granting her space to breathe.

She lunged for the door but made it inches before her arm slumped. "What..." she slurred, speaking like she was underwater.

"You can thank your brother for this."

Those were the last words she heard.

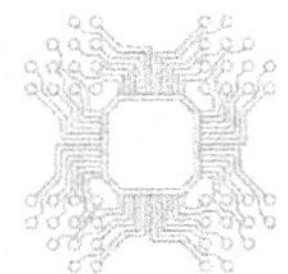

TINY MUSCLED HER WAY through the fog consuming her brain. How much had she drunk last night? A piercing pain shot through her left eye. Everything was sluggish, from her swollen tongue to moving her body. Her stomach churned, threatening to throw up a variety of alcohol and semi-digested peanuts. She must've tossed and turned because the blankets had her wrapped tight.

A sense of urgency pressed on her. What was it about today that she needed to remember? Somewhere she had to be, maybe? And what was that smell?

Burned metal came to mind. She winced and flicked an eye open. Then the other in disbelief.

Tied to a chair, she slouched forward as far as the rope would allow. Her neck pinged like she'd slept funny, but none of that mattered when she was in the center of what looked like a warehouse. No. A factory. Welders worked around her. Bright flashes of their torches were focused on autodrives and antique cars, some worth more than all her tuition combined.

A hexagonal dome of glass separated her from them and muted the sounds. Which meant screaming wouldn't be heard by anyone. Besides, they could see her, and yet, they'd done nothing to save her.

The sexy stalker had mentioned Jamie. What the hell had he done this time? She searched for a friendly face, someone who could help her escape. Beyond the floor was a staircase going up to a mezzanine level. Below that were walls with no door in sight. Besides, she couldn't escape the hexagon. A glance up showed chains on a metal frame capping the room. They would have to lift the glass in one movement to reach her. For a cell, this was quite effective.

Tears pressed at the backs of her eyes and leaked past her defenses. She was trapped by a brooding asshole. Because her slime ball of a brother had pissed off the wrong people, by the looks of things.

Men hurried in, carrying boxes overflowing with packets of blue pills, and dumped them at each welder. Realization dawned. They were stashing the drugs inside the frames of all these vehicles.

She tried to focus past the white flashes, hoping to remember as much as she could to convey to the authorities. If these dealers let her go.

Pain cinched her wrists when she struggled to free them. She slumped and glanced down for a moment. Worse than disco lights, the arc flashes made her eyes burn.

Part of her hoped the stalker from last night would appear. She needed a familiar face even if it was his. And maybe, he'd explain what the hell he'd injected her with and what he planned to do with her.

She gritted her teeth and glared at all the mean men around her.

When she got her hands on Jamie, she was going to strangle him.

A cranking of chains snapped her gaze up. The cell lifted, inch by inch. Waiting on the outskirts were two men, neither of them the stalker dude. One had a mustache and a buzz cut, his muscles straining against his ill-fitting suit. The other was an older man with his white hair perfectly styled. He wore jeans, a T-shirt, a blazer, and loafers, looking like he'd just stepped off a yacht.

As soon as the glass was high enough, he dipped under and approached her.

"My apologies for the treatment, Tinika," he said, his accent cultured. The scent of soap and cologne teased her nose. Gold rings glinted on a tooth and his fingers.

"You seem to have me at a disadvantage," she said. "I don't know who you are."

He chuckled. "Indeed. Nor shall you. Suffice it to say, your brother has stolen from me for the last time."

She grimaced. "What he does is his problem. I'm not responsible for him. I used to be, but I gave up."

She flinched when White Hair circled her until she couldn't see him in her peripherals anymore. Each sound he made shot through her senses, made worse when she couldn't anticipate his actions. He stopped to her right to cup her chin, raising her gaze to his.

"So pretty, young, and soon to be a doctor?" He tutted then released her. "My men haven't found Jamie, and until they do, you're stuck here." He glanced at Buzz Cut. "Did you send word that we have her?"

"I did," the man rumbled.

"Listen, sir, you're wasting your time. My brother doesn't care about me unless he wants tokens. He's not to be trusted, will stab you in the back, *and* throw you under an autobus. If you'd met me first, I would've warned you about him." She wiggled in the hopes that blood flow would return to her cold fingers.

"Now, that I can believe. Still, I must try, y'know, to get back what is mine."

She sighed. "I understand. It's just that I'm missing my graduation. Couldn't you have captured me a day from now?"

White Hair laughed. "Oh, dear, you have a sense of humor."

"I'm sorry." She yearned to roll her eyes but resisted. "I'm a little hungover, my arms are numb, and I need to pee."

"Loosen the ropes, Warren," White Hair said. "Take Ms. Bryant for a...pee."

She blessed him with a smile. "Thank you so much."

Again, he laughed. "And manners. Are you sure you're Jamie's sister?"

"Unfortunately, yes," she muttered when Warren freed her hands, flooding her arms with an explosion of pins and needles. She cried out, bit her lip, and refused to move.

Warren rubbed her from shoulder to fingertips. At first, she wanted to smack him, then when the sensations faded, she thought of kissing him in sheer gratitude.

"Thanks," she whispered.

He gripped her by the elbow and hoisted her to her feet. Without a word to White Hair, he ushered her through the factory to a door she hadn't spotted.

"Pee," he said, shoving her inside.

The stench hit her first, but she gulped down her disgust, and did her thing, squatting like a sumo wrestler in the hopes that she touched nothing. While she washed her hands, she stared at the window, trying to assess whether she could fit her ass through it. Her height was an issue, and she didn't know what awaited her outside. It could be a sheer drop or two ravenous guard autodogs who would see her as their next meal. Did they even eat flesh?

She shook her head. Wrong thinking.

Then again, what awaited her inside the glass cell? The loss of her fingers? Her kneecaps shot off? Worse, if they gave her some of those blue pills. Certain death for sure.

Almost disbelieving what she was about to do, she tipped the trashcan over then climbed on top of it. Not a simple feat as short as she was. Balanced on her toes, the can wobbling beneath her, she unlatched the window to peer out.

Nothing but a staff parking lot meant she could slip out and make a run for it. No fences hindered her bolt for freedom, no security guards either. She squeezed her eyes shut, grittiness from lack of sleep taking effect.

Up she lifted herself, then with a grunt, she wiggled through only to realize the error of her ways. Headfirst meant landing on her face. With her ass on the sill, she gripped the window's metal frame.

"Are you done yet?" Warren called.

She swallowed a squeak and pulled her feet through, then the strength in her arms gave out, dropping her. Hitting the ground on her back sucked the air out of her lungs. She gasped but couldn't exhale. The back of her head throbbed where she must have bounced it off the tarmac. Pain pulsed outward, worsening her headache and the nausea in her gut. She flipped onto her stomach, pushed herself to her feet, then threw up in a nearby discarded box.

Nausea coiled, bile rose, and the horrendous tang of it coated her tongue. She swallowed hard, willing her body to realize the situation. No way would she get recaptured just because she had to spill her guts. That would be all kinds of foolish.

While wiping her mouth, she eyed the window, half-expecting Warren to be watching her. When he wasn't, she sprinted along the parked vehicles, keeping them between the bathroom and the road. Her feet were stinging. The sunlight blinded her hangover-sensitive eyes, setting them on fire. Not that she dared to close them, needing to navigate the roads of an industrial area she'd never visited.

Activating her phone implant in her palm, she called the police. Tears slipped free willy-nilly, burning her cool cheeks. What she wanted to do was find a dark corner and huddle. Instead, she marched toward the city's center and prayed she'd come across a patrolling police vehicle.

"What's your emergency?" an AI droned.

"Hello?" she blurted. "I was kidnapped, am now free, and don't know where the hell I am. Please…"

"One moment, please," the AI said with saccharine sweetness.

"Ma'am, we are tracking you," an officer said a second later.

She almost cried, so great was the relief bowing her shoulders. "Please. Hurry."

"Tinika," someone yelled.

She swiveled, a sob escaping her at the sight of Warren sprinting toward her. Reacting on instinct, she bolted, crossing the streets without checking, veering around loitering homeless people or leaping over bodies she hoped still breathed. Panic drove her to use all her energy to pump her arms, while ignoring her aching feet, her throbbing headache, and her blurred vision.

She wasn't going back. A square with carved paving stones carried more foot traffic than she'd encountered this morning. She stopped at the courtyard's center and spun, trying to decide where to go next. Away from Warren, duh. So she took the straight path in the opposite direction. People in corporate wear, their palms to their ears, didn't notice her or her pursuer.

When he crossed the distance between them, she veered into a building skirting the square. The cool interior offered her some relief. Warren hesitated, glowered, and still approached.

"Um, hi," she said to the security guard behind the reception counter. "Could I wait here until the police find me?"

The skinny dude glanced at her then outside. His eyes widened when he spotted Warren.

"No, not without clearance." He nudged his pointy chin at the door.

She gaped, her thoughts reeling. A peek confirmed Warren waiting for her to leave. A glance over her other shoulder showed the path she needed to take—up a small hill to the park beyond. She could hide there, maybe?

"Asshole," she snapped at the guard.

Without another word, she sidled to the door, slipped through it, then ducked. Air brushing her head told her how close Warren had come to grabbing her. She broke into a sprint. At this time of the morning, the park grounds were empty except for two cyclists, a woman with her stroller, and a few joggers. A crowd would've been helpful.

Everything ached, from her leg muscles to her chest, tight from her ragged breaths. Sweat pooled at the base of her spine and between her breasts.

"Tiny, come on," Warren called.

She faced him while walking backward. "No, I won't be used as a pawn. Kill my brother, do what you want with him, but leave me out of whatever this is." She swiveled and slammed into someone. With a cry, she teetered, her arms flying wide.

"I've got you, miss," a man said.

The red of his uniform caught her attention, and she whimpered, lunging forward to grip his arms. "Officer?"

"I told you we'd find you."

At his familiar voice, she slid to the ground, uncaring that she sat there sobbing. "Thank you."

"Are you all right? Do you need an ambo?"

When her tears didn't soothe her gritty eyelids, she had to face the truth as excruciating agony forced her to shut her eyes. "I do need medical attention. Please." She folded both forearms across her face. "Arc eyes," she wailed.

This was her fault for not shielding herself against arc flashes. She knew better, knew the damage the radiation could do. It was for this very reason that welders had protective gear.

What followed was a blur, made worse by her diminishing ability to see.

Warren was no more, not in the crowd gathered around the ambulance, not on the outskirts of the park. He'd vanished as if demons had chased her across blocks instead of a drug lord's hitman. Would they try this again? Steal her from wherever? She couldn't say.

Swear words clung to the tip of her tongue, begging for release. Even if she spewed them at her brother, he'd shrug them off. If she told her folks, they wouldn't believe her, like a med student had a reason to lie.

She was grateful though for Parsons, the officer who'd stayed by her side. His voice had the most impact on her, keeping her in the moment and sane.

"You don't have to stay," she said to him once they had her in a ward.

The doctor had examined her after administering anesthetic eye drops. A nurse now placed padded dressings over her eyes. She'd have to endure the pain with only Ibuprofen and Proparacaine drops to help her endure.

"I will, until your parents arrive."

"You called them?" she squeaked, slumped, then stiffened when the nurse tutted.

"Had to. You're blind, Ms. Bryant," he said.

"True." She forced a smile she far from felt. "It's temporary, though—about five days. Don't get me wrong. It's going to suck."

"Tiny?" Mom cried, entering with a flurry of squeaks from her sneakers on the polished floor.

"Hi, Mom." She kept her smile in place by sheer will.

"What happened?" Mom asked, bringing with her a cloud of rose perfume.

Tiny hesitated. Burning scratched at her eyelids, drooping her shoulders. How could she tell her mom without revealing the truth that she wouldn't believe anyway?

"Fireworks incident in the city square," Parsons said. "We were lucky to find her, ma'am."

Tiny smiled in the direction of his voice. She wished she could squeeze his hand in gratitude. He'd been her hero when she'd needed one so desperately.

"Thank you, young man," Mom said. "Your father's sorting out the payment. Jamie's—"

"Don't mention his name," Tiny snapped, venom in her voice. She wanted to kill him, strangle him with her bare hands.

"Why are you angry with your brother?" Mom sighed. "This vendetta you have against—"

"How's my pumpkin?" Dad asked, his heavy tread music to Tiny's ears.

She sucked in a calming breath, uncurled her fingers, and pasted on a smile. Now wasn't the time to discuss Jamie's secret criminal life. Her parents wouldn't believe her anyway. She needed evidence or law enforcement to spill the beans.

"Better," she said. "All thanks to Officer Parsons..." He hadn't given her his first name, but she couldn't be sure, not remembering anything past the agony that had consumed her eyes at the time.

"You have a remarkable daughter," he said, which he no doubt told all the women he rescued.

"What were you doing in the city center?" Dad tutted. "You missed your graduation."

"Oh?" Parsons asked.

"Yes, our daughter's a doctor now." Pride filled Mom's voice.

"I still have to do my residency," Tiny hurried to remind them.

"Good, you are here, Mr. and Mrs. Bryant," Dr. Murray said, his gravelly voice recognizable. "I'm sorry to have to tell your this, but the damage is severe." He cleared his throat. "I want to run some more tests, which is why Tiny's been admitted for overnight care."

Severe? Chills sent a shiver across her shoulders and down her spine. No. She was fine. Dr. Murray was just being cautious. She refused to consider what the worst-case scenario could be, but her mind went there anyway.

Permanent blindness.

"Hey, sister," Jamie said, striding into the stunned silence.

Her thoughts went blank. Fury exploded in her. She hadn't planned to slide off the bed, but she did, stumbling toward her brother's voice. Tears inflamed her eyes and cheeks, matching the blaze of anger inside her. She threw a punch, missed, spun on the spot, and fell, collapsing to the floor amid shuddering sobs. Everything ached: her knees, heart, eyes. The cold registered from the tiles and the gap in her hospital gown. None of that mattered. All her hopes and dreams had shattered.

"Jamie Bryant?" Officer Parsons asked. He gripped Tiny's waist, the warmth of his hands making her shiver. Without warning, he hoisted her into his arms and carried her to bed like she weighed nothing. Then his touch and presence were gone.

"If I ever see you again, *brother*, I'll kill you," she spat at the room while someone tucked the blanket around her.

"Is it the medication?" Mom asked from a way off. "I'm so sorry. She's never acted like this."

Tiny screamed, cursed, gestured with her arms, demanded a gun, some weapon, poison. Whatever she spewed was beyond her control as if the connection between her brain and her tongue had been severed.

"Pumpkin," Dad said, his steadfastness breaking through the blinding haze of fury and sorrow.

"Let me explain, Mr. Bryant," Officer Parsons said. "But first, your son is under arrest."

"What? Why?" Mom squeaked, her footsteps tapping in a flurry of activity.

Right then, that said it all. How much Tiny truly mattered to her parents. Not that she'd ever wanted them to choose between their two children. But for farg's sake, she could be *blind* because of Jamie.

Fargen blind.

Bitterness coated her tongue, and she struggled to swallow. Throughout Officer Parsons's explanation, her parents' shock, and her brother's whining, she sat, listened, and let the hatred fester.

Chapter Five

Year: 2218

Three Years Later

Earth

Carne Corp. Augmentations

Headquarters

Ground Floor

"C.C.A. complaints, how may I help?" Tiny tried not to wince when she said that, but it was unavoidable. She was far too miserable to care.

"Yes," a woman wailed.

Tiny held her headset away from her ear, her tight grip almost cracking the plastic.

"This is the fourth time I've called about my leg. It swivels randomly and pitches me forward or slams me into the closest object. It's defective, but every time I call, I'm shunted to the nearest fitment center." The woman sucked in a sharp breath. "And they're useless, no doubt exchanging my ankle with the same shitty part. I want a full refund."

"I'll need your details. Please swipe your wrist across the phone, ma'am." Tiny waited for the information to reach her, read out in a robotic voice that often appeared in her dreams. "Mrs. Holden, you've had this model for twenty-two years and have, on numerous occasions, declined an upgrade."

"Why would I accept another ankle when the old one doesn't work?"

Tiny plastered on a fake smile through gritted teeth while she fought the frustration welling up inside her. "Because they've redesigned the functionality. Technology evolves based on the feedback from valued customers such as yourself. Why shouldn't you benefit from the process?"

Mrs. Holden huffed. "I'll give it some thought."

Typing away, Tiny beamed, sensing the end of the call. "Excellent. I've notified your closest fitment center to expect a possible visit. We truly appreciate your input, Mrs. Holden. Please feel free to inform the technician about any improvements you would find helpful. Is there anything else I can assist you with?" she added with saccharine sweetness.

"No...thank you. I think I'm good."

"Excellent. Please take a minute to rate my service. And have a lovely day." Tiny pressed and held the disconnect button. Doing so bought her a few precious moments of silence.

"I don't know how you stay so calm," Elsa said from the right.

Tiny shrugged, understanding what drove people crazy when it came to their health. "Some complaints are valid. Others just want someone to vent to." She gestured to the screaming person on Elsa's line.

"...Lost his new eyeball. He bent to buckle a boot, and his eye fell out. It rolled across a street where an autodrive ran over it. That's his sixth implant in as many months. Tokens don't grow on trees, you know."

Tiny squeezed her eyes shut in gratitude. Sure, she couldn't see anything but blurred shapes, but she still had her own 'eyeballs.' She whistled. "Different caller than yesterday's?"

"It's the third complaint this week alone."

Tiny frowned at Elsa's words. Not once did she get those kinds of clients. Hers were always for limbs far from the face. It was sweet of switchboard to screen the calls, but she didn't need them to.

Her line chimed. She tapped the answer button and forced a cheerful, "C.C.A. complaints, how may I assist?"

"Hi," a man whispered. "I didn't know whether to call you or emergency services."

She stiffened and wheeled her chair closer. "Sir, are you injured?"

"My...new appendage won't...um...soften."

She cupped the headset, pressing it to her ears in the hopes she'd understand him better. "For how long have you been suffering?"

"Four days. At first, my girlfriend loved it being so...*ready* for her, but now... It started to ache about a day ago."

Tiny jerked back. "Please swipe your wrist." She listened while the system read out his details. The reality flushed her cheeks until she gave off so much heat, her eyes watered. Her fingers flew across the keyboard while she set things into action. "Mr. Adams, please head to the nearest fitment center. I've notified them of your situation and requested emergency services to be on standby."

"Thank you," he said with a long exhale. "I love my new... Well, um, I just need help calming it."

"I understand and suggest you do not delay." When he ended the call, she relaxed and let out a chuckle. Moments like this were what made her days—a chance to help someone. "That poor man." She noted the limb on their shared notepad. Anything unusual—no names—was recorded for a giggle at Friday's afternoon socials.

Elsa's perfume drew closer. "Appendage?" She laughed. "That's one name for it. I can't believe you're a doctor and you're doing this horrible job." She cleared her throat. "Yes, ma'am, I'll need your details..."

Tiny zoned the call operators out and flicked to her search tab. Elsa was right. She needed something else that didn't drain her soul. The accessibility settings helped her navigate to a career site. Her attempts to complete her residency had been met with disaster. Every hospital she'd worked at had eventually let her go, citing their facilities weren't geared toward her disability, or they couldn't afford malpractice lawsuits. She'd figured there had to be colonies desperate for a doctor, even a blind one.

"Medical positions...in space," she whispered into her mic.

"Zero available," the search engine droned. "Notification is activated for Tinika Bryant."

She slumped. "Anything else I can do with my hands?"

She wiggled her fingers, the brush of air across her implants flashing details across her mind, such as the temperature and the carbon dioxide levels, even though her nose twitched from the stench of body sweat and someone's reheated fish. The sensors in her hands had to be petitioned with permission granted only to emergency or blind doctors. Lucky her. It also cost her parents a fortune. If the government had known she'd never hold down a medical position, she doubted they'd have allowed the procedure.

"A masseuse position on Lunar Base," came the engine's unexpected response.

"Tiny, your father's here to fetch you," the new floor manager called.

She whipped her head up and forced a smile while hitting random buttons to exit the screen. "Thanks," she squeaked while praying he hadn't seen what she'd been doing.

She gathered her stuff, sliding items into her bag by rote. Without routine, she'd forget things, so in went her jacket, lunch tin, and empty travel mug, and in that order. She powered off her computer, squeezed Elsa's upper arm, and made her escape. Thirty-two steps took her to the front of the open-plan, her hearing pricked up for certain voices to guide her to reception.

"Hey, sweetheart," Dad said, his rough hand on her wrist when he linked her arm through his. "How was your day?"

"Good," she said, letting him escort her onto the walkway. A warm breeze, thick with fumes and the smell of hot concrete, flicked her hair back. "You don't need to fetch me, Dad. I can get home by myself."

He harumphed. "Nothing's going to happen to my pumpkin."

She shivered, distrusting his and Mom's new affection toward her. Having never been granted their attention in this abundance, she didn't know what to make of it. At least, she hadn't heard how amazing her brother was, not after the whole drug-dealing fiasco. After the hospital discharged her, Officer Parsons had gone from hero to zero after that day. She swallowed past the pain cinching her chest. He'd checked up once then gone silent. Hell, she didn't even know his first name. That said it all.

Bitterness layered her heart. Still. Because of her asshole brother, she had no prospects in career or love.

"Your mom's making your favorite," Dad said, lifting Tiny onto the bus as if she were a child.

"Again?" She frowned at having lasagna every two days. "I do like other things like pizza and takeout."

"She's showing you love. Appreciate it while you can."

Tiny sank onto the seat her father guided her to. Appreciate their guilt? Accept this new family dynamic when her instincts screamed to run? She wanted to yell at them to let her have some freedom. After all, she'd enjoyed her independence during her studies. Living with her parents wasn't the future she'd envisioned. And having a blind daughter not practicing medicine wasn't the brag they'd dreamed of either.

Without a word, she let the autobus's hum lull her into a daze. The air conditioner cooled the sweat dewing on her skin. How far away was far enough? Another city? A space station or ship? Her heart skipped a beat. *Yes.* If only she could find work somewhere else... Maybe then her parents would let her live a life without their interference.

They disembarked, rode the elevator to the fifteenth floor, then headed along the long passage to their apartment. As she did this, she counted the steps while wishing she didn't automatically do that. With her fingertips on the paneling, her touch guided her past the neighbors. Heat slapped her face when she strolled into their home, Mom having not lowered the air conditioner to accommodate for the oven. Sweet vanilla hung in the air like an aftertaste, which meant chocolate chip cookies and ice cream for dessert.

"Hopping into the sol-bath, Mom," she called and veered into her room.

She closed the door and sank against it. Minutes later, she stood on the plate and let the beam warm her body as it cleaned her. Her arm beeped. She tapped her palm, pressed it to her ear, and listened to the robotic voice vibrating along the bones in her hands.

"Application accepted. Position awarded to Tinika Bryant."

She froze. *What position?* "Details please," she asked, wiping shampoo off her temple.

"Masseuse at Celestial. Expected start is 8 AM in two days."

She squealed, dancing on the spot. *Shit.* Reality settled upon her like ice water sliding down her back, and she leaned against the wall. She didn't even know how much the position paid or what the perks were. Nor did she have a clue as to how her parents would deal with this news, but that would be their problem.

"Inform the employer of my disability."

"They are aware," the voice responded.

"What are the benefits, the salary?" She waited.

"Seven thousand tokens and a room."

She almost sobbed. Half her current salary for the distance? Could she survive on so little? At least, she didn't need to worry about rent.

"Confirm acceptance of offer," she said into her palm.

"Acceptance confirmed." The robotic voice tingled and was a little distant since she hadn't held her hand to her ear for clarity.

She wrapped a towel around her head and threw on her pajamas. Then with a forced smile, she left her bedroom to announce the 'good' news.

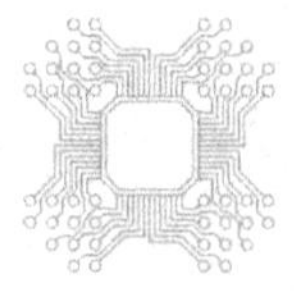

Months Later.
Lunar Base
The Celestial Spa

"I'm sorry, Tiny, but my hands are tied. He paid upfront, and with Elise falling ill, you're my last hope." Madame Madelin cupped Tiny's hand.

The implants in her fingertips told her more, flickering information across a neural pathway.

"Drink more water, Maddy," she said, sensing dehydration through the pliancy of her skin. "Now why are you worried? Who's the client? Is he a troublemaker?"

"He can be a little exuberant. I'll have Mother on guard, just in case."

Tiny grimaced. An antique AI bot dominating the unused corner didn't create a calm atmosphere for her clients. But for Maddy to offer, that told Tiny what to expect.

"Have Mother stand outside the door. I'll scream if I need its help." She squared her shoulders then tidied the towel draped over the bed's headrest. Everything around her was a white blur, but she prepped the room after every session and did it by rote now. As long as no one moved anything, she was fine.

"Thanks, Tiny. I owe you one." Maddy left, her delicate tread recognizable. 'Mr. Emerson, please, this way."

"About damn time." A man huffed when he entered, his feet thumping like his balls were too big and he had to compensate with wild leg swings.

His smell hit Tiny first: a mixture of sweat, overcooked onions, and lack of hygiene.

Her fingers twitched in protest. She pasted on a smile and gestured to the bed. "Make yourself comfortable, Mr. Emerson," she said.

"What—?" He growled. "You gave me a blind girl?"

Maddy cleared her throat. "Tiny's one of our best masseuses. I can, of course, refund your payment, if you prefer."

"As long as she's good, I'm willing to forgive and forget." He popped something that sounded like a boot strap or his pant fastenings. The stench of unwashed feet almost made Tiny gag.

"Well, enjoy," Maddy said and beat a hasty retreat.

Tiny gazed at the door, wishing she, too, could leave. Instead, she tried to breathe through her mouth while she waited for her client to strip and sprawl over the bed.

"Been a tough day?" she asked from the list of boring questions she kept on hand.

"You have no idea," he muttered, his voice garbled with his face pressed into the bed.

Covering her implants spared her from diagnosing any ailments he might suffer with. She scooped up gloves and slid them on while standing near his feet, then with two pumps from the oil dispenser, she set to work, massaging every inch of his body. Classical music filled the room, almost masking his heavy breathing.

"You *are* good," he mumbled.

She didn't let his compliment go to her head. With the number of clients she saw daily, their opinions didn't matter. This was a job, nothing more. Not what she wanted to do, that's for damn sure, but it was far better than working at C.C.A. Massage, dance, sleep, and repeat, just so she could eat. No way would she meet a man, settle down, and have a kid. Chances of that were zero. Not on her schedule.

Dad called often, begging her to come home. "A woman of thirty should be married and giving us grandbabies."

She always responded with, "No man wants a blind wife." Though it shut Dad up, his silence lasted about a month before he'd call for the same reason.

A squeak escaped her when she realized Mr. Emerson was no longer on the bed. She angled her head to listen, then focused on his panting no more than a meter to her left. Which put him between her and the door.

"Sir," she said, keeping her voice calm. "Are you dissatisfied with my service?"

Lord, she prayed he was so he would leave. Her stomach grumbled, blaming her for skipping lunch. She'd have to grab a meal before changing for her shift at the bar downstairs.

"I consider you a boon," he said, his stench closer.

She frowned. *Like a lucky charm?* "Please return to the bed so I may finish." She patted the foot end for good measure.

"I offer you a little something extra for, well, a little something extra." He chuckled. "If you're interested, that is."

She blinked at him, unsure she understood him correctly. And if he meant what she thought he did, that was all manner of 'ew.' Instead of revealing her revulsion, she went with fake ignorance. "I'm sorry. It's been a long day. If you wish to extend the package you purchased, it will mean another session. Only thirty minutes has been allotted to you for today."

She didn't expect the hand on her throat. Nor could she prevent being thrown onto the floor, hard enough to wind her. Every inch of her pinged in complaint. Had she wanted to call for Mother, she wouldn't have been able to, gasping for air like she did. All this was made worse when Mr. Emerson layered his sweaty, stench-riddled body over her, pinning her in place.

"Do you like it rough, Tiny?" he rasped in her ear, sending a shiver of disgust into the pit of her stomach.

Bile rose, but she could do nothing but squirm and kick. Her face flushed hot. A sure sign she was losing consciousness. If only his hand would ease long enough for her to draw in a breath.

A tear slipped free. This was how she would die. So fitting for the disappointment she'd turned out to be. He shifted, taking away one hand.

Blessed air, despite his smell and fetid breath, was still sweet. But the 'zip' of her uniform parting had her screaming as sheer panic fueled her limp muscles. When his hot touch squeezed a breast, she slapped at it, at him, anywhere she could reach.

The door opened.

Mr. Emerson was yanked off her and slammed against something.

She didn't care, choosing to sit up and suck in air as she clutched her uniform shut. A sob escaped her. When a heavy tread approached, she scrambled backward with her free hand extended in front of her.

"Are you okay?" a man asked, his tone gentle. And he smelled of soap, grease, metal...and hay? Not a bad combination.

"I am," she said, stroking her neck in search of bruises then wincing when she prodded them.

"Ah," the man said. Before she could react, he hoisted her to her feet, resting a hand on her hip to steady her. "He saw someone helpless," he growled.

"I am," she gritted out, dipping her unseeing gaze. "Thank you, though."

He caught her chin and tilted her head up. "I'd suggest you have your employer install cams in here to make sure you're never vulnerable."

She scoffed. "I'll do that. I'm saving to buy my own AI, y'know."

"Good." His voice softened as if he smiled.

"Oh, Tiny, I'm so sorry," Maddy said, coming in with a flurry of her skirts. "He's been permanently removed from our clientele. And I've reported him to station security."

"This gentleman saved me." Tiny gestured to where her rescuer's darker form consumed the white of the consultation room.

"Well, I'm impressed, sir. Please, your session is on the house." Maddy crowded Tiny, her vanilla fragrance drawing nearer. She nudged Tiny's hands aside and zipped her uniform shut. "Leave early. Take a nice, long sol-bath. I'll cover the extra power rations."

As grateful as Tiny was, she wanted to chat to her hero more. Under the task of removing her gloves, she sniffed. She didn't smell him, nor had she caught fading footsteps.

"You ready?" Maddy asked but didn't wait for Tiny to respond.

She gripped Tiny's elbow and ushered her down the passage to the staff elevator pod. After selecting the floor, she waited for Tiny to step inside, then walked off, her dainty tread marking her progress.

Tiny slumped against the back wall of the pod while it shot up, heading to the staff cabins. Alone at last, she wrapped her arms around her body for a self-hug. Her hero's suggestion held merit even though being attacked wasn't a common occurrence. When the pod dinged and the doors opened, she tapped the floor in front of her, just to make sure there wasn't a gap or ledge to trip her. The last time that had happened, she'd nursed a bruised shin for a week. Twenty-two paces brought her to her home, the door on the left. Her thumb on the handle unlocked it.

Two meters by seven was the extent of her privacy in the dismal lower levels of Lunar Base. She'd wanted to escape and had hoped space was the answer or the chance for other opportunities. She hadn't made it farther than the moon and wouldn't with the little she earned.

Dismissing her depressed thoughts, she splayed her fingers on the kitchen's one-meter-long counter housing a reheater with a wall-mounted boiler above it. Prepping chicken-flavored noodles wouldn't take her long. Next to the counter was the sol-bath and a slide-out toilet. On the opposite wall was a flip-down table and chair, a dry-cleaning drawer referred to as a wash-box, and hidden closets. At the very end was her bed, spanning the width of the cabin. By the flickering lights, she had to assume she had a view—wasted on a blind woman.

She slumped. That smacked of bitterness. Which she'd been working on since her parents checked Jamie into some fancy rehabilitation clinic.

She stared at the view, trying to imagine what she'd see if she could...see. All while scooping noodles into her mouth. As meals went, she'd had better dorm food. But beggars couldn't be choosy.

Who was her rescuer? She wished he'd given her his name. He was right to suggest installing sec cams. Though, she couldn't see Celestial willingly spending that much. She couldn't expect them to either.

After disposing of the container, she activated the sol-bath, rubbing her stuffed stomach. A nap maybe, then she'd dress and head downstairs to the club. She stripped out of her uniform and tossed it into the wash-box. By tomorrow morning, it would be clean and ready for her.

She swallowed, stroked her neck, then grimaced. As a blind person in a new environment, the sting of bruises was far too familiar. Other than that, she was lucky to be alive. While she sat on the sol-bath plate, she let it spin her. The scent of heat lingered but not that of sunbaked rock, nor the hint of lavender for those wealthy enough to purchase the better-quality sol-baths. She pondered the state of her life. This was it. She raised her arms so the ray could reach her pits. Her hair tickled her chin, somehow disturbed when the air flow was minimal. Gone were the days when a dye job faded. Hers was purple to match her stage persona. She didn't care what color it was when she wouldn't see it anyway. Whether it suited her face or not didn't matter either.

After her near-death experience, sleep would be elusive, so perhaps, arriving at the club earlier meant she could leave when her six hours were up. Besides, if she stayed, the last hour would settle in her mind and deepen her depression. There was no one she could talk to about it. Dad would use it as the reason she should come home—that she couldn't survive on her own, especially in space.

So, to work she'd go. Wiggling into her skintight jumpsuit took more energy than she possessed. Minutes later, with her hair gelled flat and slippers on her feet, she took the pod to the basement. The thump of a deep, resonating beat reached her. In went her ear plugs to lessen the impact of high decibels on her hearing. The bass traveled up through her feet, forcing her heartbeat to align.

"You're early," Cindy yelled, looping an arm through Tiny's to usher her to the dance cage.

"Been one of those days, babe," she said, plastering on a smile. "How's the clientele?"

Cindy snorted. "The same." She yanked on the lever to lower the cage, then helped Tiny step inside.

She was told purple lights strobed around her when she danced. It had to look good, or she would've lost this job. Informing Axel, her other boss, that she was blind had made no impact.

He'd almost sounded bored when he said, "Dancing doesn't need sight, only rhythm."

"Is my weight an issue?" she'd asked. By the rolls around her middle, she could only think she'd been stress eating. Food didn't judge.

"No," was his response.

She stood in a cage, only being lowered every hour for five minutes to rehydrate or for a pee break. Some waitresses asked her if she lost her mind up there. No, not when she wore no label. She doubted any observer would realize she was blind. None of that mattered.

Time flew by, measured in increments of pee breaks. Many songs were her favorites, reminding her of days long gone. Down she went, was ushered to the bathroom then handed a bottle of water. Here, she didn't need to count her steps. With the milling crowds, the landscape was forever altering. Axel hadn't instructed his staff to help her, but a few had taken it upon themselves to do just that. Depending on the shifts, she could count on Cindy or Liza or whichever bouncer was nearest.

With one more hour to go, Tiny sipped her water, gazing into the club at random. She had no idea how large it was, where the music came from, where the bar was, or what was below her cage. In the shifting darkness, she had to use her imagination.

Someone bumped her from behind, spilling water down the front of her jumpsuit. As welcome as the cool liquid was against her sweaty cleavage, she still hissed.

"Oh, so sorry, sweetheart," a man drawled.

Her skin itched when he gripped her hip and tugged her against him.

"Unhand me, sir," she snapped, shoving at his chest.

He didn't smell bad except for the staleness of alcohol... His beer breath fanned her face, roiling her stomach.

Instead of releasing her, he pulled her closer. "Pretty little thing like you..." When he nuzzled her throat, her bruises stung.

She whimpered while squirming, trying to wriggle free.

"Hey," Cindy said, grabbed Tiny's arm, and yanked. "Let her go."

"Go away. Lady Purple and I are just getting acquainted."

Cindy huffed, the mint-scented puff of her frustration blowing across Tiny's cheek.

Tiny stomped on the man's boot, but her slippered feet had no effect. Parts of her that hadn't been touched since med school pinged at his abuse. The urge to vomit gripped her, but she swallowed, shut her eyes, and prayed for help.

When cool air bathed her chest, the man's hands no longer touching her, she almost sobbed. *Miracles do happen*, she wanted to scream. *And twice on the same day*. A fist connecting with the man's jaw followed. She staggered back, away from the scrambling of feet on a sticky floor. When she bumped into a wall, she stilled, not sure where she was. She hadn't been this lost in a long while. Fear coiled in her belly, and she squatted, curling into a ball.

When someone seized her under her arms, she cried out and swatted at the hands.

"Getting yourself into trouble again, cupcake,' her hero said, the gentle humor in his voice welcome. "Maybe another job would be safer."

She faced the direction of his voice, on the verge of gushing her gratitude. His words sank in, and she glared, instead. Another job? Was he kidding? Did he have any idea how hard it was to find work as someone 'helpless?'

"Well, if you know of anyone hiring blind doctors, call me." Her tone dripped venom and ingratitude.

There was no helping that. Exhaustion had stretched her energy reserves thin. Her neck throbbed, her throat was scratchy when she swallowed, and her willingness to face whatever life threw at her with as much dignity as she could? Farg, that had evaporated along with her patience.

"I see," he said then laughed. "No joke intended. I may know of an ice hauler in need of a medic. You interested?"

She gaped, then snapped her mouth shut. Squaring her shoulders, she raised her chin as if to meet his gaze. "I might be."

"We don't need medical treatment that often, but it would be handy having you onboard." He caught her fingers and pulled her forward. "Name's Dieter, Finish your shift while I make a call. I'm gonna see what Captain has to say."

She smiled. "For real?"

With a grip on her hip, he sent her inside the cage. "Would I lie to a blind woman?"

She didn't get to answer when the cage cranked upward. Oh, Lord, she hoped he was sincere. Quitting would break Maddy's heart. The woman had been nothing but kind to Tiny but leaving would save Celestial a security upgrade.

She danced by rote as excitement pinged through her. She was giddy, unable to draw deep enough breaths while she considered the possibility of being a doctor. It had been her dream for so long, and if she could find her place in the universe, perhaps her life could return to normal.

She'd never be the Tinika she'd been pre-blindness, but she might recover her lost *joie de vivre*. Her heartbeat scattered when the cage lowered. This was it.

Tonight, she might be packing.

Or sobbing.

Would her hero save her for the third time?

CHAPTER SIX

Three Solar Cycles Later
The Senate
Planet of Ivoy

NENN PEERED OFF THE platform surrounding the med-tech spire. With his chores and studies attended to, he had time for what he loved to do. Far below the Amikar Cliffs were endless waterfalls and rivers, all enshrouded in gray-lilac mists. Only on rare days, when the rain didn't threaten to fall, was the beauty revealed. No matter how many times he tried, a pressing task always ended his descent too soon. He had yet to reach the bottom. A sensation in his bones said that was about to change.

He sat with his feet off the side. Chuckling at what the next hour held for him, he flipped around and caught the lip with his fingers, dangling with his arms bearing his full weight. Down he shimmied, from toe-hold to finger-hold. He zigzagged, crimping ridges, scars, grooves, and mini platforms as a way to descend. The wind whipped at his hair and cooled the sweat on his brow and bare torso. The lilac sunlight offered warmth between the breezes.

At ease, his symbiotes thrummed, but his armor remained hidden. As a maed, though his symbiotes had been manipulated to form Ivoyan armor across his skin, he hadn't gotten to use it for protection. In moments of extreme emotion, they appeared without thought. While he inched down the cliff, he practiced masking and unmasking, training his symbiotes to rise to the surface and harden.

The Qaldreth way was to dismiss the armor when in the company of other warriors. His inability to do that was a sign he hid something from his 'brothers.' Suspicion could lead to him returning home with shame upon his shoulders.

A zalziki swooped and flapped around him, squawking in dismay. Its elongated snout, the beady eyes, and meters-wide wingspan made it intimidating when it dove for him. A glance to the left confirmed he was too near its nest.

He chuckled. "My apologies, my flying friend. Let me move away…"

Under the bird's vigilance, he crossed to the right in a diagonal decline. A cooling mist tickled his bare feet. The familiar tumble of waterfalls thundered in his ears. He'd yet to reach the bottom. Moisture glistened on the moss-covered rock, making his holds slippery. Today, he persevered, choosing his path with care. Sure, a river may be beneath him should he fall, but who knew what beasts lurked in its depths? Nor did he know how to swim.

He hoped an island or beach offered safety and a chance to see what the mists obscured.

"Nenn," Caah snapped via the nodule embedded in Nenn's neck.

He groaned. *No, this is not happening.* He shoved his hand into a crevice, formed a fist, and hung there. "What, Caah?"

"Where in hell are you?" His voice crackled, implying the distance was too great for clear communication.

Nenn huffed. "Where do you think?"

"I knew it," Caah cried out. "Give me…a minute."

A muted whir reached Nenn's ears moments before bright lights blinded him. He shielded his eyes and peered over his shoulder at the velorx hovering too close for comfort.

"There had better be a valid reason for your intrusion," he said, glared at Caah, then glanced down in search of his next hold.

"You've been tasked to attend to an arrak with a faulty nodule."

"Not another maed available?" Nenn locked his arms in place to rest his temple on the warm rock.

"Would I be here if there were?" Caah had the right of it. It had to be serious to send an arrak to track down a maed.

With a grunt, Nenn gestured for him to fly closer. When the male brought the velorx's ass in line with Nenn, he pushed off the cliff wall and landed across the seat. The hover dipped under their combined weight, then leveled, its engine whining.

"A warning would be appreciated," Caah said, his white hair ruffling.

"Then why did you draw near?" Nenn asked when he'd pulled himself up until he could sit behind Caah. "Which arrak?

"Meorri aac Drafe," Caah said, shooting the velorx upward, skimming past holds Nenn knew too well. "He is at the Senate."

"I understand the urgency," Nenn said. "Assisting such a warrior cannot be delayed."

Caah hovered the velorx where Nenn had dangled his feet off the edge a while ago.

He leaped off to land on the platform. "Thank you, Caah. I will take it from here."

He strode into the med-tech spire, past the emergency wards to the barracks beyond. Inside his three-by-five room, he yanked on boots and red pants then summoned his armor. It shimmered across his obsidian skin in a pattern like a vibuy's.

He stopped at the first ward to collect a med-dev and a temporary nodule, just in case. With both pocketed, he tapped his heels to activate the power boots then launched himself off the ledge. For a male from Erasril, flying was reserved for the Zuphayr tribe.

"How much longer, Nenn?" Meorri aac Drafe demanded.

"Why? You have a female awaiting your return?" Nenn chuckled, veering to the right for the ornate platform high above Ivoy's natural wonders below.

Drafe snorted. "A female on Ivoy? Sure."

"Ivoyans are androgynous, so finding a compatible female *is* possible." Nenn deactivated his power boots as he landed on the platform, his focus on the pacing Qaldreth guardian.

Drafe Arrak was the most promising Qaldreth warrior or so Nenn had heard. Having dealt with the male before, he could only agree. He comported himself as Nenn imagined Panior would.

The warrior's grunt reverberated through Nenn's mind. The nodule buried in his neck had a limited range. This close, he caught the frustration and impatience in Drafe's voice.

He met Nenn's gaze and strode toward him. "I am attempting to banter with you. Try it before you reject the skill."

Ahh. Now he understood. Despite knowing much about Drafe, they hadn't spent time together to build a casual rapport. "Would this be from your xenology studies I have heard rumors of?"

Drafe didn't answer, just angled his head to grant Nenn easier access to his ear. His bald head was a Qaldreth feature with his black hair streaking from his temple to disappear into his gray, armored bodysuit. All males shaved their heads but allowed a strip to grow from the brow to the base of his spine. His yellow eyes also confirmed his home as being the deserts of Qaldreth—the Meorri part of his name.

Nenn raised his arm to scan Drafe's ear. "Is your ot inside?" he asked, soft beeps and flashes marking his progress. The med-dev was far superior to russmar. He planned to take it with him when he returned to Erasril.

The med-dev pinged, green pulsing for a second. Not a good sign.

Drafe stiffened. "Diagnosis?"

"Replacement," Nenn said, lowering his arm.

"Here?" Drafe's wide eyes revealed his hope.

Nenn frowned. The new nodule would need the old one surgically removed. "No, you will have to come with me."

"Curse it, Nenn. I cannot leave, not with my ot unguarded," Drafe snapped.

Nenn swallowed the urge to mutter how childish Drafe reacted for an arrak—his rank of protector or guardian. Instead, he clipped a temp-device over the old nodule. "See me when you can," he said. "I will have the implant waiting at med-tech."

"My thanks." Drafe strode off, his focus on the doors to the Senate.

Nenn shrugged, having learned not to take arrak behavior to heart. They bore much pressure guarding the ots—the highest-ranking Ivoyans. Ots were the judges or generals, the revered councilmen, those positions determined at birth and based on IQ. Then came the zi, who traveled to expand Ivoy's knowledge of the universe. A lo taught, sharing the information held in the archives. Last were the uz, the servant class. Any baby with a lower intelligence than that wasn't allowed to survive.

He curled his lip in disgust. Not the Qaldreth way but changing centuries of tradition and culture would be impossible for a maed. He kept his head down and healed where he could.

"Med-tech, confirm temp-device installed on Meorri aac Drafe Arrak. Reminder to be sent to the male should he not schedule a full replacement."

"Acknowledged, Giniiri aac Nenn Maed."

Nenn huffed. *Task done.*

A boom jerked him to a halt. He hovered, gawking at the burning Senate platform tumbling to the city below. He charged forward, not sure what he could do. When he neared, he spotted Drafe diving over the side, chasing a falling Ivoyan—his blue uniform that of a servant.

A glance at the Senate confirmed it was beyond salvation; debris dripped down like globules of lava. Already, salvage ships caught chunks of metal and stone before it hit the forests and rivers below. Nenn's mind reeled. How had this happened? Who would dare? He didn't know of any enemies. Nor could he fathom how'd they'd breach the shield around the planet of Ivoy.

Many Qaldreths blasted in, answering Drafe's calls for aid.

They surrounded him when he landed on a sec-ship, the uz in hand. Questions bombarded Nenn through the nodules, louder when he, too, approached the crowd. Another med-tech or maed attended to Drafe, so Nenn sought the uz vomiting over the holographic guardrail.

"Do you require healing?" he asked the Ivoyan.

He straightened, his black eyes wide, but the tint of orange on his cheeks had faded to a peach. "I am well, Maed," he said. "If not a little shaken." He glanced at the gathered Qaldreth. "Though why the protector saved me, I cannot say."

Nenn activated his wrist and scanned the uz anyway. Drafe must have rescued him for a reason. And Nenn had no doubts the Q.C.C. would want to question them both.

One by one, the Qaldreth commanders or udaps landed, barging through those gathered around Drafe. Too many voices bombarded Nenn, so he switched off his nodule, unable to bear the onslaught. Only when a sava or security officer collected the uz did he glance at the platform.

The crowd of warriors dwindled.

"We are to convene in the council chambers," someone said when he reactivated his nodule.

He grimaced, expecting the next hour or so to be most unpleasant. The Qaldreths flying toward the chamber looked like a swarm of tiaez, their feet ablaze. He landed on the platform and strode into the dark passage where images depicting tribes and their homes were carved into the stone walls. Qaldreths of every color filed onto the staggered steps, all gazing at the curved dais where seven udaps sat. Under the circumstances, scowls marred every face in attendance.

Nenn unmasked from the waist up, baring his skin. Bright beams poured from the yellow, stained-glass lights up high, mimicking the suns on Qaldreth. All yearned for real sunlight and warmth—no one more than a Giniiri. Nenn's symbiotes reacted with eagerness as if he would return home soon.

"Meorri aac Drafe Arrak, you have been brought before the council in the direst of circumstances." Meorri aac Kish Udap paused, his face contorting in disgust. "By the grace of Ivoy and Osnir, you were welcomed as a karu, to train under those who *earned* their place to be protectors." Kish Udap scanned the room, his lips curling further.

Nenn could only imagine what ran through the udaps' minds. The planet was in chaos, losing a significant number of Ivoyan ots. With so many dead, the zi would be called to duty from their travels. As far as Nenn knew, all the ruling ots had been in the senate. With the younger ots still in training, the zis would have to rule.

And the Qaldreths would be blamed for having failed to foresee this.

Nenn studied Drafe who stood tall. Exile would be known to all generations of symbiotes. His family would never live down the shame.

"Worse, instead of rushing to save *the* Luharp Vadril Ot or any high-ranking ot, you rescued Vizen Aehort Uz...a servant." Grumbles rippled through the council and the witnesses behind him. "What say you, Drafe Arrak?"

Drafe opened his mouth to speak.

"Giniiri aac Nenn Maed claims your language implant failed, explaining your presence outside the Senate." Borven aac Eran Udap gestured to Nenn to come forward.

Nenn jerked back, then hurried over the steps, not wanting the council to think he delayed out of doubt.

Drafe bowed his head to acknowledge Nenn.

Nenn stood beside him and met the udaps' gazes. He raised his chin so his voice would be clear. "It is defective, Great Council. I attached a temp-device until his can be replaced."

"Happenstance led you to abandon your ot?" Zuphayr aac Srim Udap hummed, his white hair draping over his temple. With the air tribe's crisp blue eyes so reminiscent of Qaldreth's sky, he peered at Drafe.

Nenn kept his shoulders stiff even though their focus wasn't on him. Slumping would draw attention and raise suspicion.

"I rescued the only witness, Great Council, and yes, my implant did malfunction, causing Luharp Vadril Ot to suffer alongside me. Unable to bear the shared pain, he instructed me to seek medical attention." Drafe inhaled, his nostrils flaring. "I ensured he was well-guarded, tasking Meorri aac Saha Karu to protect him. Under the circumstances, twenty-two arraks, twenty-three karu, and a dozen sava were sufficient protection against a corpse."

The council nodded.

"You are wise to mention the protectors, the trainees, and the additional security, Drafe Arrak. Had I been in your situation, I would have acted the same," Kish Udap said.

Nenn smothered a wince. Any udap complimenting a warrior was not to be trusted. Not that it smacked of evil intent, but praise was rarely given.

"This was an attack none of us foresaw." Srim Udap scanned the chamber, his gaze lingering for a moment on Nenn. "An illogical strategy is required. You will share your symbiotes with the uz, Drafe Arrak."

Gasps rippled across the room. Kish Udap slapped the stone desk, and silence prevailed.

Nenn peered at Drafe out of the corner of his eye. The male didn't react, as expected, despite this shocking news. To share his symbiotes with an Ivoyan was only done when a warrior graduated to protector. The higher the Ivoyan's rank, the more honor the warrior would bring to his tribe. Like Drafe had with Luharp Vadril Ot, Ivoy's revered ruler. An uz would bring no honor. And until that uz died, Drafe wouldn't be able to protect another Ivoyan.

"The acting Ivoyan leadership has demanded justice be served. You and your uz will travel the galaxy and hunt down the culprits." Kish Udap pinched his brow. "All findings will be reported to me."

Drafe straightened. "As you command, Kish Udap."

"You leave when the symbiote transfer is complete, your implant replaced, and a ship fueled." Eran Udap swept out his hand. "Choose your crew. Additional security will be provided."

"Do not take this mission as leniency on our part." Kish Udap nodded at his council members. "Fail this, and dishonor and exile won't be the worst of your punishment."

Nenn had expected exile, so if this wasn't that, then what was this mission? A chance for Drafe to regain favor or die trying?

Drafe frowned. "I thank you for this opportunity, Great Council." Offering his back to the Q.C.C., he addressed the chamber. "One from each tribe would suffice. Riermus aac Vaen, Zuphayr aac Gusin, Jeerlud aac Juunn, Borven aac Igar, Giniiri aac Nenn, and Awayar aac Caah."

Nenn froze and sucked in a sharp breath, even as his hearing dampened. To be chosen was an honor and a death sentence. Those who jogged to the dais scowled. No doubt, they, too, felt as Nenn did.

"So noted." Srim Udap banged his fist on the desk.

The Q.C.C. followed, announcing the end of the council.

Nenn studied the warriors around him—a few he knew.

"You are a lucky male," Vaen snapped. "Not that I thank you for dragging me along."

"Same." Juunn's green eyes flashed. His brown hair ruffled, revealing his displeasure.

"Is this punishment for making you wait for the temp-device?" Nenn rocked on his heels, a smile teasing his lips.

If anyone could make a success of this mission, it had to be Drafe. And, according to his studies, an uz wasn't as stupid as most of the Qaldreth thought. They just weren't savants like the ots.

Drafe chuckled. "You were there, Nenn. I assumed you would want to see justice done."

"As Osnir is my witness, Drafe, the killers will pay. To stand aside, let you go off on this mission alone, my children's children will forever curse my name." Nenn grasped Drafe's forearm.

"You believe we can find them?" Vaen arched a golden brow, glowing against his dark gray skin.

"I do." Drafe clenched his jaw—an indication of his determination. He met Nenn's gaze. "Besides, you are the only maed I know."

Nenn chuckled. "Fair enough."

"Yet again, you escape justice." Ulvus shoved through the males to glare at Drafe.

Nenn jerked back. The venom in this sava's voice was alarming. He resisted the urge to come between the male and Drafe. An arrak could defend himself.

Vaen did though, offering Drafe a shoulder while he tried to usher the angry male away. "Ulvus, now is not—"

"You should not have been accepted as a karu then awarded an ot. Now, this." Ulvus growled. "Kreta curse you, Drafe."

"Ah, Meorri aac Ulvus Sava, it is good that you are wishing Osnir's blessings upon this journey." Kish Udap parted the males gathered. "For you, too, shall be tasked to assist Drafe Arrak."

Ulvus's cheeks paled, but he offered a nod.

Nenn grimaced, dreading having to spend a minute in the negative male's presence.

Vaen's golden eyes dulled to brown when he glared at Ulvus's disappearing back. "Foq, I'd prefer to bring all the untrained karu than that idiot." His tone dipped, keeping his words to the gathered circle.

"Same." Drafe chuckled. "A vasquva would be a more helpful addition."

Vaen snorted then slapped Drafe on the shoulder. "Have Nenn see to your implant. I will ensure the ship is prepped." He paused, tossing a glance over his shoulder. "May Osnir bless your symbiote transfer with the uz, Drafe. Let us pray the servant survives it."

Nenn winced. Killing an uz, though only of servant class, would be frowned upon, especially after the day's events.

When he'd first arrived, he'd toured his new home as much as he was allowed to. Deep in the belly of the council spire was the transfer chamber. Venai stones cast flickering lights across the floor, showing the way. The walls were carved but without inlay to distract from the seriousness of the act—the sharing of symbiotes between Ivoyan and Qaldreth. Nenn tried not to focus on the fact that he would never have such an honor. Maeds served a different purpose.

Inside the chamber were two S-shaped stone tables, one for the Ivoyan, the other for the Qaldreth. A Jakar, or priest, with black markings on his temple, would oversee the procedure. He'd wound each male whose arms would be extended, almost touching. Two streams of blood, the Qaldreth's clear, the Ivoyan's blue, would travel toward each other and merge into the other's veins. Some mentioned how painful the process was; hence, Vaen's hope the uz survived. If the transfer didn't take, that wouldn't bode well for the mission.

The Jakar would wrap a strip of garak leather around their wrists, binding them together. A chant would follow, low, droning on, vibrating through the stone. Almost like Tugo singing at the base of their cavern.

If successful, the bond aligned their thoughts and memories and would remain until one of them died. In silence, Nenn led the way along the wide, story-filled passages of the Q.C.C. and passed the steps to the chamber. Weak lilac sunlight filtered through the stained windows. Still, it caught the gold inlay in the stone walls, telling great tales of defeated monsters worthy of any legend.

He chose an empty ward and gestured to a chair.

Without a word, Drafe lowered himself.

Nenn sprayed anesthetic across the warrior's neck and waited four seconds for it to take effect.

He grinned. "I am excited to see other stars and species. There is much I can learn." He leaned closer and plied out the temp-device and its damaged counterpart, leaving a gaping hole in the muscle. With a delicate touch, he embedded a new one into the same spot. A quick scan of the med-dev healed the skin around the circular device. He dabbed to remove the blood smears, then shifted back, with the old nodule and the temp-device in his palm. "Whore."

Drafe growled and leaped to his feet.

Sensing danger, Nenn's symbiotes activated his armor. He threw out a hand. "My apologies, Drafe. That is the only word I know in Ivoyan."

Drafe relaxed and offered a tentative smile. "Then the new nodule works."

"Good. I assume the uz is awaiting your presence in the transfer chamber?" Nenn nudged his head at the door.

"I assume the same. Until we depart." Drafe strode out.

Nenn hadn't lied when he'd said he was excited. What awaited him was adventure and a chance to climb other mountains and cliffs across the universe. Despite the benefits he could imagine of this unexpected adventure, he didn't want to be in Drafe's shoes if they failed.

CHAPTER SEVEN

Year: 2218

Mula Pesada

Tiny rocked on her heels, her excitement too much to contain for her to remain still. Dieter, however, was all calmness, his presence pressing in on her from the side.

"You're a doctor?" Captain Themba asked, his voice rough over what sounded like a paperback being paged through. She had to be wrong, but no, the scrape of a page turning said it all.

"Yes, sir. I lost my eyesight about three years ago." She winced at the lingering memories and the bitterness coating them.

"Saving up for implants?" He licked something. She prayed it wasn't his fingertip to flick a page like a book wasn't worth thousands of tokens.

"No, sir." She clasped her hands in front of her. "Sure, augmentation has its pros. I'm just not comfortable having them in my skull. One of my previous jobs was in Carne Corp. The augments complaints department. Eyes... They're the most defective."

Oh, the stories she could tell: an arm just fell off, a knee bent backward for no reason, a heart stopped beating, and the usual my-fake-limb-killed-my-spouse.

Captain chuckled. "Fair enough. You get a percentage of the haul if you do your part. Nikko's your line of command. And no sex between employees. It's my ship, my rules."

She gaped then snapped her mouth shut.

"Someone as pretty as you?" Captain lowered his voice as if he shared a secret. "Don't let Dieter or Trent sweet talk you into anything. And if you're uncomfortable for whatever reason, see Nikko."

Dieter shuffled on his feet, maybe nervous about the implication.

"Will do." Bubbles of joy filled her belly, making her giddy. She couldn't remember when last she'd been this happy.

Captain flicked another page. "Welcome to the *Mula Pesada*, Tiny."

Heat flushed her cheeks, and she hurried to say, "Thank you so much, Captain."

Dieter ushered her out, waited for the door to close on the captain's cabin, then laughed. "See. What did I say?"

"You came through for me. And that's why you're my hero." She dipped her head to hide any traitorous expressions. The man didn't need to know she had a bit of a crush on him. "So, do I get to meet the crew now?"

"First. Computer, grant Tiny access as per standard employee protocol."

"Acknowledged," a feminine but robotic voice coming from the ceiling said.

"Nice," Tiny said. "How kitted out is the med bay?"

"Oh, Captain and Nikko splurged on that. The crew's the life and blood of the ship. Blah, blah."

"Hey, I benefit." She hitched her thumb at herself. "Are we going to stand here all day or what?"

"Are you giving me shit?" Dieter asked, but his tone hinted at teasing.

"Yup," she said then giggled. "I can't thank you enough, Dieter. This is... You're so..." She pinched her lips to stop babbling.

"Tiny, sweetheart, you're doing us a favor, remember. We score big by having a full-on doctor on our crew. Come. Let me introduce you, show you around, then get you settled."

He took her hand and rested it on his forearm. Together, they strolled on what sounded like metal grates. "If you get lost, just ask Computer to guide you. I'm pretty sure you'll learn the routes soon enough."

The aroma of butter, vanilla, and sugar preceded the mess. Tiny stopped to inhale. "What is that?"

"Cake," a woman said. "Hi, I'm Leah. Welcome." A hand gripped and released Tiny's shoulder.

Tiny drew in another deep breath. "Did you say cake? Like with frosting, real flour, butter, sugar—"

"It's my birthday," a young man said from her right elbow. "I'm Grunt."

"Well, Happy Birthday," she said, tossing a smile in the direction of his voice.

"I just want the cake," another man said, his baritone clear. He made a sucking noise like he flicked something across his lips or smacked them together. "Name's Trent."

"As long as the captain gets a slice..." Another man came from behind her, his tread heavy. "I'm Nikko."

"Oh," she said, bowing her shoulders. "My boss, so to speak."

He chuckled. "In a way. Captain spends most of these trips in his cabin and leaves the day-to-day running to me."

"I'd do the same if I had paperbacks." She tightened her hand on Dieter's arm.

He jerked then led her to the side. "It's a bench. Can you slide in?"

She nodded, patted the air until cold metal met her fingertips. From there, she sat, only to bump her elbows on the edge of a table.

"Sorry. Forgot to mention that," Dieter said, joining her. He nudged her with his hip until she scooted up. "You won't fall off. The bench rests against a bulkhead."

She grinned, throwing out a hand to feel for the wall. "Good to know."

"Here we go," Leah said, the scrape of a plate across metal telling Tiny what she meant. "Tea, coffee, water?"

"Coffee?" Tiny gasped. "I haven't had any in years."

"Coming up," Nikko said, slump-stomping when he passed her—like he had a slight limp. The low whirring of beans grinding came moments before the rich aroma of coffee filled the space.

"Oh my word, that smells incredible," she said, drawing all the air she could.

Dieter caught her hand and placed a fork in it. "Eat up, Tiny."

She inched her hand across the table's surface, searching for the plate. When her knuckle knocked against it, she gripped and pulled it closer. "I'd just like to say, this is the best welcome party ever. No offense, Grunt."

"None taken," he said from opposite her, his mouth full.

With her left hand, she flickered her fingers until she encountered moist softness. There, she thrust in her fork until she hit the plate. "Too big a bite?" she whispered to Dieter.

"Nope, there's no such thing," he teased. "Just use your hand if you're struggling. Shove the cake in your mouth like a toddler."

She laughed. "My first time eating with my new crew and my table manners fly out the nearest porthole?"

"No judgment here," Grunt said. "Leah bakes the most delicious cakes, so you'll be forgiven for being a pig."

"I haven't had a bite yet," Tiny said, then put the fork down to find the cake with her hands. She brought the piece to her mouth and popped it in. A groan slipped free. She squeezed her eyes shut and savored the gooey sweetness engulfing her tastebuds in waves of ecstasy. "So good," she mumbled.

As a crew, they ate in silence, and the experience was made more enjoyable after a sip of coffee. Dieter added cream and sugar, just like Dad used to make it for her.

Tears pressed at the backs of her eyes. "I've died," she said. "Pinch me, someone."

"I'll take that as a compliment," Leah said, her voice filled with pride.

"You should," Tiny mumbled between licking her fingers.

"Well, you'll have to learn, too. No excuses. We all take turns to cook, bake, and churn butter," Nikko said.

"Really?" Tiny cried out, her thumb still in her mouth. "I get to make butter?"

Dieter nudged her thumb aside and shoved a napkin into her hand. "Usually, we have the new employees take care of the animals, but in light of your lack of sight—"

"Like a cow?" she squealed.

"Two," Grunt said between slurps.

"Oh, please, I'd love to." She bounced on the bench at the chance to look after an honest-to-goodness animal. When she was a young girl, she'd wanted a non-robotic pet, but in the city and with her parents' wages, they were never granted a license.

Dieter chuckled. "We'll see."

Sweet from her toes to behind the ears, Tiny let Dieter lead her away. She hadn't had that much sugar in ages, and her poor body didn't know how to handle it. Nausea coiled, bile rose, and she swallowed, determined not to throw up that delicious slice of cake. What a waste that would be.

"The med bay is close to the bridge." Dieter ushered her into a cold space, a chill summoning a shiver.

It had been a while since she'd worked in a sterile environment. After so many years studying, she'd become used to it. Now, in space, with climate control a constant temperature, being cold was rare.

Silence met her ears.

"Where's what?" she asked, sweeping out a hand.

"Oh, no, you can't ask me that," Dieter said. "I know nothing about these machines. I fix engines and other...stuff, not these."

"So if parts break?" She faced his general direction.

"We make a stop at the first repair port." His feet shuffled. "I'll leave you..."

"What?" she squeaked.

"Ask Computer if you need anything." His disappearing footsteps confirmed his abandonment.

"Right," she huffed. "Cake, then whatever this is." She stood still, listening, with only her breathing filling the space. With her limited sight, she caught vague shapes and not enough to reveal their purpose.

Was this what her life would be like? As shitty as working at Celestial had been, she'd gotten to interact with people. In space, with the expanse of nothing around her, she'd never been lonelier.

"Um, Computer," she said, raising her chin to address the ceiling.

"Yes, Tiny."

"Give me a breakdown of the equipment in the med bay."

"Certainly." While the computer droned on, guiding her from machine to device, the full responsibility for the crew's well-being settled on her shoulders.

"Anything medically wrong with the crew that I need to know about?"

"Trent's recovering from a fix addiction. He hasn't lapsed in four months, twelve days, seventeen hours—"

"Anyone else?"

"Leah's allergic to penicillin, and Captain has a weak heart. Grunt should be wearing his eyeglasses, but he doesn't. But in general, they all suffer from the usual degradation from anti-gravity on human physiology."

"Thank you," Tiny said and moved between the machines, running her fingers over them to familiarize herself.

Exhaustion burned her nostrils and irritated her eyes, making them gritty. She'd gone from finishing her dancing shift to packing her bags to being interviewed and eating cake on the *Mula Pesada*. Who ate cake in the small hours of the morning? Or had 'morning' been a Lunar Base construct?

"Computer, what time is it?"

"1400."

"Ah," Tiny moaned. "That makes sense. What time's my shift over?"

"You have no shift. When medical aid is needed, then you are on call."

"Shit," she whispered. Serves her right for not asking. And with a somewhat healthy crew, hours and hours of doing nothing loomed. "That means I can take a nap." She winced. "One hour on the job and I'm caught sleeping. Besides, where?"

"Your assigned cabin is in the staff quarters. Shall I lead the way?"

"Please." A beep came from her left. She followed it. "Are my things there already?"

"Yes. Dieter delivered them."

From beep to beep-beep, she strolled along the passages with her one hand touching the wall. She counted how many steps were needed until the computer told her to turn left or right. Too many changes in direction generated a low-key stress headache at the base of her skull.

She dismissed the fear knotting her stomach. Her first time heading to her cabin wouldn't be easy, and she shouldn't expect herself to grasp it right away. Besides, like Dieter said, she had Computer to guide her.

"Your cabin is to the right. Mind the step down."

She grinned. Yes, she had Computer. When her foot slipped, she shrieked, throwing out her arms in a flail. Smacking her forehead on something metallic drew a cry, with the throbbing agony summoning tears. She sniffed, splayed her fingers on the wall and banged her knuckles. Despite the sting twitching her fingers, she stroked the offending thing and realized it was a handwheel. She gripped and spun it, the whirl so satisfying that it almost distracted her from her heartbeat pulsing in her temple. With a hefty pull, the door didn't open. So she shoved, and it thunked as it swung wide.

Stale air with a hint of sweat hit her nose. She'd hazard a guess the previous occupant was a man.

"You okay?" Grunt asked from behind her.

She jerked back. "Sorry, didn't mean to—"

"Scream? Bang your head?" He chuckled. "I'd say get that checked out, but that would be pointless since you're the doctor. Your bag's at your feet."

She laughed. "My thanks. I'd have tumbled over it for sure."

"Silly of Dieter to leave it in the way."

"Full-sight folks don't think about ordinary habits being an issue." She tried to shrug, gave up on it, then prodded her temple with gentle fingers. A fresh bolt of fire lanced outward. "A bruise."

"And an egg," Grunt said, shuffling his feet like he was about to leave. "Computer, grant Tiny permanent access to Room '402.'"

"Access has been granted to Tiny and a full sterilization done. Security is also restricted to Tiny."

"Thorough as always, Computer," he teased.

"Wait, tell me, what do you do for fun?" Tiny flicked her wrist before stroking around the forming egg. "All this time on my hands..."

"I listen to audiobooks, play games, tweak Computer, that sort of thing. You need anything, let me know. I've been gathering a treasure trove of soap operas, audiobooks, music, and all legal."

"Yes to all of that." She clasped her hands at her chest and beamed in his direction.

"I'll leave you to get settled. I'm one door down which I'll keep open in case you need me."

Her heartbeat fluttered at his thoughtfulness. "Thank you."

"Grunt, tell me what you see." She didn't usually ask people to do this, but she was drained, and it was taking all her energy to stay up.

"Sure. It's a four-by-four cube with a single bed to the left, and a closet, hidden toilet and shower to your right." He caught her hand and rested it on cold metal. Narrow ridges registered on her fingertips. "Those mark each one." A swish was one of them opening or unfolding. "This's the closet with your very own blanket."

She gaped at his retreating footsteps. "Shower?" she squeaked. "As in real water?"

"Yes," he called from afar.

Farg. She didn't have soap and hadn't washed her hair in years.

And how had he known about her desperation to nap? Had he listened in on Computer's conversations when he 'tweaked' it? She shoved her bag aside with the sweep of her foot, then shut the door. Whatever Grunt did wasn't her problem, nor did she have anything to hide. Stroking the area of the wall, she found the open closet and a scratchy blanket. With that in hand, she shuffled around the small space until her knees knocked the lip of the bed.

One final pat to confirm the extent of it, and down she went.

Chapter Eight

"What do you mean we have found one?" Nenn asked, looking up from his hand of teyor cards. This was his fifth attempt to complete a round successfully. And every damn fail, it was either the blues or the greens that snagged him.

He tossed in his hand and arched a brow at Vaen, who slid onto the bench beside him with a plate of roasted kurrula. Its wings were a little undercooked to Nenn's liking. Giniiri preferred banaari or vibuy to be charred.

"Using calculations, Aehort Uz located one of those capsules that exploded the Senate." Vaen sucked on his thumb before turning the cooked bird to bite into its breast. He crunched through the tiny bones, almost making Nenn wince in empathy.

"Incredible. I assume we are tracking it?"

"It landed on an uninhabited planet." Vaen pulled a jar of water closer. "Drafe's directing Caah to power up the shuttle. He sent me to find you."

Nenn jerked back. "Me?" With a grunt, he gathered his cards, stacked them, and shoved them inside their leather sleeve.

"Yes. If there is a body inside, we will need a maed to analyze it."

"Logical," Nenn said, except he knew nothing about the species that had been in the explosive pod.

"No rush. There is still time." Vaen lowered his gaze to his plate, saying no more.

Nenn rose, intent on finding Drafe. Vaen's 'uninhabited planet' didn't say much about what awaited them. A jog took him to the bridge. Displayed on the forevids was a pretty blue planet, coated in white swirling clouds.

"We head out soon." Drafe glanced at Nenn, his lips thin.

"What is wrong?" Nenn shifted his focus between him and the planet.

"The reading of the pod is not clear. We could be descending into danger. Cliffs surround—"

Nenn gasped. "How high?"

Drafe shook his head. "Now is not the time to—"

"An hour at the most. Please, Drafe, we have not been on solid ground in weeks."

"Let him be," Aehort said from the doorway. "I fear what awaits us is disappointment."

Drafe grimaced. "Very well. We find the pod, and only then can you do your climbing."

Nenn grinned and bowed his head at Aehort in thanks. As he'd known, an uz was far smarter than most Qaldreth gave them credit.

"Wear your boots, Maed. You will need them."

"Again, thank you, Aehort Uz." Nenn stepped back to allow Aehort access to the console.

"Disappointment?" Drafe muttered.

"You shall see." Aehort left, his gait graceful as his long legs carried him from the bridge.

Drafe pressed a button on the console. "Vaen and Ulvus, head to the bay." He straightened. "Caah, travel with or remain behind?"

"With," Caah said, rising. "I shall place the *Aroagni* on auto."

"Glad to have you," Drafe said with a small smile.

Nenn hesitated. The male was under much pressure to succeed for them all. "I can skip the climb if—"

"No, Aehort is right, Nenn. An hour is not much of a delay. And if it is for your well-being, then I insist you do what brings your heart joy."

"And you are right," Caah said. "I look forward to ground beneath my feet."

Drafe strode from the bridge. Nenn followed.

"Why do I get to go?" Ulvus whined.

"I am hoping a giant snow beast swallows you whole," Drafe said by way of greeting. "Vaen, is everything prepped?"

"It is, Arrak," Vaen said, placing emphasis on Drafe's title, no doubt as a reminder to Ulvus.

Nothing any of them said changed Ulvus's bitterness. Nenn had once asked the male what the source was and received a glare for his efforts. Should any danger befall him, he doubted the sava would come to his rescue.

He smothered a smile. Perhaps Drafe spoke the truth about the snow—

Nenn swiveled on a heel to hang out the door. "Did you say snow?"

"Yes, with cliffs made of ice." Caah strode past him to settle at the console.

Nenn gaped at the male as he powered up the shuttle amid flicks of his fingers across buttons. "Ice?" Excitement formed a grin he couldn't shake. He glanced at his boots and nodded. Aehort had been right. His bare toes on the cold surface would make for a hazardous climb.

"Get in," Drafe said, snapping Nenn from his daze.

He did, then paused at finding everyone seated. The only chair available was to the right of Aehort. He took it and strapped himself in. Caah reversed the shuttle and shot off, veering and dipping toward the planet. The shields endured the breaching of the atmosphere amid flames and sparks with barely a bump registering. Blue skies then thick clouds filled the forevids. Vaen released a sigh. His soft smile hinted at longing. Nenn expected the Riermus male to miss mountains, not air.

"It is the mist-like appearance," Aehort whispered, dipping his head to Nenn's to do so.

"My thanks," Nenn said, trying not to reveal his shock. How had Aehort known what he was thinking?

"Probables," he said, jerking Nenn to the side.

"Am I that predictable?" he asked, twisting to meet Aehort's solid-black gaze.

"Yes, but do not be offended. We find comfort in the familiar."

There was wisdom in that even when the habit was harmful or dangerous like pock jumping. Not for the last time did Nenn think about Tugo and how his friend was doing. The symbiotes would flood him with knowledge the moment he stepped foot on Qaldreth. Until then, he had to remain in the dark. That alone had been hard to deal with as if he'd been severed from everything he knew and cast into silence.

Caah skimmed the shuttle along flat fields of white. In the distance, a hazy silver-blue marked mountains. The sight was breathtaking. Having seen only Erasril and Ivoy, this landscape was beyond Nenn's ability to imagine. Beauty was in the shades of white and blues, in the crevices slicing across the ice sheets, in the deep blue of the cliffs descending into the abysses. He doubted magma sat at the bottom. Only freezing water, more ice, or the depths of hell awaited the unfortunate. Still, he'd descend one of those if given the chance.

"The good news is that the...pod is at the base of a mountain," Caah called across his shoulder. "You need not go far to find something to climb, Nenn."

"You are not serious," Ulvus spat, settling his yellow gaze on Nenn.

"Sava, you will guard the shuttle," Drafe said, his tone calm.

Ulvus scowled. His eyes darkened to amber. He opened his mouth to speak, but Caah touched the shuttle down. It skidded for a bit, scraping the underbelly.

"Sorry," he said. "The heat from the re-entry caused a slick landing."

They jerked to a halt with a sickening crunch.

He slapped the console, and as the door opened, he leaped to his feet. "The air is breathable," he said, winced, then hurried out. "And cold," he called.

Nenn shivered at the blast of frigid winds swirling through the shuttle. He double-tapped the nodule in his neck to form a shield that would last for two hours. When it covered his body, heat flowed over his skin and summoned a moan. He unstrapped and trailed Aehort who glided across the snow without leaving more than his footprints behind. Drafe crunched beside them. Not even ten meters away sat a red object.

Drafe stared at it, then squatted to examine it. "It does resemble the pod in the Senate." He scanned their surroundings. "It splintered upon impact. Spread out, Vaen, Caah, Nenn; find the other pieces."

Nenn headed toward the mountain, his calls merging with the others when they located anything red. Until he found a body.

"Drafe, over here." Nenn removed his med-dev and ran it over the crumpled and stiff corpse. "The readings are as per the archives. This one is male. It appears he was dead before the pod crashed."

"How would you know that?" Vaen asked, leaning over Nenn's shoulder.

"No blood around his body. Had he died after impact, he would have bled out from his injuries." Nenn withdrew his ceremonial dagger and sliced the body's arm. "They bleed red." He parted the flesh to show anyone curious. Then with a nod, he sheathed his dagger.

"Interesting." Aehort hummed. "Once you have gathered the information, you may attempt to climb."

Nenn stilled. *Attempt?* He raised his chin to study the summit of ice towering before him. From left to right, he searched for footholds, any ridge he could crimp. A few shone through in a solid black stone he couldn't name. But to reach those, he had to get through a meter or two of icicles formed along the bottom.

Excitement charged his heartbeat. He splayed his fingers across the ice and felt nothing, no cold, no texture. With a scowl, he double-tapped his nodule, dismissing the shield. The cold seeped into him within seconds. Under his touch, the chill stung his fingertips.

"Summon your armor." Vaen asked, "Want a step up?"

Nenn did as instructed and urged his symbiotes to solidify across his skin. They kept a little of the wind at bay and still allowed him to register the textures beneath his touch. With his dagger in hand, he stabbed the ice at knee-height to form a toe-hold. Up he climbed, slower than he would've liked. Worse, what lay ahead was an overhang of icicles he couldn't see a path over. On either side were thinner, sharper spires he doubted would bear his weight.

His arms burned, and his armor flickered like his symbiotes were failing. Exhaustion shot along his back and settled at the base of his spine. He glanced down and frowned. His males and Aehort had returned to the shuttle to await him. The door was shut, too.

He'd need more than an hour, and perhaps an ax or a pick would be beneficial. Spikes on the tip of his boots would also speed this up. Failure bowed his shoulders. Yet another climb he couldn't complete.

This time because of lack of preparation.

He hung by one hand to return the dagger to his belt, then he shoved off the rock, planning on using his power boots. Aehort had said to wear them. How much did that male discern? Probables, he'd said. Didn't that mean statistics? And Nenn didn't know anyone else who climbed like he did. So what data was out there on this?

In midair, his boots remained deactivated. He shouted, flailing as he plummeted. In a panic, he slammed his heels together. One spluttered then shot him upward in an uncontrolled spiral. He spun; his vision was white-blue-snow-sky. If he didn't learn how to fly with one boot, he'd crash land beside the corpse.

Taking a deep breath, he pressed his heels together to center the propulsion. Then he threw out his arms until he stabilized. Once he had that stabilized, he tilted to the left and rolled. Again, he settled himself, praying to Osnir that his power boot would last. With a gentler tilt, he veered toward the shuttle, a dark speck on the horizon.

He was coming in too fast. If he switched off the blast too soon, he'd hit the ground hard. He swooped and dipped until he was a meter above the snow. Preparing for the worst, he tapped his heels and dropped the moment the thrust ended.

The shuttle loomed. He threw up his arms to shield his face and hit...nothing.

Drafe and Vaen caught him on either side and skidded alongside to slow his speed. He stopped an inch from the shuttle's side.

"Thank you," he said, sucking in deep gulps of air.

"Now, that was brilliant." Vaen laughed. "I have never seen anything more foolish."

"Indeed," Nenn muttered when he entered the compartment on shaky knees. "I did not anticipate—"

"We know," Caah said, tossing a grin at him.

Ulvus folded his arms across his chest and glowered. Nenn was just grateful the male hadn't said something, as well.

"Juunn will be upset he missed this," Vaen was saying.

"I filmed it," Caah said, closed the shuttle door, and powered up.

"You could have warned me," Nenn whispered to Aehort when he sank into his previous seat.

"A lesson you needed to learn."

Nenn swallowed a snort. Well, he'd learned many: how to climb ice, how to fly with one boot, and how not to try any of this with his males watching. And more than that was the importance of paying attention when Aehort spoke.

Chapter Nine

Year: 2219

Lunar Base

'GIBS SWIVELED HIS SEAT to face his…new partner. He folded his arms across his chest and activated his enhanced vision to monitor her temperature and pulse. "Who the frack are you, and who did you blow to land me as your partner?"'

Tiny gasped. "He did not say that," she muttered to herself with a pawn gripped in one hand. She ran her fingers over the squares and placed the pawn. "Pawn C7 to C6."

The marked board and pieces were a gift from Grunt. In all this time, she had yet to beat Computer.

"Knight G1 to F3," Computer intoned, sounding bored.

She patted the board, found the white piece, and moved it.

'Chapter Five,' the audiobook continued. *'Gibs's jaw still stung, and his reflection in the metallic coffee table hinted at the bruise forming. Thrusting his gray-laced black hair off his temple, he blinked at his hazel eyes and his unshaven jaw. Laugh lines implied he'd once been happy in life. He twisted his lips in derision, drawing his gaze to the bruise again.'*

Tiny applauded at Gibs getting punched for his rudeness. "Good for you, Naomi."

"Tiny, you got incoming. You won't believe this," Dieter said, his voice loud in the quiet confines of the med bay.

"Computer, pause audiobook." She set the knight down. The pieces were heavy, made of stone, and on one side, Grunt had carved 'B' or 'W' so she'd know what their colors were.

"I'll kill her, I swear," Leah cried out, stomping along the passage.

"Now, now, Leah, it's not her fault. It did look like we were picking on a weakling." Trent's heavy boots preceded Leah. "Tiny, busted fingers. The rest of us, a couple of bruises."

"Computer, x-ray, and give me the info," Tiny said, gesturing to Leah to place her hand on the sterile table.

"Distal, middle, and proximal phalanxes broken on three fingers. Hairline fractures in the metacarpus." Computer's monotone didn't calm the tension in the room.

Tiny nodded, prepped a pain injection gun, and let it rest on the table. The warmth pouring off Leah's hand told her where she'd rested it on the table. The heavy breathing from her right said from which direction. Tiny thrust her hand out to catch Leah's wrist, then with swift movements, she jabbed the gun into her forearm.

Leah hissed.

"Sorry," Tiny said, having not meant to cause further pain. "Some people hate needles."

"I'm some people," Leah said through gritted teeth.

"Let me know when you can't feel anything," Tiny said.

"Heat is spreading like warm water," Leah said.

"Good." Tiny offered her a gamine smile. "Shouldn't be too long now."

A minute later, she stroked Leah's hand from her wrist to the forefinger and grimaced. "Feel that?" she asked when the heel of her palm nudged a bone that wasn't supposed to be there.

"No," Leah said.

Tiny got to work, gently nudging the bones into place, using the sensors in her fingertips to guide her. In ancient times, surgery would've been needed. But these days, as long as the med-tool was updated, it would align the bones more neatly than a scalpel could. And to imagine, she'd studied for years to be able to use either. She splinted the index and middle finger together, then the ring finger and pinky. Once done, she ran the med-tool over the hand just to make sure. It encouraged the body to heal itself and quickly, too.

"Done," she said. "Come see me if you continue to feel pain."

"Thanks." Leah slumped off.

"Trent? Who else?" Tiny waved the med-tool.

"I got kicked in the chest. Nikko got punched. The only person not injured is Grunt."

She faced Trent. "Want me to scan you?"

"Nope. I deserved this. Little thing like that... I didn't expect her to wallop me that hard." He chuckled. "Damn impressive."

"Farg no," Nikko said from the doorway.

Tiny jerked back, having not heard him approach. "How's your face?"

"Scan away." He neared her, caught her left hand, and held it to his face.

She smiled, thankful for the consideration. Where she cupped his jaw helped her run the tool over him. "Need pain meds?"

"What I need is a shot of brandy," he snapped. "That wasn't pleasant."

"What happened?" she asked.

"Some woman thought we were bullying Webb and intervened. She had skills way beyond the norm." Trent sucked on something then rolled it along his teeth, making a clicking sound. "She did solve the problem, though, when she realized she'd messed up."

"I don't give a farg about that," Nikko growled. "She hurt Leah bad. That's not right in my book."

"Nikko, Captain wants to see you," Computer said.

The man huffed and stormed off.

"It was epic. I wish you could've seen it, Tiny. She moved with speed, her attacks were precise, and she didn't even generate a sweat like kicking three people's asses was commonplace for her." Trent bounced from side to side, excitement in his rushed words.

"Nikko and Leah are livid, though," Tiny said, packing away the med-tool.

"Yup, which means pizza and drinks tonight," Trent called when he left.

"He's not wrong," Grunt said, drawing a squeak from Tiny. "Sorry, didn't mean to startle you."

She splayed her fingers across her chest, her heartbeat thundering against her rib cage.

"She's smart, too—knew I was recording her. Had me delete it, but I kept the backup. There's something familiar about her, Tiny," Grunt said, his tone distant. "I'm going to do a little digging."

"Good," she said. "Let me know what you find out."

"Will do," he said, strolling down the passage.

Well, now that was entertaining. Tiny hoped she didn't run into that woman. She'd be a sitting duck, unable to see the strikes coming. And as pathetic as her self-defense skills were, even had her eyesight been 20/20, she'd have been in a worse state than Leah with her broken fingers. No, here on the *Mula Pesada* was the safest place for her.

"Computer, resume audiobook."

'He'd chosen the crudest words, pushing Naomi too far, but he needed to see what she was made of, to test her boundaries. Grudging admiration engulfed him in warm waves

he dismissed with desperate bitterness. There was no finding his partner attractive—he wouldn't stand for it.'

Tiny picked up the bishop and chuckled. "Oh, it's too late for you, Gibs."

He sliced a glance at Naomi. She held her back ramrod straight and had crossed her slender legs at the knees. Her pinched ruby lips announced her foul mood, and he'd caused it. One day, over a beer, he'd explain his reasoning. But he wouldn't apologize. Not when some sick frack toyed with his career, assigning a rookie to him.

He glared at her while fondling his aching jaw. She had a mean right hook.

Amid laughing, Tiny commanded Computer to pause. That was enough for today. What she needed was a hot, sweet cup of coffee and perhaps an early night curled up in bed while binge-listening to her current space-opera fave. It didn't take her long to find her room and settle in for the night.

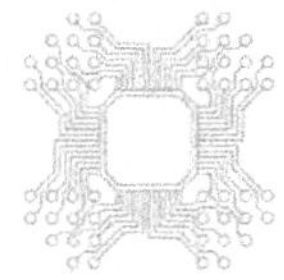

THEY SAY IT'S A luxury to awaken without alarms. Did that include pounding? Or was that her head? Tiny gripped her temple and sat up, knocking the half-eaten popcorn onto the floor. A whir preceded the house-cleaning bot, so she dared not put her feet down until the thing was done.

"Tiny." Someone banged on her door again.

"What?" she snapped.

"It's your turn to do breakfast," Trent yelled through the thick metal.

She scrambled to her knees, then froze. "Gimme five."

"Sure. I'll stall Nikko. No problem."

She winced and grabbed the clothes she'd tossed aside. Quick fumbles showed her what she'd picked up, and sniffs told her whether she could wear them one more day before they went into the wash-box. She whipped off her pajamas and shimmied into leggings and a baggy T-shirt. Though not *Mula Pesada* uniform, it would do for now. She'd change after stuffing her stomach and savored one…no, two coffees. When the bot clicked off, she bolted for the boots she left at the door. Sliding into them but not bothering to do them up, she thumped to the mess to start on the morning meal.

Scrambled eggs, toast, sauteed mushrooms, sausages were on the menu. She had the toast on and the sausages sizzling while she beat the eggs into a creamy batter with sprigs of parsley, salt and pepper, and a splash of Moo's milk.

Dieter had named the poor cow. She tried not to find his sense of humor entertaining.

"He's never going to see you as someone to date," she snapped, whipping the eggs with a little more gusto than she usually did.

Her arm throbbed then cramped. She banged the door when she shoved the bowl into the microwave and hit the first button for one minute. Every time it dinged, she stirred the eggs until they were cooked. Turning the sausages, frying the mushrooms, and toasting more slices of bread had to be done with a little more care, lest she burned herself.

"Smells so good," Grunt said when he strolled past her to the fridge.

"Thanks." She flashed him a tight smile.

She gripped the counter, drew in a deep breath, then squared her shoulders. With or without Dieter, she'd find her happily-ever-after eventually. Or at least get laid. She huffed at her silly hopes, grabbed the eggs, and slammed the microwave door.

"Whoa, someone's in a mood," Trent said, striding in. "Need any help, babe?"

At his sweet offer, she melted, letting her anger fizzle. "I didn't sleep well," she lied.

"Too many space operas. What are you listening to?" he asked, sliding along the bench when she placed the sausages onto the table.

"Space Guerillas Attack," she said, her tone casual.

"Oh, no," Grunt gasped. "That has forty-two seasons."

She beamed. "I know."

"Morning," Leah growled.

At her usual foul mood, illogical anger flooded Tiny and ripped away her good mood. If she hadn't signed a contract, she'd return to Maddy. Any female companionship, no matter how hazardous the job, was better than nothing at all.

"Is everything on the table?" Tiny asked and stepped back when the spicy-sweat smell of Nikko came too close to her.

"Looks like it. Want to sit by me?" Grunt shuffled.

She threw out a hand to stop him. "No, thanks, I'm not hungry. I'll feed the animals."

She left amid their cries of surprise, and a "We don't need milk," from Leah.

Alone time would give Tiny the space to figure out where her frustration, sadness, anger, and despair were coming from. Being a doctor in space wasn't as wonderful as she'd thought it would be. She didn't get to be useful often. Making breakfast and tending to the animals had become favorite chores, a way to contribute.

The miasma of chicken shit mixed with pigs and cows assaulted her nose. She winced, swearing she could smell colors. Throwing out a hand, she trailed the wall to the rear of the pens to the pigsty. Thankfully, Dieter was a man of habit, leaving the scraps bin in the same place. A tap of her toe confirmed its location. She grabbed and emptied it into the trough, also located with a nudge of her foot. The pigs grunted and snorted, almost in greeting. The chickens puck-pucked around her while she sprinkled their feed from a bag she'd taken off the wall.

Finding the two cows was harder since they moved around. She had only to pause and sniff to locate them. Dieter would feed them later and muck out the stalls. Both tasks were beyond her abilities. She found a cow's hindquarters and rubbed along its back to the head. It bumped her, not hard enough to knock her off her feet, though.

"Hey, sweetheart," she crooned. A skim of the collar identified which cow she'd found. "Spots, honey, how have you been?" She pressed her temple to the older cow's while rubbing her behind the ears.

When the cow stomped her feet, Tiny leaped back. "I get you. I also need some space, y'know. Where's Moo?" she called and received no response.

No surprise there. With a sigh, she stretched out her hand and walked, searching for a wall she could follow out. Maybe she could learn a new skill though her mind blanked on what. Regardless of her decision to stay or leave, she had to wait until they docked somewhere nice. She didn't want to try surviving on a destitute colony or a run-down orbiting station.

As she saw it, Maddy was her only option. Which meant dancing again.

Tiny sniffed, willing the tears not to fall. Maybe artificial eyes wouldn't be *that* bad. Bile rose to merge with the lump in her throat. If she could get over her revulsion, the next hurdle would be the cost. She doubted she had enough tokens for half an eye, let alone two fully functioning eyeballs. So on the *Mula Pesada* she had to stay because Celestial had barely paid her enough to survive.

She hurried past the laughter coming from the mess and headed to her room. A quick shower to clean away chicken shit clinging to parts of her would be the first order of the day. Hopefully, when she was ready for her coffee, the mess would be empty. She wanted no one to bother her. Today, she was determined to force herself to face the fact that she was alone in the universe, and she had to plan accordingly.

She stripped, tossed her clothes into the wash-box and activated the spray, letting its warmth run over her. Having not known about the nonexistent water rations, she hadn't thought to buy shampoo or soap, for that matter. Rinsing was all she could do until they next stopped at a station. She pulled on her uniform, stamped on her boots, and this time, buckled herself in.

'Onward and upward,' her father used to say.

He probably still did, but she hadn't recently spent enough time with him to hear it again. The mess was quiet when she snuck in, heading for the coffee machine. She pressed all the right buttons and rocked on the balls of her feet while it percolated. In went milk and too much sugar—a sheer luxury—before she trudged to her 'office.'

"Morning, Computer," she said. "Anything new to report?"

She had the computer monitor the crew in case of medical emergencies, like the captain on the cusp of a heart attack, or Dieter jerking himself off with too much force and causing a friction burn. She snorted at her unkind thoughts. It wasn't his fault he didn't find her attractive, and she shouldn't change the way she treated him based on that fact. Still, it was hard.

Becoming blind had pulverized her self-esteem. That made no sense since she was the same old Tinika, just without her vision. On sad days, she was so grateful she'd taken lovers during her studies. She'd need those memories to sustain her, even the not-so-pleasant quickies.

"Morning, Tiny. No incidents to report. Should I resume your audiobook?"

She sighed and slumped in front of her chessboard. "Please."

She scooped up a pawn and ran her thumb over its head. Thank the Lord for Grunt. If she didn't have the space operas and Gibs to live through vicariously, her life would be dismal indeed. No, she needed action. She leaped to her feet and grabbed the sterilization spray to clean her med bay again.

"Lord Fields will see you now."

He jerked back, snapping his gaze away from his partner. The receptionist wore a bronze-colored suit sharp enough to draw blood. He jumped up, running a hand over his uniform, conscious of each wrinkle. Beside him, Naomi glowed with grace and vitality with her hands shoved into her pockets in nonchalance. Where she was golden, the Renovare receptionist was somber—midnight-black hair, dark walnut skin, and coffee-colored eyes. Her beauty was striking, so he glared at her, too.

"Thank you." Naomi gestured to the woman to lead the way.

He made the same gesture to Naomi. It wasn't as if he had an attack of chivalry, having dragged his manners from antiquity. No, he needed to see her hands, anticipating another strike. Her fury festered, and if he was lucky, he'd make it home with just a tongue-lashing.'

"New crewmate for you to document," Nikko's voice penetrated the med bay. "Dieter is showing Vic the rounds. And breakfast was delicious. We missed you, though."

"Pause audiobook," Tiny grumbled and set the spray aside.

Weeks would go by without a change in her day-to-day life, then bam, she had injuries and someone to assess.

With a long exhale, she stacked out everything she'd need on the still-damp table. Time ticked by. She shuffled on her feet then huffed, sinking into the chair again.

"Resume audiobook."

"'I am Ms. Anna Zeta, and I will escort you to Lord Field's office."

"He's meeting with us personally?"

Gibs hissed at Naomi for beating him to the punch. He wrapped his fingers around her wrist and tugged with as much gentleness as a pissed-off divorced male could muster. "Let me ask the questions, rookie."

Naomi stared at his grip, then raised her gaze to meet his. "Of course, Detective Shaw." Instead of stepping back and breaking his hold, she closed the distance between them, her breasts an inch from his chest. "Synth." She nudged her head at Ms. Zeta.

Not liking Naomi's citrus scent tantalizing his nostrils, he released her wrist. Nor did he like the fall of her hair feathering across his shoulder. He shrugged off her tendrils as if they held magical powers, as if where they touched, they enchanted.'

Footsteps preceded the guest. Dieter's stomps were recognizable, but the more delicate tap-tap told her she was about to meet Vic.

"Pause," Tiny said but didn't jump up, just in case Dieter strode past the med bay for the bridge.

A waft of sunbaked scent with a feminine musk made Tiny smile. Yes, she needed someone other than Leah to chat to. As much as she tolerated the taciturn woman, talking to her for too long became tiresome. The topics up for discussion were restricted to weapons, work, or food, and Tiny was never to ask personal questions. That hadn't been a pleasant experience. Leah had avoided Tiny for days, all because she'd asked if Leah had a *nice* childhood.

"I thought Dieter would never bring you." Tiny beamed at the doorway.

"Had to see the chickens first." A woman chuckled. "But we saved the best for last."

Such sweetness lifted Tiny's hopes. "Wait outside, Deets." She rose from her chair to slide her hand along the steel table.

"I'll check on lunch," Dieter called, but he hesitated. A few moments passed before he marched down the passage.

Ah, now that was telling. Tiny forced a giggle, wishing she had such an effect on her hero. "I see you're making an impact..."

"Sorry about yesterday. I saw bullies scaring the shit out of a weakling."

Tiny froze, then checked if she gaped. Vic was *that* woman? What bullying? No, Nikko and Dieter wouldn't do that. It all had to be a misunderstanding.

"Nikko's scowl is quite intimidating, or so I'm told." Tiny pointed to the med bay gown. "Please strip and put that on."

"Nudity doesn't bother me."

Fair enough. It wasn't an issue for Tiny either. "It may appear like I'm intruding on your personal space, but I see through my hands. I apologize if they're cold."

The texture, the amount of information her fingertips gathered, the super-fine scarring said so much, not to mention, the clear delineation of muscle.

"Mm, you are in prime condition. The implants are new and well done. I've never encountered such a masterpiece of craftsmanship." Tiny grinned.

"How do you know about the implants?"

Tension thickened the air, but Tiny dismissed it, finding it hard to believe Vic would hurt her, regardless of yesterday's antics. She held up her hands. "Cybernetics respond differently to flesh. Yours are almost imperceptible, along with the barest of scars. Your new limbs must have cost a fortune."

"Yes." Though it was a one-word answer, humor laced Vic's tone.

"I've documented everything. You may dress." Tiny sprayed her hands, sterilizing them. She bit her lip, not sure what to say. Dieter's interest in Vic made sense. The woman had the body of a goddess. "Be gentle with him. He's a sweet man." Tiny winced, wishing she'd shut her mouth.

The rustle of fabric and the magnetic clips of boots snapping into place confirmed Vic was dressing. "Who?"

Tiny squeezed her eyes shut, then blurted, "Dieter."

"I'm not interested in him." Vic's smothered voice had to mean she was putting on her shirt.

Tiny released her breath in a whoosh. Thank goodness though that didn't mean Dieter would turn to her for some…companionship. Despite it being forbidden. He hadn't even tried. That smarted, too.

"Does he know?"

"Know what?" Tiny didn't look up, choosing instead to fiddle with her tools.

"That you like him?"

Tiny gasped and glanced at the door, grateful he stomped. "No," she mumbled.

"Why not?"

Tiny dropped her chin to her chest. How to explain to a woman, a new crewmate, how shitty she felt about herself and why? No, she didn't want to go down that path when all she'd hear were platitudes.

"You're beautiful as you are, Tiny. He would be a fool not to see that."

Tiny snorted, tears pressing at the backs of her useless eyes. "Right, and now that you're here—"

"Tell him I have someone."

"You do?" Tiny snapped her head up.

Vic hummed. "In a way."

Tiny inched closer to sniff. "Is that the man I smell on you?"

Vic laughed. "What does he smell like?"

"Sunlight, hot rocks, sheer masculinity?" Like real sunlight, the kind only experienced on the outskirts of the domed cities. Dad had taken her once to the sand dunes, spinning tales of seas that were now dead.

"Yes," Vic said, her voice husky. That sound alone told Tiny she spoke the truth. Whoever the man was, Vic was attached emotionally.

Tiny's twitching fingers nudged a vial. "I'll send you the results of your bloodwork."

Vic strode to the door, her faint footsteps now etched into Tiny's memory. "Mind if I visit you?"

Tiny froze, unsure she'd heard her correctly. "Sure."

"You're the only one without a hidden agenda." Vic sucked in a shuddering breath. "Here, I can be myself."

Hidden agenda? Like what? "You're welcome anytime, Vic. I'm alone for the most part." Damn if Tiny didn't sound sad.

She almost squeaked when Vic clasped her hand. "See you later?"

The door swished open, and the familiar smell of oil and grease told Tiny who stood in the doorway.

"Sure," she said then waved at Dieter. "Bye, Deets."

CHAPTER TEN

Year: 2219
Meeting the Humans
Lunar Base

THEY WERE SO CLOSE to finding out who sent that foqen pod. Nenn shuffled his feet, on guard duty with Vaen at the end of the *Aroagni's* ramp. They'd found the source of the species in the pods, going by the term 'humans.' Which was why Aehort had opted to dock on a moon orbiting a pretty, blue-white planet. Drafe and Aehort had left with the human ambassador, being diplomatic.

Nenn winced. He hated being polite when anger fueled his veins. Every pod they'd found had been in pieces or charred bits. The genders varied, and the injuries were odd, like parts of their bodies were missing.

Before him, stretching as far as he could see, were bridges traveling many levels up, higher than Erasril was tall. Thousands of humans strolled across them, riding those boxes up and down, or they zoomed around in their little yellow shuttles, servicing or refueling the docked ships. The platforms were in crisp white but grayer to black the farther they descended. A dome showed part of the moon's dull, craggy landscape and a wall of stars behind a blue planet.

After the last failure of a climb, he didn't dare ask for two hours to attempt to summit one of those towering peaks—attempting it being the issue. He gritted his teeth. One day, he'd succeed without interruption or ignorance on his part.

"Some are too pale," Vaen muttered, scanning the crowds on the various plat-forms—all buzzing with activity. "Their males look...weak."

"Not every male is a warrior, Vaen." Nenn smothered a yawn. "Compare us to their more trained males."

"I am," he snapped, gesturing to two uniformed males on guard; their gazes shifted between him and Nenn while clasping toy-like weapons to their torsos.

"What are you planning?" Nenn asked, folding his arms across his chest when he leaned against the frame of the bay door.

"How best to take them down if Drafe and Aehort do not return," Vaen said, snapping Nenn's gaze to him.

Nenn wasn't sure how to respond. Here, he dreamed of exploring the moon around him; whereas, Vaen planned war.

Nenn cleared his throat. "As superior as the canons are on the *Aroagni*, I am certain they are insufficient for the task at hand." He swept out his arm to encompass all around them. "Besides, these humans might be the victims. It is their bodies in the pods, after all."

Vaen glared at him. "Do not fight me with logic, Maed."

"Ah." Nenn chuckled. "You seek to vent." He tapped his chin. "I would introduce a biologic to kill them swiftly."

Vaen laughed. "That is brilliant."

Nenn shrugged. "I have vowed to heal first, not massacre. Just remember, if I am to do this, it must be for a noble cause."

"Same," Vaen said, staring ahead.

Nenn released a slow exhale, grateful Vaen agreed with him.

A female sprinted past them, her pale-yellow hair streaming behind her. She leaped into a male's arms then latched her face to his. Nenn's stomach knotted. He didn't know whether it was from disgust or intrigue.

"Is that how they greet each other?" Vaen whispered.

"I do not know."

Vaen shuddered. "Let us pray to Osnir that we need not do that."

The two humans walked off hand-in-hand. They gazed into each other's eyes with…affection. Nenn's heart twanged in longing. The face latching, no. Finding his love mate, yes.

Splitting the crowds with his head high above the average human was Aehort Uz. Beside him marched a scowling Ulvus.

"Where the foq is Drafe?" Vaen asked, glancing at Nenn.

"No idea," Nenn said with a shrug.

"Do you know anything?" Vaen snapped.

Nenn laughed. "That I am not an ass like you."

Vaen huffed and called out to Aehort, "Where—?"

"With a human female," Ulvus barked, revulsion curling his lip.

Vaen jerked back, his brow furrowed. "Drafe would neve—"

"Aehort Uz encouraged it," Ulvus grated out.

"I did and with reason, Ulvus Sava. Victoria Harper-Barnes will come to play a pivotal role in finding the killers." Aehort peered down his nose at Ulvus then glided into the bay. "Drafe Arrak will not be long. Nenn and Vaen, remain at your posts until he returns."

"As you command, Aehort Uz," Vaen said.

Ulvus stamped his foot and stormed inside.

"What happened to cause such bitterness in that male?" Nenn nudged Vaen. "You are closest to Drafe."

"Ulvus won the rite of Uhann by brute strength, and yet, he dishonored his tribe by stealing from Drafe then lying about it. For that, his tribe took his hand as per their laws. Drafe showed such calm and control during his defeat that the Ivoyans accepted them both."

"Ah, so the animosity runs deep."

"As it should when one hates oneself." Vaen tapped his chest. "To side with Drafe would paint Ulvus's actions in a negative light. Had the male confronted his behavior, he would not have stayed a sava. His inability to deal with his weakness adds to his self-hatred."

"And the cycle continues."

"Indeed." Vaen clasped his hands behind his back and stretched. "I first met him when he was a karu. He wore a new hand, a gift from the Ivoyans."

"Yes, they have that skill." Nenn had recognized the medical miracle of Ulvus's orange hand although he'd yet to see the procedure performed.

"Is it a perfect mirror of his other hand?" Vaen raised his hand, curled his fingers into a fist, then unfurled them.

"It is. How can you match a missing limb?"

"And yet, he is not grateful." Vaen shook his head. "I have often pondered how Ulvus's mind and sense of honor works."

"Or he has neither?" Nenn winced, not liking to talk ill of anyone even if the male was Ulvus. "My thanks for sharing, Vaen. I now understand better."

Companionable silence descended. More face latches occurred, some between male and male, or female with female.

"Is that hygienic?" Vaen asked, gesturing with a flick of his wrist.

"I doubt it is." Nenn tried not to stare. Each time it happened, that knot in his stomach tightened.

"I want off this moon station and onto the next phase," Vaen huffed.

"You wish to return to Ivoy soonest?"

"I do. We might earn honor for our tribe on this mission, but it is not guaranteed. Whereas, serving Ivoyans while they rebuild their leadership is."

Nenn succumbed and yawned. "If this is successful, you may be able to choose which ot to serve."

Vaen smiled. "Truth."

A furious Drafe stomped toward them, parting the human crowds. Never had Nenn seen the male lose his calm.

"What has you so miserable?" Vaen demanded, hurrying forward to meet him.

"I...lost something," Drafe mumbled.

"Oh?" Vaen studied him. "You have your blaster and a strange black strip around your wrist."

Lifting his hand, Drafe twisted his wrist, his eyes widening, and at last, a small smile formed.

"Ulvus is most displeased with your departure." Vaen trailed him, waited for Nenn to pass him, then smacked the button to shut the bay doors. He bolted ahead to fall into step beside Drafe. "Aehort awaits you in the command room."

"I know where it is. You need not escort me." Drafe glared at Vaen.

Nenn froze. Drafe's reaction was uncharacteristic of him. Nenn sniffed, picking up a mating and a sunbaked female. She must have been incredible or the worst though by the way Drafe reacted, like a child forbidden to pock-jump, Nenn would hazard the former applied here.

He gazed at the display vid showing the humans streaming past the *Aroagni's* ramp. Had Drafe gotten to face-latch? Nenn hummed. When the male had calmed, he'd ask.

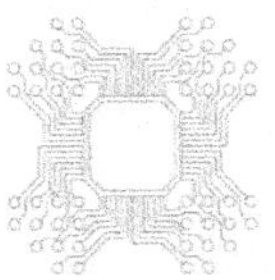

Nenn sucked on his fingertips then smacked his lips. Drafe's salty tulsig cakes were heavenly, nothing like what he'd eaten at home. The replicate could make anything Qaldreth warriors could ask for, and yet, for the most part, they stayed true to their traditions. Nenn had tried garak, kurrula, and awayar but not os-ayy. Garak was a wilder meat compared to banaari. Kurrula were small birds with bones to crunch through, and awayar had a slimy texture. Os-ayy were hard-shelled insects with too many feelers and legs and a juicy interior. He shuddered at the thought of slurping from the carapaces even if they were a pretty iridescent blue. He'd rather eat onis, the potent black moss clinging to the overhangs of volcanic rock.

To the right of his plate sat a stack of teyor cards. This was what his life had become, filling his time with games, climbing, and the occasional maed work. What he should start was some sort of contest, pitting Qaldreth against Qaldreth. As entertaining as that thought was, suggesting such an event would be selfish of him. The number of injuries would increase...all to alleviate his boredom.

He snorted and sipped from a jar of hot water.

"What has you huffing to yourself?" Juunn asked, sliding onto the bench in front of Nenn.

"I need something to do. Got anything for me?" A weight lifted off his chest at revealing what he'd been struggling with since they'd left Ivoy.

Juunn chuckled. "Was just going to ask you if you wanted to spar?"

Nenn leaped to his feet. "Yes, please."

Juunn rose, too, but he threw out his hands, palms outward. "Nothing too violent. We cannot afford to wound our only maed."

"I do not find your warning funny," Nenn said and grinned. "Where is Ulvus?"

"Sulking," Juunn said, leading the way to the activities room. "Thank Osnir. His continuous 'helpful' comments are unbearable to endure."

"The Ivoyans must have seen worth in the male to agree to train him." Nenn ignored Juunn's wide-eyed gaze.

"True, and to invest their med tech on his hand. Had I been in his shoes, I would be grateful for the opportunities offered to me."

"All the udaps know who he is, though," Nenn said. "Would they be able to name you or me?"

Juunn laughed. "Being a pain in someone's backside is not the way to bring honor to your tribe."

Nenn shrugged. "We cannot say he is not trying, no matter how controversial."

Juunn paused in front of the climbing wall, a specific feature Zuphayr aac Gusin Taed had built for Nenn. From a meter off the floor to the ceiling, pieces of metal forming hand or footholds were scattered at reachable distances. Every now and then, he shifted them, changing the difficulty. The thoughtfulness swelled Nenn's heart. That Gusin had done so without asking was more precious.

"I must admit," Juunn muttered, "to reach the top gives me a sense of accomplishment." He glanced at Nenn. "I have not been doing it as long as you have, but I have noted how it requires strength, agility, balance, and focus."

Nenn grinned. "Next time we land somewhere, I could use backup."

Juunn snorted. "After the last incident, that would be wise."

"I thought you were going to fly into space all by yourself." Caah chuckled from the wet pod, his head poking out the top. From the Awayar tribe, his skin was used to moisture. In space with the climate control, he suffered the most.

"I thought so, too." Nenn laughed. "If anyone asks, I was testing the range of the power boots."

"Indeed." Juunn nudged his chin at the wall. "Gusin's changed it, has he not?"

Nenn studied the placement of the notches and bounced on his feet. "Yes," he said, eagerness tearing through him.

"Well, go for it," Caah called.

"But..." Nenn gestured to the mounted weapons on a side wall.

"We can spar after we have mastered the new course." Juunn toed the first foothold, his booted foot struggling to find grip.

Nenn unclipped his boots and set them aside. Barefoot, he nudged Juunn back and lodged his toes in place, putting his weight on the biggest of the four. He hesitated, learning where to crimp and when to do dynamic moves. Everything fell away; only the next hold mattered. When his head bumped into the ceiling, he snapped out of it and glanced at Juunn halfway up.

Nenn released his breath, his chest swelling with pride. "You are doing well," he said, reversing his footholds. On the descent, he met Juunn, who'd scrunched his face in concentration.

When he passed, Juunn tossed out a smile. "Do not leave. I might need healing."

"Fair enough," Nenn said and dropped.

"This is foolishness," Ulvus muttered when Nenn stepped back from the wall, his gaze on Juunn.

"Is it?" He frowned, glancing at the belligerent male. "Have you tried it?"

Ulvus jerked back, his lips twisted in derision. "Of course not."

"Then you cannot comment," Nenn said with a dismissive flick of his wrist. "A male with no experience brings no value to the table." He angled his head and met Ulvus's yellow gaze. "Did your tribe not teach you this?" He tutted and settled his focus on Juunn almost near the top.

Ulvus blustered.

Nenn didn't glance at him. "Until you have experience in anything, I will ignore everything you have to say."

Rather than deal with Ulvus, he strode across the floor to lean against Caah's pod. Its smooth surface was cool to the touch.

"Tell me, Caah, is the water cold?" The mere thought of an unheated bath made Nenn shiver.

Caah chuckled. "Not as cold as I would prefer."

Water sloshed inside, then the pod's lid split in the middle. Caah dragged himself out to stand there, dripping wet and naked. Nenn paid him no attention when Juunn climbed down the wall. The blade of a sword slapped Nenn on the arm. Caah inched backward, a towel in hand. Nenn faced the male who wielded the sword.

"As a sava, I have extensive experience in weaponry." Ulvus offered Nenn the hilt. "I challenge you, maed."

Nenn laughed. "I do not have the fighting skills of a sava. I heal warriors. That is my calling and the vow I swore to the Ivoyan Council." He smacked Ulvus's hand aside. "But a sparring I can do."

Ulvus grinned, a twinkle sparking to life in his amber eyes. "Accepted."

While he mounted the sword to the wall, Caah sidled closer to Nenn. "Are you certain?" he whispered, the towel looped around his neck.

"No, but this seemed safer than Ulvus anywhere near me with a sharp stick." Nenn waited in the center of the activities room, the padded mat beneath his bare feet. "Boots on or off?" he asked Ulvus, swaggering toward him.

The male shrugged, a smile still in place when he rolled his shoulders. "Your choice."

Juunn tossed Nenn's boots toward him. "Save your toes for climbing," he said.

Nenn smirked. "Logical." He stamped on his boots then clipped them in place. "What are the rules? I would not suggest to the death. Arraks can perform a sava's duty, but none on this ship can heal."

"Very well," Ulvus said and lowered into a crouch, his fingers touching the floor. "Ready?"

Nenn huffed, uncaring that Ulvus seemed ready to kill him. As a maed, they were taught far more than healing. Priority one was to be able to subdue a bigger male. No maed should heal if his life was in danger.

Ulvus took his silence as confirmation and charged.

Nenn raised his arms above his head and waited for the brute to grab and lift him off the floor. Despite his arms squeezing the air out of Nenn's lungs, he smiled at the male then slammed the heel of his palm between Ulvus's upper lip and nostrils.

He cried out.

In an instant, Nenn was released. Ulvus's eyelashes fluttered and his forehead tilted to the ceiling. He staggered back before slumping.

"What the hell just happened?" Caah asked, kneeling beside the sprawled sava whose soft snores declared him well.

"That was brilliant." Juunn laughed, an arm around his torso. "I will be sure to show this to Vaen and Drafe."

Nenn shrugged and pulled the med-dev from his pants pocket. He nudged Caah aside to run the device over Ulvus. Blood dribbled from his nose and pooled on the floor. A muted crunch meant a broken nose being repaired.

"You may have won that round, but Ulvus is a mean male." Caah pointed to the mess. "I shall meet you there for a celebratory drink." His bare backside jiggled when he strode off.

Igar's voice filled the room. "Nenn to the command center."

Nenn leaped to his feet and hurried toward the bridge, veering to the left to where Drafe and Aehort chatted. He waited to be acknowledged.

Aehort nodded at him. "Take a sample of Drafe Arrak's blood. Test it extensively."

Nenn schooled his expressions for the instruction was odd. Drafe was in excellent health with no apparent injury. "Yes, Vizen Aehort Uz."

Drafe angled his head, granting Nenn access to flip his med-dev, the tail end an injection gun. Into the tiny glass capsule trickled clear blood. He stared at it as he exited, unable to fathom what could be wrong with it. The maed bay was between the mess and the activities room. He slotted the med-dev into the analysis machine and started the process.

Moments later, he blinked at the results. Robotic creatures had fused with the symbiotes in Drafe's blood. What they did, Nenn couldn't say, not without the required equipment. He introduced a biologic, in too small an amount to kill. The symbiotes formed armor, while the robotic creatures attacked the 'intruder.' He gaped and tried again, a larger dose this time. Again, the shield-and-destroy response rolled out before his eyes.

He forwarded his findings to Aehort Uz and wondered if he had the right to ask Drafe how he'd gotten the 'parasites.' Now, he had two things that intrigued him: this and face latching. With a shake of his head, he strode to the mess, intent on enjoying a container of wine.

Chapter Eleven

Tiny inched toward the med bay's door, angled her head to listen, then swiped her hand across the pad, sealing the door. "Computer, my beats, please."

Vibrations traveled up her feet, the base thumped around her, and her heartbeat aligned with it. She let the music move through her, urging her hips to swing, to swirl. With her hands in the air, she allowed the tribal rhythm to consume her. Song after song, she moved, lost in the moment without a care in the world. When sweat dripped off her chin, her T-shirt clung to her, and thirst drove her to order a bottle of chilled water, she stopped to catch her breath.

"Computer, halt my beats."

The deafening silence settled on her shoulders and slammed her back to reality.

"Analysis complete," Computer intoned.

"Good. Read them to me."

"Victoria Barnes's blood contains an overabundance of nanites. This is to be expected with her recent implants. However, these nanites are not decreasing in number and dying off as designed. In addition, an unknown organism has merged with them and may be the reason for the nanites' extended life."

Tiny blinked. "Say again."

Computer repeated the results.

"Any record of wounds, puncture holes, or do you think Vic drank something?" Tiny pinched the bridge of her nose. "If no to the first two, the last wouldn't work either."

"Her assessment revealed no unnatural holes in her body."

Unnatural holes? Tiny rolled her top lip, trying to hide a chuckle. Though why she bothered, she couldn't say. Computers couldn't be offended. "Which leaves natural holes?" She laughed. "Thank you, Computer."

She plucked at the collar of her shirt, using it to fan herself. Vic had said she had someone. Did she mean sexually? "Could this unknown organism hide in sperm?"

"That is the most plausible. It is not destructive and seems to have formed a symbiotic relationship with the DNA and nanites."

"Print a 3D representation of it."

"In process," Computer said.

Tiny stood before the printer and waited, sipping her water as she pondered this organism's existence. "No known record of it?"

"I have trawled all medical archives with no success."

Excitement flared into a blaze of energy. She bounced on her toes then winced when her calves cramped. "Order a vitamin boost."

Without Computer, she would've had to fiddle with the gun's settings, slot the nozzle into place, and pray she hadn't chosen the incorrect solution. She ran her hand over the face of the refiller to familiarize herself, angled the gun into the pocket, then pushed it in until it clicked.

"Refill in process," Computer said. "Booster shot ready."

Tiny unclipped it, grasped the grip, then pressed the nozzle to her forearm. A quick pinch was all she needed to endure. That sharp pain couldn't compare to the days of agony from her scorched eyes.

"Model complete."

She laid the gun on the table then glided to the printer, running her fingers along the counter's edge. A pat confirmed her location in correlation to the model. With a delicate touch, she broke the structure off its support struts until a smooth, wormlike shape filled her palms.

"This has memory T-cells?"

"Affirmative," Computer said.

"And it entered through natural holes..." Tears pressed at the backs of her eyes. "I haven't had anything enter my natural hole for so long," she wailed.

Why was seducing Dieter so hard? Every time she had any proximity to him, he treated her like a kid sister. Maybe it was time to give up on getting dirty with her hero. Maybe she needed to find another possible romantic interest. Trent? He was sweet to her, too. Grunt came across as too young, so he was a no. Sure, Captain had been specific, but with the way Leah's voice hitched when she spoke to Nikko, some folks were getting it on despite the no-sex rules.

"We can replicate the organism if you wish to inject it."

Tiny sniffed and offered the ceiling a watery smile. "Thanks for the suggestion, Computer, but I think I'm good."

She could order a sex toy if need be, but it couldn't compare to the intimacy she so desperately craved. "Damn blindness," she muttered.

The door slid open.

She yelped and clutched her chest. A whiff identified the intruder. "Vic, you scared the shit out of me."

"Sorry, Tiny. Did you get the results from my bloodwork?"

Tiny frowned. "Yeah, but they make no sense. Computer, explain Vic's bloodwork results."

While the computer repeated the findings, Tiny dried her eyes using the hem of her T-shirt.

"What?" Vic gasped.

"There is no clear indication of how they entered your system. Removing them will be impossible since they have fused with your DNA," the computer continued in a monotone.

"What?" Vic thumped against something.

"It is unusual. The nanites encourage your body's healing process and are integral to post-implantation. It now appears that they will remain indefinitely."

"Thank you, Computer." Vic neared Tiny, bringing her sunbaked scent with her. "What doesn't make sense?"

"The existence of these organisms, Vic. When you enter a public area on the Lunar Base, a sterilization spray neutralizes all manner of bugs. Yours are...foreign. I can tell you that." She held up the worm. "Although they carry the memory cells we find in human brains."

"Right." Silence settled before Vic drew in a sharp breath "Am I dying?"

"No, they're not harming you. They're communalistic since I can't see what they gain in this symbiosis. They're repairing minor damage to your liver and kidneys—the natural decay from a diet with insufficient hydration and nutrition."

"Okay, fine, great, but can this explain the shimmer?"

"The what?" Tiny frowned. "As in glitter? You're glowing?"

"Kind of. Nikko punched me, and I didn't feel it."

"Oh, dear." Tiny giggled, wishing she could've seen it. "That must've irritated him."

Vic crossed to the door. "According to you, I'm well, and I don't need to panic."

"Yes, and I'll have to inform the captain." Tiny offered Vic her back to type on a small console. "Only the captain. Medical results are considered confidential."

"Good to know."

"We are traveling to the best medical facility in the galaxy..." Tiny paused as butterflies exploded in her stomach. A chance to visit a place few medical students got to? She considered herself lucky. "Maybe we can get them to assess you?"

"Thanks, Tiny. I'll find Sarg and let him punch me again as a peace offering for abandoning him on the training mat."

"Enjoy." Tiny waved the worm even as her fingertips registered its molecular substance. "Shit. I forgot to ask if she had sex with her man."

"Probable," Computer said.

A heavy tread reached her from the passage. Nikko. He walked past, so he wasn't in need of medical treatment. Dieter's drag-step followed him. Then Vic's delicate footsteps headed to Tiny.

"Listen here, babe, gonna show you a few self-defense moves if you're up for it."

"What?" Tiny squeaked. "I'll get my ass handed to me."

"True, but what I'm trying to trigger is Dieter's protective instincts. Want to work with me on this?"

"Hell yes." Tiny grinned. "I can handle a punch or two if it gets me laid."

"That's my girl. Listen for my signal, then we'll meet on the mat." Without waiting for her response, Vic sauntered off like she hadn't just brought a little hope to Tiny's lonely existence.

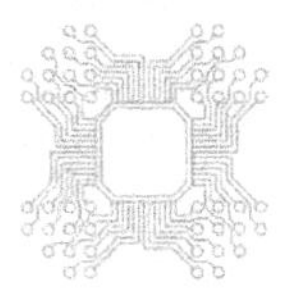

DAYS PASSED BEFORE VIC set her plan in motion. Tiny had barely a moment's warning. Nor had she expected the woman to spring it on her in the middle of breakfast.

"Meet you in five?" She squeezed Tiny's shoulder.

Tiny nodded, brushing her hair off her face. Silence reigned, and she swallowed, aware she was the center of attention. "I messed up a test, so Vic agreed to let me scan her again."

When the conversation continued around her, she picked at her half-eaten toast, too aware of Dieter sitting beside her. Time ticked by, her leg bounced, and she tried to participate, but the words lodged in her throat. Her cheeks flushed when anyone spoke to her.

Desperate to get this over with or, better yet, to talk Vic out of this crazy idea, she hurried to the gym. When she approached, she caught Vic's chuckle.

"I can call you anything I damn well please, and there's nothing you can do about it. Now, as I see it, you can help me bring her out of her shell and find her a good man to love her. For that, you need to step aside."

Dieter's familiar tread paced.

Tiny hesitated, not sure if she should announce her presence or eavesdrop. But because she couldn't see them didn't mean they wouldn't spot her. "Oh, am I bothering?" She slipped into the room and waited, prepared to make a run for it.

He crossed to her then gathered her hands, his touch unexpected, even as he tugged her forward. "Are you sure you want to do this?"

Now was her chance to say no and leave. A part of her, though, wanted to know if there was a chance with him, or had she wasted all this time hoping he'd notice her? "Yes. I'm an easy target. It's why I don't leave when we dock."

"I can protect you."

She smiled and cupped his cheek. "What happens when you want to find companionship? Why would I play the third wheel?" She grimaced but lifted her chin. "I need affection, too, Dieter." She offered him her back and faced the room, using Vic's breathing to locate her. "Shall we, Vic?"

"Sure. What I'll teach you can only be done if they touch you." She clasped Tiny's wrist. "I have you; now try and get away."

Vic wasn't hurting Tiny, per say, but wriggling and pulling didn't free her, only bruised her wrist. Panic set in, stealing her ability to breathe. On the cusp of crying, she dropped to her knees, using her weight in the hopes it would force Vic to release her.

"Okay, stop." Vic tightened her hold, drawing a whimper from Tiny. "Register where my thumb is. Can you feel it?"

Tiny nodded, trying to think. Vic pressed her thumb to the underside of Tiny's wrist.

"Good, now, instead of yanking, curl your wrist inward and tug down."

Tiny did as instructed, and when she broke free, she squealed. She swayed her hips in a happy dance. Dieter chuckled from the sidelines. Heat flushed Tiny's cheeks. She'd half-forgotten he watched.

"Now, I'm going to breach your space. Don't be alarmed. Listen for my breathing; that will tell you the location of my face." Vic pinned her body to Tiny's. Her scent engulfed Tiny. The earlier panic reared its head.

She relied on her technique to keep her grounded.

Five sensory connections around her.

The mat under her toes, cool and warm.

The gentle waft of air from the filtration system.

Dieter's heavy breathing.

Vic's scent.

And the bruising sting around Tiny's wrist.

"Your chin is about here." She touched Vic's jaw.

"Good. Can you guess the location of my upper arms?"

Tiny thrust out her hands and caught Vic's arms.

"Great, you're doing well. Slowly, lift your knee."

Despite being able to dance for hours, Tiny wobbled when she tried to balance on one foot.

"Tighten your grip on me. Use me as leverage." Warmth filled Vic's voice.

Squeezing as Tiny found her balance, she raised her foot and nudged Vic's inner thigh.

"Good. When someone tries something you don't like, do that, and knee them in the groin. It hurts just as much for a woman. Leap back, though, because they will double over."

Tiny went from one foot to on her ass, a gasp escaping her when she hit the mat hard.

"What the farg, Vic?" Dieter kneeled beside Tiny, his presence pressing on her senses.

"She could be bumped while crossing a bar, Deets."

"Vic's right." Tiny threw out her hands and found his.

The roughness of his skin changed when she slid her fingers along his forearms to his neck. Rising onto her knees, she looped her arm across his shoulders and used him to stand. Heat poured off him, and his huff fanned her face. She was close enough to kiss him, if she could find his mouth with hers. This was the nearest she'd been to him since he'd saved her at Celestial.

"Why the farg would she go to a bar? The men there are assholes." He leaped to his feet.

The loss of stability sent her whirling. Before she could fall again, he scooped her into his arms, sending her sense of balance reeling.

"Stop giving her these ideas, Vic. You're done. This is...done."

Tiny clung to him, having not been carried since she was a girl. "Deets—"

"No, this is stupid. You're safe here." He lowered her feet to the floor and guided her hand to the counter. The smell alone told her he'd brought her to the med bay.

She folded her arms across her chest and glared in his direction. "I need sex."

His breath hitched, and a growl slipped out. "No, you don't."

"Deets," she whined. "You're dooming me to a life of celibacy." This overprotective brother act was starting to irritate her. She gritted her teeth then changed tactics. "I know Captain said no sex, but do you think Trent would be—"

"Maybe. I can't speak for the man, but he's better than a stranger."

Ice drenched her, curling around her soul with a numbing grip. Dieter's response said it all. "Thanks," she managed. "I'll get around to asking him." Tears slipped free, forcing her to turn away from him. "I have work to do... If you don't mind."

"Oh—" He shuffled, bringing his grease, sweat, and subtle cologne with him. "We could...if you want."

Fury fired through her veins and stiffened her shoulders. *Farg no.* She wasn't so desperate that she'd be his pity fuck. "There's the door."

She clung to the counter and waited for him to leave. Only when his footsteps faded did she allow the sobs to escape. Her chest squeezed tight, her throat burned, and so did her tears where they traveled down her cheeks to wet her shirt.

Dieter was her hero no more.

CHAPTER TWELVE

Year: 2219

On Ceres

Orbiting the Planet Jupiter

SEATED NEXT TO DRAFE was the only opportunity Nenn had had to fire his questions at the male. They were en route to some dwarf planet called Ceres to investigate the contents of a pod they'd captured.

In his tribe and with the symbiotes, all knew who was mated to whom. Here, in the wilds of outer space without the Qaldreth soil beneath their feet, Nenn could only hazard a guess what had happened between Drafe and Vic. And if they'd shared...time together, then it had to have happened on the Lunar Base.

He leaned in and whispered to Drafe, "As a maed, I would like to know how the robotic creatures got into your body?"

Drafe glanced at him, his eyes brightening to a blinding yellow. "None of your business."

"Fine, can you explain the face-latching to me?"

Drafe jerked back, his scowl turning ferocious. "The what?"

"Vaen and I observed the way the humans greeted each other." Nenn glared, not prepared to demonstrate what he meant on anyone, especially not the crew.

"Kissing is what it is called." A smile formed, changing Drafe's demeanor to approachable though Nenn knew better than to push. "It is most enjoyable."

"Oh." Nenn stared at the moon's marbled-gray landscape whizzing past.

"Laying with a human is worth it, if you get the chance."

At Drafe's words, Nenn's focus shifted. "Thank you." He grinned. So, Drafe *had* mated with a human female. "Does she have your symbiotes?"

"Yes, though she calls them organisms." Drafe chuckled and turned his focus elsewhere, ending the conversation.

When Caah landed the shuttle miles from any civilization, they waited. A frowning Aehort stayed seated, staring at the hovering pod in the center of the shuttle's compartment. Drafe rose and tapped his throat, activating his shield. The crew did the same. Nenn lingered, choosing to trail Aehort Uz to where Vaen had pulled the pod meters away from the landed shuttle.

Its red exterior hinted at the danger within.

"The last one detonated after a few hours of breaking the seal." Drafe met each male's gaze through his shield.

"Work fast. Gather what information you can, and do not disturb me." Aehort's eyes rolled back when he splayed his palm above the capsule.

Vaen opened the pod, needing Caah's help to do so. Inside lay a naked female. Nenn inched closer, intrigued by her unmottled gray skin. She could've died days ago. If he compared her to the humans on Lunar Base, parts of her were missing, exposing metallic bones.

"Mm," Aehort hummed. "She endured great pain." He winced. "Even in death, her cries for mercy fall on muted ears."

"Her body has been enhanced." Nenn ran his arm over her, scanning and recording details visible and unseen. "Every inch, including her organs, has been altered. What remained human was removed." He jerked back when he caught a glimpse of her five-fingered hands, so similar to a Qaldreth's bone structure.

Caah frowned, shifting on his feet. "I do not like this. Some of her enhancements have been stripped from her." He gripped the edge of the opening. "The pod has been fitted with an explosive device. I would need to remove it for Gusin to study it." He spun the holographic representation of the pod shining from his arm. "If I hazard a guess, once the pod is unsealed, there is a time limit to reseal it before it explodes."

Drafe stiffened as if preparing for battle. "That makes sense. If they have to open a pod, they need a bypass."

"They expect these pods to be destroyed upon impact." Vaen stroked a lock of her brown hair, though he'd feel nothing through the shield. "Why do this? Why not burn or bury the bodies?"

"Burying would require soft soil, a mine, or a cavern." Nenn captured his conclusions on his arm. The why was logical to him. The Borven searched for caverns to entomb their dead which often meant expeditions some didn't return from. Fire was the simplest solution if they had access to a crematorium. "They would need immense fuel reserves."

"This near to Jupiter?" Drafe gestured to the massive planet.

Nenn shrugged and deactivated his arm.

"Hydrogen gas is volatile, and mining it would be hazardous." Caah ran his forefinger across the human's skin.

Drafe lunged forward to peer at the female. "What the foq?"

Nenn hoped Drafe would explain his alarm. He didn't.

"Place the sensors, Caah. Let us have done with this rock." Vaen peered at the surrounding hills too low for Nenn to bother climbing. "We have an Ivoyan in the open."

Drafe grimaced. "We wait for Aehort Uz. Spread out."

Nenn marched to the outskirts of their circle, peering at the moon's surface. Massive craters showed much impact from passing asteroids or meteors. Drafe stayed by Aehort's side without moving or commenting. A slight breeze tossed Nenn's hair across his temple. What about the female had shocked the arrak? He studied his findings, noting the thin scars marring her body. With his gaze on the horizon, he let his mind wander.

Aehort gasped then headed to the shuttle. Nenn kept his back to the pod until he could enter the shuttle.

"Caah Arrak, hurry," Aehort Uz commanded, snapping Caah to attention. He bolted for the pilot seat and powered up the shuttle.

"What is it, Aehort?" Drafe asked but didn't receive a response.

No doubt sensing the urgency, Caah pushed the engines to get them to the *Aroagni* faster.

Into the tense silence came Gusin's voice through the language implant in Drafe's neck. Nenn caught every word. "Drafe Arrak, we have a problem."

Drafe tapped his neck to ask, "What is it, Gusin?"

Aehort's head dipped from exhaustion, his skin mottling from orange to amber. "It has begun."

Nenn unbuckled to run the med-dev over the Ivoyan, encouraging his remarkable physiology to self-heal faster. Qaldreths served the Ivoyans even when it was just a headache.

"We have collected a stranded human." Gusin paused. "Ulvus Sava intends to interrogate."

Nenn focused on Drafe. A human? Weak, vulnerable, and in Ulvus's clutches?

"Foq. Caah, get us back now." Drafe shoved past Nenn to thrust the level, shooting the already straining shuttle forward.

Caah laughed, steering as he ran his fingers over the control, issuing commands to the full-pulse engines. "The bay is prepped for landing. Ulvus Sava has the human trapped near the airlock." He landed with a solid thump.

"I will return to my quarters." Aehort rose to his feet with a nod to Nenn then Drafe. "No escort is needed."

Nenn waited, not sure whether he should follow Drafe, who'd bolted before the ramp had lowered. If a maed was needed, Nenn would be summoned, but for now, he'd deal with the exhaustion aching in his shoulders. First, though, would be to assuage the lesser pain cramping his stomach.

Aware Gusin hovered, Nenn ordered his meal from the replicate in the galley. He took his plate of charred audinna and sank onto the bench. His steaming jar of usturo tisane perfumed the air.

Gusin sat opposite him and pinched a kurrula between forefinger and thumb. "What did you think?"

Nenn popped a strip of mushroom into his mouth. "About?" he asked while he chewed.

"The female in the pod."

"Caah recorded her. What more do you need to know?" With sticky fingers, Nenn pulled his jar closer for a sip. He smacked his lips when the hot liquid tingled his tongue.

Gusin bit into his meal, the bones crunching. "She seemed young."

Nenn paused. "Indeed," he said.

"Any idea how she died?" Gusin licked his fingers clean before gulping his water.

"Heart failure. No other signs of distress, no injuries, just the parts missing from her limbs."

Gusin slumped, resting his elbows on the edge of the table. "Good. I pray to Osnir that her death was painless."

Nenn kept silent. Aehort had said she'd suffered.

"Vic, this is Giniiri aac Nenn Maed and Zuphayr aac Gusin Taed." Drafe smiled at Nenn and Gusin, a human female beside him.

Nenn gawked, his mind reeling at having a human on the *Aroagni*. A pale-yellow braid draped over a shoulder. Her body was tiny, compact, but rippling with strength. She met his gaze with warriorlike boldness.

With an odd wiggle of her fingers in greeting, she sat next to Nenn, bringing with her a feminine scent so sweet, he longed to inhale it deep into his lungs. "Those are your names?"

Drafe laughed. "Your family name is last; our tribe name is first. Aac means from, and maed, taed, arrak, uz, and sava are ranks."

Now, that is intriguing. Nenn glanced at Gusin who'd frozen in place, a kurrula hallway to his mouth.

"This is a military ship." She gestured to their armored pants then chuckled. "You're so colorful. Is there a significance to your red and blue hair and matching eyes?" She smiled at Drafe when he set water, tulsig cakes, and garak before her.

"Each tribe has a color. None know why." Nenn grinned, delighted to have met her. He tore another strip off his audinna. "That's the Giniiri in my name."

"It also means from which clime we stem." Gusin finished the last of his kurrula. "Giniiri is the volcano tribe. Zuphayr is where the sky meets the water."

"And Meorri?" She hesitated to eat a tulsig cake, but when she did, she moaned, her eyelashes fluttering. Thinking her in pain, Nenn almost pulled his med-dev from his pants. "This is *so* good," she said, gazing at them, honesty in her expression.

When Drafe didn't react with any alarm, Nenn released a breath and carried his empty plate to the disposal. "Drafe is from the desert tribe." He gripped Drafe's forearm then left, eager to research kissing now that he'd met a living human female.

His room, dark and hot, was reminiscent of his home in Erasril. His bed was like a rock ledge, but the indoor waterfall instead of a pool he'd had to get used to. At least he could set its temperature to scorching, which he doubted Caah did. The ceiling was speckled with fake venai stones, mimicking the formation of stars above his beloved volcano. He stripped off his pants and boots, setting them in alcoves in the 'rock-hewn' walls.

Exhaustion pressed on him. The day had been eventful, rattling his perceptions of the universe he barely knew. Change and death were life's constants, yet he hadn't expected both to be so swift and impactful. His father had gone from a hug to the fire, forever altering Nenn's course. They'd abandoned a dead human on Ceres and returned to a live one in their ship.

He stepped under the water, hissing when it engulfed him in heat. Tilting his face to the spray, his thoughts circled to Vic. He hadn't expected her softness or her core of controlled strength. Something niggled. He squeezed his eyes shut, focusing his mind. What was it?

His breath caught. Vic had the same hairline scars as the female in the pod. No wonder Drafe had reacted with shock. Not all humans carried the same scars. Did that mean she had hidden implants? Nenn itched to scan her and study the results. How did her body handle the robotic creatures *and* symbiotes? Was she exhibiting symptoms?

Judging by her and Drafe's exploits, humans and Qaldreth were compatible, but could she bear children?

Did Aehort know any of this?

Nenn scoffed. An Ivoyan, even an uz, had intelligence far beyond a mere Qaldreth's understanding. Aehort had steered them well thus far, his insights phenomenal. Nenn deactivated the spray, rubbed his body with a towel, then sprawled on his bed. He tapped his tablet and typed in the word 'kiss.'

Streams of video footage showed acts of kissing, their varieties, and for the most part, how to do it. His gut tightened when a female swirled her tongue into a male's mouth. He'd never seen the like.

And as Osnir was his witness, he wanted to try this kissing with every fiber of his being.

Chapter Thirteen

Year: 2219
Mula Pesada
En Route to Europa

Tiny froze, angling her ear toward the ceiling. "What did you say?"

"Victoria Barnes has been lost to space."

A crushing weight squeezed Tiny's chest, and she staggered back, throwing her hand out to catch the counter. "No, it can't be." She pressed a fist to her mouth as the tears flowed. "Oh, Vic," she sobbed. "When?"

"Hours ago."

"And you tell me now?" she yelled between sniffs and wiping her cheeks.

"So you heard?" Dieter asked, startling a squeak from her.

"Just," she rasped, wishing he'd come closer for a hug. She wasn't going to ask for one, though. "How...did this happen, Deets? Don't we have safety nets in place or restraints?"

"Some freak accident, so Nikko says."

Ice drenched Tiny, her ears ringing, her mind spinning, because behind those words lay a tone far too friendly. "Losing a crewmate doesn't devastate you?"

"Nope." Dieter laughed. "I say good riddance."

Hope shriveled inside Tiny's heart, and the full realization of where she was and with whom she worked slammed into her. Unexpected deaths were investigated by port authorities, delaying departure and costing a fortune in docking fees. Safety was paramount. For an accident to happen, especially on an ice hauler, human error had to be involved. Which implied intent. And judging by his jovialness, he had to have been involved in something like this before. Would he dispose of her if he thought her a liability?

"You wanted her gone," she whispered.

His hand on her elbow made her skin crawl. "She lied to us, Tiny. She's an escaped gladiator and was wanted by Carne."

She blinked. *Well, now, that explains so much about the snippets Vic let slip.* "I'm used to nudity," she'd said, and those almost imperceptible scars, her state-of-the-art cybernetics, and her love of food... Still, Vic had shown Tiny nothing but kindness.

"But—" She cleared her throat. "Handing her over to Carne makes more sense." She shook her head. "Who else is 'happy' about this?"

"Leah and Nikko."

Nikko hated being lied to. So his lack of remorse was almost forgivable. But why Leah? "Is it because of the busted hand?"

"Yup." Dieter tugged as if to draw Tiny into his arms, but she pulled way, choosing instead to sink into the chair.

"I...can't believe you're so blasé." She raised her chin despite the pain inside her chest threatening to swallow her whole. "It's like I don't know you. And here I thought you my hero." She curled her fingers into fists and rested them on her thighs, gathering her courage. "You're nothing but a cold-hearted ass, Deets."

He growled. "You're either for us or against us."

She stiffened. No way could she afford to burn bridges when she was trapped onboard. Nor did she have anyone she could confide in. She had no idea how far up the chain this disregard for life went. Surely not Trent or Grunt? Not Captain either... Was he even aware of what his crew got up to?

"For, of course. Just pissed you didn't try to rescue her. Carne might have offered a hefty reward—dead or alive."

Dieter chuckled. "Yeah, but Leah wouldn't let me. Nikko didn't try either, and I ain't the boss," he said like that excused his inaction.

"I better stay on Leah's good side." Tiny wiggled her brows in a weak attempt to be funny and put Dieter at ease.

"Me too. You never know with her. What Nikko sees in her..." He cursed. "Sorry, wasn't supposed to reveal—"

"I know about their rule-breaking," Tiny said.

"Phew, Nikko would chew my ass off. Well, I've got to feed the zoo. See ya later." He stomped off, leaving her alone at last.

"Computer..." She paused. What could she ask? What really happened? Did she want to know? No, she preferred to believe Nikko. For now. Knowing the truth meant she'd have to lie, and without her sight, she couldn't read expressions. But she wanted off this hauler. So much for finding her place in the universe.

"Yes, Tiny."

She slumped and let the tears fall. "Play the audiobook."

'Chapter Twenty-One. Date: 2170.14.10. The Colony.

"No, no way." Naomi shook her head, fastening her uniform with nimble fingers. "I'm not moving in with you, Gibs."

"Then live with Davis if it's me you dislike."

"Dislike? After the way I kissed you?" She snorted. "It's a no because I like my privacy."

He trailed after her stomping form, loving the sway of her ponytail and hips. Having her beneath him was only a matter of time, and he could wait, flex his patience for a bit.'

Tiny zoned out, unable to focus. She'd have to replay this part when she didn't need the computer's voice to comfort her. Disembarking at Europa was her only chance to escape. Could she do it without letting anyone know? And she'd signed a fargen contract.

"Oh, Dad, what have I done?" she wailed like a disobedient child.

She'd been 'safe' at Celestial. Would Maddy take her back? She barked out a hysterical laugh. Here she was, making a difference. What a fool to think a blind doctor could be of value...

Nor did she dare contact her family, unsure whether her correspondence was being monitored. She rose... Who could she trust? She had to risk speaking to someone.

"Pause audiobook and rewind to chapter twenty-one for next time," she said and left, trailing her hand along the walls. She'd need access to Earth or Europa. Instead of heading to her room, she paused outside Grunt's door. It opened before she could knock.

"Come on in, Tiny." He shut the door behind her, a solid thunk making her shiver in its finality.

"I..." She hesitated, unsure how to phrase it.

"You heard about Vic and now believe you're not safe."

At his words, she whipped her head up, settling her gaze in his direction. "How—"

"I see everything onboard." Grunt sighed and sat, his chair squeaking beneath him.

Farg. It's as bad as I thought. Tiny squared her shoulders. "How do I get off?"

"You can't," he said. "Europa waystations aren't accepting applicants or refugees. You'll have to wait until our next port."

"The whole moon's not available?" She bit her lip, fighting the tears stinging her eyes.

He hesitated. "'Fraid so. You can do it, Tiny. Stay in the med bay and don't involve yourself in anything other than medical." He rose, his chair wheeling back. With a gentle touch, he patted her cheeks with a soft cloth. "I'll set Computer to warn you with a safe word..."

"Celestial," she whispered, not sure whether she could believe Grunt. But why would he lie? Why would he deceive her when there was nothing to gain from it? "The last place I called home."

"Very well."

She caught his hand close to her face. "Who else can I trust, Grunt?"

Silence met her question. He dropped his arms, drumming his fingers on his thighs. "Captain's ignorant, but don't go to him; he lives in the past. Trent's the muscle with his own demons to deal with. If the shit hits the fan, come to me or him."

Relief engulfed her in a flood of warmth. She smiled. "Thank you." She turned to leave. "Is my correspondence monitored?"

"No." Grunt chuckled. "Do you want me to?"

Her shoulders relaxed at the 'no,' then twitched when he offered to. A laugh escaped her. "Not at all. Just didn't want anyone reading about my whining to my parents about my inability to adult."

"This isn't on you, Tiny. You've been an excellent addition to the crew, one I don't need to worry about." He ushered her to his door with a hand on her elbow.

"Thanks again, Grunt."

"Don't mention it...when anyone's within earshot."

Alone in the passage, she stood there, her thoughts spinning. What was he worrying about? Sure, she got hiding this little conversation from the others, but it felt so...clandestine. Her moral compass was being tested. She scowled and crossed to her room. Never had she needed to spin the handwheel and lock herself inside. Today, she did.

Trent had mentioned once that each cabin was an escape pod in case of emergencies. She could be shot into space while she slept.

"Breathe," she muttered when her heartbeat stuttered. "No one's out to kill you."

With the way her mind raced, it took her ages to drift off.

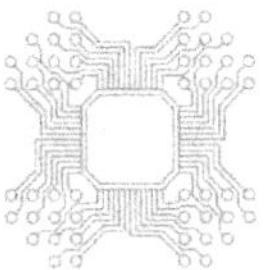

NENN JERKED AWAKE AND lay there, reeling from having finally reached the bottom of the Amikar, even if it was in his dreams. Instead of an isolated pool with a waterfall cascading into it, large tongues tumbled over each other when they spilled onto the shore.

He sat up, sweat drenching his chest. That was an odd occurrence for a Giniiri used to extreme heat. Which meant, as his heart pounded, his reaction was emotion-based. He swung his legs off the bed and rose, summoning his symbiotes to cover the bottom half of his body in armor. Barefoot, he headed to the mess, his tablet in hand. A cup of asturo or strips of vibuy might calm him.

The silence of the ship pressed on him like the quiet of a forgotten cave. He ordered his meal and sank onto the bench. While he nibbled or sipped, he flicked through his conclusions, analyzing where the missing implants on the human bodies should've been. The precision of the scars along her skin couldn't compare to the haphazard tearing of the muscles and tendons where the implants had once been fitted. Screws and metal brackets remained. No blood stained them, an indication she'd been dead when they stripped her.

A male padded past the table to order something from the replicate. Nenn recognized him by the smell alone.

"What has you awake?" he mumbled and bit off a piece of vibuy.

"The pod exploded." Drafe paused then leaned against the counter.

"So I heard." Nenn met his gaze. "Yet, you left the loving arms of your female?"

"Mm, I have a dilemma I need to work through." Drafe sat opposite Nenn, nursing a jar of water.

"Care to share?" Nenn flipped his tablet over and shifted his bowl for Drafe to rest his arms on the table.

"She does not want to involve herself out of fear. Revenge is driving her to take the hauler, but after that is completed, she might...leave me." Drafe slumped, his shoulders bowing.

"You want a way to keep her?" Nenn arched a brow. "Drafe, she is not Qaldreth—"

Drafe growled.

Nenn raised his hand to silence Drafe. "Let me finish." He popped the vibuy dangling from his fingers into his mouth. "She does not know our ways and cannot be held to our expectations." He paused to swallow. "In addition, she is a warrior who will not be subservient to you. Perhaps all you need to do is ask her, warrior to warrior."

"That *is* our way." Drafe frowned. "To ask."

Nenn swallowed a laugh, aware of Drafe's dismay. "No, I mean, explain it to her, how staying with you will change her life."

Drafe rested his chin on his hand. "She knows nothing of our homeworld. It is right that I share this with her."

Nenn hid his grin by sipping his steaming asturo tisane. "If you are serious about having her for your love mate, then yes."

"Wise, Nenn." Drafe straightened, a small smile forming. "Do we have any Ivoyan data vids on Qaldreth?"

"We do." Nenn gritted his teeth, smothering his urge to curse. Males could be such fools. "Images are wonderful, but memories spoken from the heart have greater impact."

Drafe's frown darkened. "She has my symbiotes and access to all Meorri history."

"Yes, but she has not learned to commune with them." Foq, it had taken him ages as a young male. His mother had despaired that he'd never learn. "You are rushing the most beautiful thing to occur to a warrior, Drafe."

"I know." He slumped, dipped his gaze, then leveled it on Nenn. "I want it done. I want her to be mine with no chance of her walking away."

Nenn laughed. *At last, the truth.* "You are feeling insecure. It is not the way of a fearless warrior."

Drafe glared at him. "Foq, Nenn. Wait until you meet your female."

Images of tongues attacking him swept across his mind. It took all his focus to offer a shrug. "I hope to be as senseless as you." He pushed aside his empty plate, then licked his thumb. "On a more serious matter, her besting Ulvus has enraged the male. I will guard your back."

After Nenn's demonstration, Ulvus had stayed clear of him. But when she bested Ulvus, he'd directed all his anger and frustration at her. Nenn was partly to blame for Ulvus's vindictive state of mind and would protect her, as well.

"Ulvus is predictable." Drafe downed his water and rose. "Thank you for the advice and warning, Nenn."

Drafe's nonchalance made Nenn smile. There went an arrak who'd tackled Ulvus on more than one occasion. Nenn had managed to avoid the male for the most part, but who knew if he was just biding his time?

He sighed at his cooled tisane. If Drafe mated with the human, Nenn didn't know how the Q.C.C. would react. He leaned back, a decision forming. No matter what lay ahead, Nenn would make damn sure he and the males onboard the *Aroagni*, Ulvus excluded, sided with the couple.

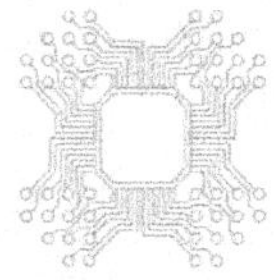

"ALL PERSONNEL HAVE BEEN allocated full access to all areas, including the engine rooms. Do not...disturb me, even if it's life and death." Captain's voice snapped Tiny awake.

She blinked, trying to understand the reason for the announcement. Where hadn't she been allowed to go before? Not that she'd need to know when her room, the mess, the zoo, her med bay, the bridge, and hydroponics were the only places she frequented.

She scrambled out of bed and hurried through her ablutions. Did she sneak out of her room? Yes. She listened with care to make sure no one crept up on her despite her stomping along the passages. The air in her lungs had solidified, like a pressure built, and the effort to inhale became a mission, so she veered to hydroponics, hoping to find some peace. Stroking the leaves while crooning at the plants gave her a sense of normalcy. The organic smell alone bathed her in peace.

"Oh, no," she whispered when her thumb brushed along a jagged leaf. "You poor thing." With clippers in hand, she glided her fingers along and snipped the leaf off, placing it in a bucket she'd later dump in the compost bin.

Focusing on not cutting off a finger kept her mind on the moment and not on the fact she'd survived a night without being jettisoned. And despite the aroma of bacon wafting from the mess, she'd avoided spending any time with Nikko, Leah, and Dieter. If she didn't need to 'act' happy or lie, then she wouldn't put a target on her back.

Approaching footsteps made her pause. The cadence was like Vic's except for the heavy treads accompanying it. Was she losing her mind?

"Hi, Tiny."

She froze, her breath hitching. "Vic." She faced the door, wishing her vision returned for a moment. Seeing was believing, so they said. "I thought you... Nikko said we'd lost you to some freak accident."

Dragged into a hug, she almost dropped the pot. But the sunbaked perfume that was Vic engulfed her. She succumbed and squeezed back.

"You did. My tether was cut."

Tiny gaped. As she'd suspected. Oh, Lord, let it not be of Dieter's doing. She couldn't be that wrong about the man. "Cut?"

"Yes," Vic muttered. "Carne's ship passed us, so I rushed inside to warn Nikko. I was a fool to think he was friendly. To my face, sure, then when he sent me out again, he made sure I didn't come back. Thankfully, I was rescued by Qaldreth warriors on their own mission somehow tied to Carne. Which leads us to believe there are prisoners onboard the *Mula Pesada*."

"Us? Wait, did you say warriors?" Tiny angled her head, zeroing in on the breathing. "Three?"

"One at a time, introduce yourself," Vic said.

Tiny stiffened, drew in a shaky breath, then faced them. Farg, she hadn't even brushed her hair. At least she'd showered and wore clean underwear. Mom would be so proud.

Someone stepped closer. "I am Meorri aac Drafe Arrak. Vic is my female."

"Oh." Tiny gasped then gasped again when he took her hand. "Does that mean what I think it means?"

"More than you can know." Vic hugged her from the side. "Nenn, you're next."

Excitement swelled inside Tiny, summoning a grin. "Describe them for me, Vic. Oh, I do love the way they smell. Like I'm in a biodome on Ganymede, filled with rich soils, succulent plants, trickling water..." She took a long sniff. "Volcanic rock."

Silence met her request. Tiny frowned. Had she said something wrong?

"Only Drafe and Nenn are near to you; the others... Besides, we're out of time. Will you help us?" Vic asked in a rush.

Tiny folded her arms across her chest and waited, tempted to tap her foot for good measure. She wasn't going to budge until she had some idea of who she was helping.

"Fine," Vic huffed. "They have obsidian skin. Their hair runs from their brows to the base of their spines. All are muscled, strong, and skilled. Drafe's a warrior guardian. Caah's a tech guru, I think. Nenn is like you, a medic."

"He is?" Tiny swiveled, widening her eyes to peer at the smudges. Not that she could tell anything apart, but right then, she wished she could.

"Can you not see me?" Nenn gathered her hands in his, sending a zing up her arms. He was hot to the touch, and the urge to snuggle against him was a little overwhelming. "Loss of sight is no more where I come from. Allow me to heal you."

She scowled at the offer. Just like that? Let a stranger operate on her? "With implants?" She shivered. "That's a no, thank you."

Nenn's husky chuckle coiled heat in her core. "We regrow your eyes and encourage the optical nerves to reconnect. I will return for you when our mission is complete."

Tiny leaned toward where she thought Vic stood and whispered, "Is he for real?"

"Yes." Vic laughed. "Now, will you help us?"

"Sure. What you need is access to the engine rooms. Security was restricted, but last night, Captain just up and gave everyone full-access status. He did sound...odd. Anyway, that means I can appoint you as our new captain." Tiny giggled. Served Nikko right for kicking her friend off the ship.

Vic arched a brow. "That could work, but won't Leah notice?"

"Why would she?" Tiny scoffed, ignoring the sliver of fear sliding down the nape of her neck. "She's probably got her boots up on the console and her nose buried in smut." Tiny offered a smile at the room in general. "Computer, set all crew to staff access only, and grant Vic full control."

"Control granted, Captain Vic."

"See. Easy as that. Computer, locate all storerooms." Tiny gestured to the console, hoping Computer was showing *Mula Pesada's* floor plans. "I would start there." She raised the pot to bury her nose in the aromatic rosemary leaves. When a thought struck her, she stiffened and peered over her shoulder at the door. "But Vic, what if you're wrong?"

"Then we leave the ship without bloodshed," Vic said.

Tiny squeaked. *Farg.* What had she done? First do no harm, that's what she'd sworn to do. "Don't hurt...anyone."

"Especially Dieter?" Vic teased.

Tiny swallowed a growl. "No," she pursed her lips, "go ahead. Kick his ass."

"What the farg?" Vic cursed. "You're coming with us. Pack what you need."

Tiny gaped. Sure, she'd wanted off the ship but to where? For all she knew, she was going from the pan into the fire. "But—"

"Do you want to stay on the *Mula Pesada* if it's true, Tiny? Wouldn't that make you complicit in whatever the hell Nikko's up to?"

Tiny slumped and placed the clippers in the bowl. "No, you're right. I'll be ready."

They stomped out except for one. She waited. Hot hands clasped hers again. She offered Nenn a tentative smile.

"I am pleased to have met you, Tiny." He pinched her chin and angled her head with the gentlest of nudges. "I look forward to learning all there is know about you."

Then he was gone, taking his volcanic touch and smell with him. She shuddered, sucked in a sharp breath, but didn't move. She stood there, hugging herself. With a gasp, she hurried to her room to pack. It didn't take her long. Accumulating pretty things had fallen to the wayside many months ago.

With careful steps, she headed to the med bay, bag in hand, to collect her chess set. No way was she leaving it behind. She'd just dropped her bag in the corner and sank into the chair when Leah approached.

"Your turn to man the bridge," she snapped.

Heat splashed across Tiny's cheeks at almost being caught with her bag in hand. That would have raised suspicion for sure. "Is it that time already?"

"Whatever," Leah said. "Get your ass there. I need to piss."

"Oh." Tiny scrambled to her feet, waited for Leah's footsteps to fade, then darted onto the bridge.

She couldn't see the console and its many buttons or figure out what they did. What she did do was listen to the beeps. A single beep seconds apart meant all was well. Anything else, she had to notify Nikko or Leah.

Manning the bridge was dull work. She couldn't listen to her audiobook for fear she'd miss a bad beep, so she sat there, spinning the chair until dizziness drove her to stop.

While she waited for her cybersickness to dissipate, she sifted through worst-case scenarios. This could all go bad, fast. She needed backup. "Computer, patch me through to Grunt. Secure the channel."

"Grunt is unavailable."

Farg. "And Trent?"

"Asleep. Do you wish to wake him?"

She slumped. "No... No, thank you."

She gripped the edge of the console and prayed everything worked out in the end. Never had she been so helpless, with Vic's and the warriors' arrival ramping up the tension in her shoulders. More than her life was in her hands. And that included the prisoners, *if* they existed. She'd better act normal like everything depended on it.

Because it did.

Leah couldn't suspect a thing.

Chapter Fourteen

Nenn trailed Drafe along the narrow passages, the walls touching his upper arms. He frowned, casting a glance at the too-low ceiling. For such a big ship, the *Mula Pesada* was too cramped for his liking.

A melodic croon snapped his gaze ahead. Over Drafe's shoulder, Nenn caught a flash of pale purple—the color of russmar in spring. The delicate curve of a cheek led his gaze to a pointy chin on a short human female. Something squeezed his chest. Breathing became irrelevant.

He shifted between Drafe and Caah, inching closer to admire her better. In a loose tunic over tight pants to barely covered feet was a female in full bloom, softness in every part of her body. There wasn't a thing about her he didn't like. Even her smile snagged his attention, so vivacious and joyful.

Finding out she was a medic, too, made his thoughts spin. *And* she was blind. How did she function without sight? Never mind, the Ivoyans would heal her.

He tried to ignore the bounce in his stride, more energized than was wise. She'd be with them when they returned to the *Aroagni*. Without hesitating, he tapped his implant.

"Gusin, prep the room next to mine." His familiar face... No, his voice might put her at ease.

"Why?"

Nenn scowled, unable to explain the need to have her near. "Just do it."

Drafe angled his head, no doubt catching Nenn's instruction but said nothing to gainsay him. Down ladders Vic took them until she stopped in front of a door. She pushed the lever, bending it in half.

Nenn froze in disbelief. How had she... He tested the solid metal bar. With those scars, she had to have implants. Studying their placement would reveal what had been stripped from the dead female.

Vic's scowl had Drafe laughing. "I am not trying," he said, throwing up his hands.

Nenn squeezed her arm. "Foq, Vic, I need to take a look at you when we return to *Aroagni.*"

She shook off his touch and raised her chin to the ceiling. "Computer, unlock this door."

It thunked, leaving a gap. Drafe and Caah teamed up to peel it open.

Despite the stale air, the heat pouring over Nenn made him smile.

Along the passage, Drafe sprinted from door to door until he stopped at the fourth one. He spun the wheel and yanked on the door. His expression darkened.

Nenn peered around him at the gray pods stamped with a red symbol—just like the one they'd investigated on Ceres.

At the evidence, Vic rasped, "Find the prisoners."

Nenn hurried along the passage, Caah with him. They took turns peering through portholes to the contents in the rooms. Caah stiffened then gestured to Nenn to look. Many human faces filled his line of vision.

"Found them," Caah said, touching his implant.

Drafe and Vic nudged them aside to peek through the circular window.

"Farg," Vic moaned, stepping back.

Caah gripped the wheel and spun it, the whir deafening in the silence.

As soon as he swung it wide enough, someone called out, "Who are you?"

"Victorious?" a woman gasped, staggering forward to grab Vic's hand. Her bedraggled garments hung on her, many sizes too big. "Did Carne send you to save us?"

The stench of piss and sweat burned Nenn's nostrils, but as a medic, he'd been trained to shut off any distracting sense. He did so now. Though, his fingers twitched with the urge to remove his med-dev to heal those with obvious injuries.

"Carne?" Vic stroked the red symbol on the woman's sleeve then sank to the floor. "No, I'm not their favorite person; neither are you. They're using you to test augmentations on, then when they're done with your body, they'll jettison you into space in an explosive pod."

"No," a few muttered.

"I knew it," others said.

"Pods? Explosions?" A man limped toward them.

Drafe sidled along the wall, keeping himself between the stranger and Vic, who jumped up to squeeze the older man's arm.

"Yes," she said. "We located the medical facility they're taking you to. Computer, patch me through to Tiny."

"Patched through," the monotone feminine voice said.

Vic glanced at the ceiling. "Tiny, we found them."

"Tiny can't help you, bitch," a female said, hatred in her tone.

Ice slammed into Nenn's chest. What had she done to Tiny? Pressure built inside him until a roar consumed his hearing.

"Now I'll get the chance to kill you," the female snapped. "Jettisoning was too insipid for what I wanted to do to you."

"Where's Tiny?" Vic demanded.

Nenn lunged for the door but paused, listening and praying his female was fine.

"She'll be dealt with soon enough."

Relief flooded him at that promise. Tiny lived. He could work with that.

Vic nodded at him, and he bolted. "If you want me, Leah, come and get me, but then again, you never had the balls. Unable to face your weakness, you cut my tether, didn't you?"

He sprinted from the passage, through the door, then froze at the ladder. "Computer, direct me to Tiny." He prayed to Osnir the ship heard him.

Lights flickered in the direction he needed to go. Some levels looked familiar, but he didn't take the time to confirm this. Tiny needed him. How could anyone hurt such a joyful female? He gritted his teeth and hurried, desperate to make it in time. To save her. Everything in him, including his symbiotes, urged him on. He burst onto the bridge but found it empty. Back along the passage he went, pausing to peer into the first room on the left.

There, sprawled on the floor, was Tiny. Bright red blood poured down the side of her bruised temple. Ripping his med-dev out of his pants, he kneeled beside her and ran it over her wound. The results flickered and beeped, listing her blindness, bruising, bleeding, swelling, and unconsciousness. All he already knew.

He cupped her cheek to angle her head, granting him easier access. "Please, Tiny, *hirihadie*, wake up."

Minutes passed, his ears honed for any approaching footsteps. He was vulnerable on the floor, but more than that, he didn't want this Leah female to take him by surprise.

Tiny's moan was the sweetest he'd ever heard. When her eyelashes fluttered, he pocketed his med-dev and slipped his arm under her neck to lift her onto his lap. The cold, hard floor would be harsh on her soft body. He shouldn't have noticed, but the way she filled his arms was unlike anything he'd experienced before. Peace consumed him while his malehood stirred with an eagerness he hadn't expected.

She raised her hand to her wound. "What...happened?"

"I do not know. Leah—"

"Nenn?" Tiny gasped.

"How do you feel?" he asked.

"Um...good," she said then struggled to sit up.

He let her with some reluctance.

"Leah hit me, didn't she?" She rubbed her fingers together, smearing her blood across the tips.

"I think so. Come, let us clean you." In one smooth movement, he had her on her feet.

She threw out a hand and caught his arm, holding on tight. "Where am I? My med bay?"

"Yes," he said and ushered her to a bed. He released her to hoist her onto it.

"Quit lifting me," she muttered. "I need to get my bearings."

"You are on the bed."

"I can tell," she said and gestured to a drawer. "Antiseptic wipes are in there."

He fetched a few thin pockets, set them beside her, and placed one in her hand. She tore it open, pulled out a white sheet then dabbed her face.

He smiled, took the cloth from her, and nudged her fingers aside.

She clasped her hands on her lap, her eyes wide and her gaze distant. "Where is she now?"

"Vic is dealing with her."

Tiny shivered with bumps forming across her skin. "I don't want to know how." She dipped her chin. "And I do." She glanced at Nenn. "Is that awful of me?"

"No, the female attacked you. It is right to be hurt and angry." He inched closer, settling between her parted knees to share his body heat with her.

"Computer...who's dead?" She held her breath, her concern in the paleness of her face.

"In order: Leah, Dieter, Nikko."

A smile teased her lips. "Trent and Grunt are alive?"

"Yes."

She kicked out her feet in a little wiggle, laughter tumbling from her. But her joy dwindled too quickly. "Things are messed up," she said. "I was hoping *Mula Pesada* would be my home, but with my crewmates trying to kill Vic and keeping prisoners for whatever reason... I need off this ship." She gestured to the corner of the room. "I'm almost packed."

"Good, I would love to show you my home." Nenn paused, caught her chin, and tipped her face to his. His chest expanded at the thought of showing her Erasril, sharing roast banaari, or a hot pool... "I have prepped a room for you onboard my ship."

He ran the now-pink cloth over the blood staining her purple hair, marveling at her smooth skin and how small she seemed to him.

"Thanks, I think," she said, offering him a tentative smile.

His strokes slowed. What he wanted to do was cup her cheeks, to lower his head, and press his lips to hers. He didn't, though, despite the urge driving him. "May I scan your eyes?"

She stiffened, and against his thumb under her jaw, her pulse leaped. "With?"

"My med-dev. It encourages healing and records information."

She angled her head, her brow furrowing in thought. "What do you hope it will find?"

"The extent of the damage. I would prefer to know upfront whether the Ivoyans can heal you. Giving you a false hope...angers me." He growled the last two words, unable to calm the volatile emotion burning through his veins. To be this outraged over something so simple was illogical.

She touched his forearms then slid her hands to his elbows. His symbiotes exploded in a hive of activity, peeling away his armor to grant her access to his unprotected skin.

"Will you share your med-dev's findings?" she asked, unaware of how much her caress shattered his control.

"Of course," he managed through gritted teeth.

Her shoulders dropped an inch, and she released a long exhale. "Then, yes, you may." She straightened her spine and waved her fingers at him. "If I can scan you?"

He chuckled. "With?"

"I have implants in my fingertips."

He grabbed her hand and focused on the hexagonal pattern of scars across her skin. "This is...incredible." He removed his med-dev and ran it over them, then gaped at sensors tinier than her pores. "I am most curious what they will reveal to you. I am, after all, unknown to your species."

"True," she said and splayed her fingers on his chest.

Again, without his instruction, his symbiotes retreated. His breath hitched when her touches summoned an unbearable heat in his core. He cleared his throat and raised the med-dev to her eyes.

"Were you born blind?" he asked.

"Oh, no," she said, feathering her hands up his throat. She found the implant and circled it. "What's this?"

"A language implant and communicator. It allows me to understand and speak your language, as well as reach my males within a short range."

She tapped her palm. "Mine is here. I can call my parents or friends." She ventured lower, trailing her fingers over his right pec. "Your..." She gasped and repeated the motion on his left pec. "Where are your nipples?"

He couldn't help himself and glanced at her breasts filling her tunic. "Males do not nurse babes."

She gaped. "Fascinating and true. I'm sad for you; it's such an erogenous zone for humans."

"Good to know." He swallowed past the lump in his throat and gripped the med-dev tighter to calm his trembling hands.

Heat radiated off her cheeks, so he scanned there, found nothing amiss, and returned to the task.

"My eyes used to be green," she said. "I'm told they're white now." Sorrow leaked into her voice, and a tear dewed on her eyelashes. "I stopped caring about my appearance a while ago." She caught a lock of her hair. "This was to match my dance outfit."

He smiled. "Now I am curious. You have a specific garment for dancing?"

Again, her cheeks warmed. "I...didn't make enough tokens at my day job, so at night, I danced at a nightclub to earn a little extra." Her stiff shrug in no way implied indifference. "I was in a cage and high up, so unbothered for most of the time."

"What color was your hair?" He placed the med-dev on the bed beside her and buried his hands in her locks. Cool, silky strands wrapped around his fingers.

"Brown. To get this color, they had to genetically modify the melanin. It's permanent for now." She flashed a smile. "What color's your hair?"

"All Giniiri are red-haired and red-eyed."

Her lips parted. "I wish I could see that. Is Giniiri your last name?"

"My tribal name." He massaged her scalp, checking for bumps he might have missed.

A poor excuse indeed when the med-dev would have listed a 'hidden' head wound. But touching her... There was nothing like it. No experience he could compare it to. Drawing on his dwindling control, he scooped up the med-dev and ran it over her eyes again. He had all he needed to know, but he didn't want this intimate session to end.

A throat clearing snapped his gaze to the door.

Vic grinned. "Am I intruding?"

"Not at all, Vic." Tiny glanced at Nenn, a small smile teasing her lush lips. A little green shone through the white of her eyes. Perhaps the med-dev had done more than he'd anticipated.

"How are you feeling?" Vic strode deeper into the room. She bore no injuries. But according to Computer, she'd taken care of Leah.

"Good. Nenn has a soft touch." Tiny's cheeks pinkened again. He frowned, planning to research the reason why. "You've been busy."

"I have?" Vic cast her gaze at her feet. "Aehort?" she gasped and flicked her focus at the door.

"Vic? Are you all right?" Tiny inched closer to the edge of the bed like she planned to slide off. Nenn filled the space between her thighs, blocking her. "Nenn, scan her, too."

"I'm fine." Vic tried to stop him with her hands raised.

He offered her a cloth to wipe the blood off her arm. As Drafe had said, she had his symbiotes and robotic creatures, so only healed skin remained.

"I know I told you to come with me," Vic said, "but you can stay with Themba. If you want."

"Nenn invited me to travel with him to his home." Tiny pursed her lips, drawing his gaze there. "I'm undecided. You?"

Vic exhaled in a whoosh. "I, too, will be going to Ivoy."

"Oh." Tiny grinned. "Then, of course, I'll go. I didn't want to be a burden nor the only human onboard their ship."

Nenn admired her bright smile. This... Yes, he loved it when she was like this.

Vic crossed between them to squeeze Tiny's shoulder. "Tiny, sweetheart, you helped us free the prisoners. You're not a burden." She winked at Nenn, though what that meant, he couldn't say. "Since you're in Nenn's capable hands, I'll return to the bridge. I'm sure there's much to discuss. When you're feeling better, please care for Themba. He's…" She winced. "Not well."

Tiny threw out her hand, finding Nenn's chest. "Captain's sick? Computer, status on Themba's heart."

"He is suffering from arrhythmias."

Tiny shoved Nenn aside and leaped off the bed. "Come, let us pay the ex-captain a visit." After grabbing a few things from drawers and cupboards, she marched down the passage.

He trailed her, content to watch her ass swing. Aware his temperature spiked and his koq throbbed, he willed his symbiotes to aid him, cooling and calming where needed. Though, he didn't mind suffering through both.

"You don't need to come with if you have other things you—"

"I choose to follow you." He smirked. She had no idea how true that was.

Her breath hitched. She said no more, just angled her head, listening to beeps.

"Do you know where to go?" he asked, wishing he could help her, but the cursed passage was too narrow for side-by-side.

"No, but Computer can take me there," she said, tossing a smile at him over her shoulder.

He said no more.

Chapter Fifteen

When Tiny entered her ex-captain's room, Themba was sobbing. She'd had to override security to gain access.

"Captain," she said, with no response.

"Someone has died," Nenn whispered from her right; his presence like an immovable wall. "A vid is playing on the wall."

"Oh." Now, Vic's hesitancy made sense. *He's not well*, she'd said. Pain had been in her voice. Maybe she'd known the person who'd died?

Tiny tapped the injection gun, choosing a mild tranquilizer. But when she took a step to where the crying came from, Nenn grabbed her hips and swung her, pinning her to his body.

She gasped and clung to him, her mind blank.

"There is debris on the floor," he said, his breath hot against her temple.

Beneath her fingers was solid muscle. Red hair and eyes? She liked the sound of that. And the texture of his skin was a mixture of warm suede and velvet. How could he be walking around shirtless in cold space? The thomp-thomp of his boots on the grated flooring said he wasn't fully naked, but still. While drawing in deep breaths to calm her erratic heartbeat, she pressed her temple to his chest. His scent filled her nose—sunbaked rock and metal.

"Thank you," she croaked. "Lead me to him, please, or press this gun to his neck."

Nenn shifted back but gripped her elbows. Then his touch was gone, along with the gun she'd squashed between her palm and his arm.

The swish of the injection ended the crying, no doubt surprising the catatonic captain. Sniffles then silence consumed the room.

"Computer, status?" she asked, reaching out a hand for Nenn.

When he grasped her fingers, something fluttered inside her: a sense of permanency, hope, promise... Whatever it was, it took all her concentration not to dwell on it.

"Heartbeat stabilizing."

"Take me to him," she asked Nenn.

Up he lifted her, summoning a squeak from her. He wrapped his arms just under her butt, leaving her clutching his shoulders. Before she could chastise him, her feet touched down. He released her, and the sweep-clink from the floor told her he brushed things aside for her.

Against her knees was the hard edge of a bed. She patted the air until she met Themba's hair. Under her fingertips, she registered dehydration, no doubt worsened by alcohol—he reeked of it. What she'd given him would help him sleep and wouldn't be affected by anything he'd consumed. Maybe in the morning he'd feel better?

"Computer, monitor him, and notify me if anything changes. Please lead me to the med bay." A beep sounded to her left.

Hot fingers laced with hers, and with a gentle tug, Nenn drew her toward it. "Computer, deactivate the vid."

At his thoughtfulness, she smothered a smile. She trailed him, happy to do so. Just because he was a medic wasn't a good enough reason to blindly trust him. Yet, he'd healed her, stayed with her, and been nothing but kind. No way would she entertain the thought that he did all this to get into her pants.

She shivered and ignored her nipples puckering in anticipation. No, she wouldn't seduce the man, nor would she broach the subject. She'd waited, bided her time, hoped Dieter would make the first move. How quickly she'd forgotten the lessons learned from her promiscuous past. An interested man would move mountains. One who didn't care wouldn't even bother to get to know her.

And she wanted it all: a knight who swept her off her feet, seduced, cherished, and...loved her? Finding that for a normal woman was hard, but for her, unable to read expressions, she was at a disadvantage from the get-go.

"My chessboard's the last thing I need to pack," she said when the familiar smell of her med bay surrounded her.

"I shall leave you here," Nenn said.

"What? Why?" she asked, taking a step toward his voice.

"We are on a mission to find killers. As a medic—"

"I get it," she muttered, flicking a dismissive wrist. He couldn't babysit her forever. She pursed her lips, desperate to understand why she didn't want him to go.

"I will return for you, *hirihadie*."

"If you live," she snapped, then scrunched her face at her angry tone.

He chuckled: low, husky, and sexy. "I am hard to kill."

"When you're shirtless?" She huffed. "At least put on some protection. Or...don't go." She winced, shut her mouth, marched to the chair and sat.

"Tiny," he said, his body warmth at her knees. "I *am* armored." He cupped her cheek, holding her still. "My symbiotes form it when I am in danger."

She layered her hand over his. "Your what?" A ping shot across her temple when she tried to unravel what he'd said.

"Inside every Qaldreth are symbiotes that carry the memories of our ancestors. Anything we do is recorded for all to remember."

"T-cells," she whispered, her eyes widening.

She leaped to her feet, then darted around him to grab the 3D model. "Like this? Vic's got these in her."

"Yes," he said, laughter in his voice. "Our symbiotes." The model left her hands. "This is brilliant. Is this how you 'see?'"

His admiration made her soul sing. "It's fascinating to hold it," she hurried to say to hide her breathlessness.

"Do you have one for Vic's robotic creatures?"

"Her what?" She frowned. "Do you mean her nanites?"

He hummed. "Is that what you call them?"

"It is. I can ask the printer to make a model for you." She raised her chin to the ceiling. "Computer, print a 3D representation of a nanite found in Vic's blood."

"Starting job now," Computer said, accompanied by the whirring hum of the 3D printer.

"I like your med bay. Mine is not as well-fitted." He caught her hand and stroked across her fingertips.

Somehow, she doubted that. "But you have that med-dev."

"It is designed for urgent care on battlegrounds." He caressed her knuckles, around her wrists, then to her elbows. She pinched her lips, trying to hide the goose bumps rippling through her even as she relished being touched. "For serious injuries, a pod fitted to the wall slides out when summoned. It caters for the full height of an Ivoyan."

"Oh," she gasped, splaying her fingers across his torso. Judging by how high she had to lift her arms, he was far from short. "How tall are you?"

"Six feet. An Ivoyan reaches seven feet on average."

She smiled. Here was a world she'd never encountered. Everywhere she went were humans. Qaldreths and Ivoyans were aliens, proving there was life in that black expanse humans had yet to discover. "Do you come from Ivoy?"

"If you mean was I born there? No. My home is Qaldreth. I am Giniiri—the volcanic tribe."

Her jaw dropped. No wonder he smelled like hot rocks and gave off such heat. Was that normal? Did all Qaldreth burn hotter than humans? What type of upbringing did he have? Were there parents, siblings, or was he raised by a village? How did he become a medic? What made him choose such a path? How did he get to Ivoy?

"Is your world advanced enough to space travel?" Out of all her questions, that slipped out. She almost stamped her foot in frustration.

"No. The Ivoyans collect those who pass the rite of Uhann." His tone lowered as if the subject hit a nerve. "That was...not a good day for me." He cleared his throat. "A discussion for another time."

"I'm sorry, Nenn," she said, sensing something horrible happened to him.

"*Hirihadie*, you have nothing to apologize for." He cupped her cheek, drawing a shiver from his hot fingers.

"Nanite model complete," Computer announced.

Grateful for the distraction, Tiny snapped the model off its stilts. The hefty structure of a nanite came to life in her hands. Having studied them, what she held felt right: a hexagonal ball with nozzles protruding off each flat side. She handed it to Nenn, who'd crowded her from behind, warmth pouring off his body with his breath fanning her shoulder.

"Yes, this is it," he said, his voice filled with awe.

"When you say Drafe has these, what do you mean?"

"The nanites have fused with the symbiotes, forming something...new."

Her mind reeled. "Have there been any symptoms or side effects?" She gaped, her eyes widening. "When you said your symbiotes form armor, what does it look like? Do you sparkle?"

He barked a laugh. "No. Why do you ask?"

"Vic said Nikko punched her, but she didn't feel a thing. That something shimmered over her skin."

Silence met her words. "That…is impossible," Nenn whispered. "I had to learn how to summon my armor."

"Oh, it just happens. I don't think Vic knows how to control it…them."

A moan snapped Tiny's head up. No, she'd heard wrong.

"Please," Vic groaned.

A flush crawled up Tiny's neck. She didn't dare glance at Nenn, but she couldn't sit there and listen for who knew how long. With or without Nenn beside her. "You better not be doing what it sounds like. I may be blind, but I'm not deaf."

The kissing stopped; whispers and laughter followed. Vic and Drafe hurried past the med bay. Nenn didn't say anything, and Tiny was at a loss, too. She gathered her confidence around her, strode to the bridge, and sank into the seat in front of the console. With no one here, someone had to be on duty. Nenn trailed her, bringing his quiet presence with him.

He didn't draw near but stayed by the door. His shifting gave her the impression he leaned against the wall, his arms folded. She liked the imagery even though she couldn't confirm whether her imagination had run away with itself. Tingles rippled along the right side of her body; that sense that someone was watching her. She angled her head to focus on the singular beep as tension built in her body. Heat coiled, desire throbbed lower, her nipples puckered, and her breathing became shallow. She squeezed her eyes shut, stuck in this situation. Glancing at him would reveal nothing to her without her ability to see his expression. Nor would she ask him what he was doing.

"You are beautiful," he said.

She gasped, succumbing to the pointless urge to face him. "You didn't just say that." Her heart zinged in sweet joy at his unexpected compliment.

"Why not?" He approached, sending a bolt of anticipation through her.

"Um…" What could she say? They barely knew each other? It wasn't normal behavior? That meant nothing to an alien. She dipped her chin, hoping to hide her confusion.

"Why does your face change color?" he asked as he stroked a cheek. "I like the heat, and it is a pretty pink."

"Oh." She whipped her head up, then closed her eyes at having to explain her embarrassment. "A blush forms during overwhelming emotion or exertion."

"Emotion?" Warmth filled his voice. "Such as?"

She winced and swiveled the chair to break away from his magnetism. Who would've thought his touch could scatter her wits? She smothered a borderline hysterical giggle. "Shame, awareness, attraction, anger..."

"Attraction." He hummed.

She huffed at him snagging on the truth. "It could be any of the others."

"Shame when you do not concern yourself over your appearance? Anger carries different mannerisms and posture and is often accompanied by yelling. Awareness? Yes, that is possible." He rested his hands on her shoulders and dug his fingers into the tense muscles, drawing a moan from her as he worked on the knots. "I would blush for you."

She stilled, her body buzzing with pleasure. "Why are you charming me, Nenn? You cannot think I'll have sex with you after knowing you for such a short time."

His breath hitched. "You intrigue me, and I plan to discover everything about you on our return to Ivoy, when matters are settled here." His fingers gentled. "As to sex...or mating, that is what I very much want to try with you."

Her face burned. She opened and closed her mouth, unable to form words, never mind speak them. His honesty was brutal, but she had to admit, she appreciated it after crushing on Dieter and Office Parsons.

"Glad to see you two," Vic said, striding onto the bridge. "We're getting ready to take the facility."

"I'm staying, of course," Tiny said and didn't glance at Nenn still grasping her shoulders.

"I will be heading moonside with you, Vic." He slid his hands down to squeeze Tiny's upper arms, captured a lock of her hair, then tucked it behind an ear.

Her pulse exploded into an erratic beat. She forced herself not to react. Perhaps some time apart would end this insanity.

"Good. I like knowing there's someone I can trust on the *Mula Pesada*, Tiny. How's Themba?" Vic asked.

"I administered a calming drug. It will knock him out for a while. The computer is monitoring his vital signs." Tiny paused, turning the chair to 'look' at Vic. In doing so, Nenn moved with her, his hand once more on her shoulder. "Nenn said there was a vid playing of someone dying?" She frowned. "I'm sorry for his loss."

"Thank you." Vic exhaled like someone about to attempt something momentous. "Computer, ship-wide broadcast. *Mula Pesada*, this is the captain speaking. Report to the docking bay. The shuttle leaves in ten."

Vic and Drafe left the room. Nenn didn't.

Tiny waited, dread crushing her chest. He could die down there. As a doctor, she cared. She'd sworn to heal as many as she could. But for some odd reason, the thought of Nenn injured sent sheer panic through her. She bit her inner cheek, praying she didn't reveal her anxiousness.

"Be careful," was all she allowed herself to say.

"I will be." Softness brushed across her temple. He lingered for another moment then marched out.

She touched her forehead, her breathing nonexistent. *Did he kiss me?*

She scoffed. No, she'd imagined it. But wow, what a wonderful fantasy. She grinned then remembered what awaited them moonside. "Computer, can you monitor the team heading to Europa?"

"In the shuttle, yes; on the surface, no, I do not have access."

She slumped. So much for that. What she needed to do was keep busy. "Status of the crew?"

"Trent is pacing, his heart rate ramped. Grunt is working at his console. Themba is asleep. Various other crew suffer from malnutrition and minor injuries."

"The other crew?" Her eyes widened. *The prisoners.* She leaped to her feet and hurried to the med bay for the multi-tool and the injection gun. Time to get to work.

Chapter Sixteen

Year: 2219

Moonside on Europa.

Nenn stepped into the shuttle, wishing he'd stayed with Tiny. She fascinated him, with her pink cheeks and sweet smiles. Not to mention the way she managed to do her job despite her blindness. Her strength was to be admired.

Telling her she was beautiful had been as much a surprise to him as it was to her. He'd stared at her, memorizing the curve of her face. Her breasts rising and falling with her ragged breathing, her pulse ticking at the base of her throat, and her nipples tenting her tunic had proved she wasn't immune to him.

Foq. His lips tingled from where he'd pressed them to her temple. Her skin had smelled so good that he wanted to inhale her exotic perfume until it saturated his senses. At least, the taking of the facility had been relatively quick. He'd healed where he could, calmed those traumatized, and returned to the rusted box, grateful he hadn't needed to carry anyone onboard.

He drew in a deep breath and slapped the side. Its flight worthiness had been confirmed on the trip down. They hadn't gone up in a blaze of fire despite the shuddering frame and whining engines.

The human pilot, Sonja, kept it powered up until Caah appeared behind her. "Dez is staying. The facility is secure if you wish to disembark now," he said.

She tossed him a tight smile. "I'm returning for the others."

"Told you she'll fly," Caah said to Nenn when he leaned against the interior bulkhead beside him.

Nenn arched a brow, still finding it odd that a species would genderize inanimate objects.

"I wish to remain on the *Mula Pesada*," Caah said to Drafe when Sonja launched off the moon. "Without having to ask the Q.C.C. for permission. You know how long they take to debate."

Nenn gawked at Caah, finding his request unexpected yet understandable. Had Tiny insisted on staying, he might have done the same. Something stretched between them he couldn't identify like she was his to protect. He almost snorted at that nonsense. She'd survived without him and would continue to do so.

He studied Sonja, wondering if any female would inspire the same intensity of emotion. She didn't have the softer curves and vulnerability that Tiny had. Having not seen another female comparable, he couldn't say if this attraction was solely for Tiny.

Drafe gathered Vic close. "I shall inform them it was my decision." He didn't glance at Caah. "Your skills are needed here, and you will serve as a bridge between humans and Qaldreth. If the Q.C.C. wish to send an ambassador, they may do so at their leisure."

Caah beamed and gripped Drafe's forearm, snapping his attention from Vic. "My thanks, *darasaho*." He returned to Nenn's side, brimming with eagerness. Calling Drafe 'brother' said much about the crew's opinion of the arrak who had chosen them for this seemingly pointless mission.

"Drop us on top of the *Mula Pesada*, Sonja." Drafe gestured at the massive ship dominating the forevids.

"What?" she squeaked. "Okay, if you say so." With deep concentration, she veered the shuttle left.

Nenn had no intention of going anywhere without Tiny. He'd told her he'd return, but escorting her along the outside of the ship to reach the *Aroagni* was a no. It would endanger her, and she didn't have a nodule to survive in space.

"Get the *Aroagni* to send a shuttle for pick-up," he said to Drafe. "I do not want my female walking across a ship, not until I have repaired her vision."

Drafe chuckled. "Protecting her is your right, Nenn." He pulled Vic toward the door, crowding it.

"Thanks, Caah, and good luck." She smiled.

Sonja clipped a mask on, covering her face, then opened the side door. Nenn, Caah, Drafe, and Vic double-tapped their nodules, summoning their shields. Out Drafe and Vic leaped, landing on the *Mula Pesada's* exterior. The door shut, and the shuttle shot off, aiming for the starting point of this adventure. Sonja powered off the engines and skidded the shuttle under the retracting arm. A thump followed then a jerk before the door groaned across.

"How did it go?" someone asked when they marched down the ramp.

"We did well," Sonja said with a laugh, glancing at Caah. "Des says to choose: Libertas or *Mula Pesada*."

Nenn gripped Caah's forearm. "I shall leave with Tiny when the shuttle arrives."

"On its way," Vaen snapped, his voice buzzing through the nodule. "This is madness, Caah. Insanity."

"And yet, I am compelled to stay. Osnir urges me to do so," Caah said, his fingers pressed to his throat.

"Well, incoming," Vaen growled. "Let whoever know—"

"Granting access to bay 7A," Computer said. "Follow the flickering lights. Bay doors opening now."

"Well done." Grunt beamed, striding toward them. "My company's pleased with our success. Nenn, if your people need anything, reach out to me."

Nenn bowed his head, tossed a final glance at Caah, and headed for the med bay. His feet carried him there like they had a mind of their own. Something fluttered in his chest, exploding warmth through him. Tiny would be in his arms soon.

She sat at a table, her hands in her lap, her gaze distant. "Nenn?" She faced the doorway.

"Yes."

"Oh," she gasped, a smile teasing her lips. "It went well?"

"The facility has been freed." He strode across to her, gathered her hands in his, and guided her to her feet. "My shuttle has arrived. Are you ready?"

Her eyes widened. "I thought—"

"You are coming with me." He wouldn't tolerate indecision now.

She grinned, squeezing his fingers before releasing them. "I am. Just glad we're not space walking."

He lifted her bag. "Bay 7A."

"Computer, show me the way," she said then followed the beep. "I'm going to miss it." She didn't glance over her shoulder at him.

"Your planet? People?" He kept his gaze on the back of her head, forcing himself not to stare at her swaying hips no matter how much he wanted to.

"The computer. I couldn't have done this job without it." She flicked a dismissive wrist as she turned left, then right along a passage. "I was saving tokens to buy my own AI. Do you have any like that on your ship?"

"No, but then I plan to heal your vision."

She stumbled and caught herself with a thrown-out hand. "I hope so," she whispered. "Though if you or the Ivoyans can't, I won't be angry with you, Nenn. I promise."

Pain cinched his chest as if Kreta had thrust her claws into him to crush his heart. He didn't know what to say to Tiny, but her acceptance drove him not to give up. Somewhere, a species had to heal her. If not the Ivoyans, then another world? Would he travel the universe for her?

Certainty poured from every symbiote.

She paused when they reached the bay. "Um, is there a ladder?" In her path was the railing but far lower than where she patted the air.

"Yes. Stay here. Let me deliver your bag." He gripped the ladder and slid down, sparing no effort to drop her things inside the compartment. Vaen glared at him but didn't say a word.

Nenn sucked in a breath when he returned to Tiny's side. "I can guide you."

She shook her head. "Are you strong?"

He frowned. "Yes, why?"

"Throw me over your shoulder." She nibbled on her lip, drawing his gaze there. "Is that okay?"

"You will not mind?" His fingers twitched at the opportunity to touch her.

"Nenn," she said. "Why would I suggest—"

He grasped her by the hips and bent her over his shoulder. She squeaked, her fingers digging into his back as she clung to him.

"Warn me," she rasped.

He took each rung with care until his boots touched the bay floor. But he didn't lower her. Instead, he strode to the shuttle, up the ramp, then stopped by a seat. He ran his hand from her plump backside, along the delicate curve of her spine, to between her shoulder blades before flipping her to the front of him.

She filled his arms to perfection. He stared at her flushed face, her parted lips, the way her fingers dug into his upper arms.

"Ready?" Vaen called, shutting the door before Nenn could respond.

Nenn glared at him while ushering Tiny into a seat, buckling her in.

"Who's that?" she whispered, leaning forward to do so.

"Riermus aac Vaen Arrak." Nenn lowered his voice, a smile widening his mouth. She was too adorable. "And he can hear you."

"Oh. Sorry. Is he another medic?" she asked, gripping and releasing her knees when Nenn stepped back.

"Arrak stands for guardian. I am a maed."

"Ah, the ranks are on the end of your name," she said, staring a little over his left shoulder. Her heartbeat pulsed at the base of her jaw when Vaen reversed the shuttle out of the bay.

Nenn caught her chin between his forefinger and thumb, then swept a caress to her pulse. She raised her unseeing gaze to him, making him doubt she couldn't see him.

"You're not hurt?" she asked, her eyelashes fluttering when he ran his touch to her ear then along her neck to her collarbone.

"I am well."

Her breath came out in a rush. "Good. Describe your ship... Please. What does it look like? That sort of thing."

"It is beautiful, looking like a polished volcanic rock in the shape of a horizontal teardrop."

A smile twitched her top lip up. "That's beautiful. Quite poetic."

He squatted before her instead of sitting beside her. "Vaen's bringing us in."

"That quickly?" She lifted her chin. "Thank you for fetching us, Vaen."

"Not like I had a choice," he muttered, but to her, he said, "I serve Qaldreth."

"Did Nenn force you to come?" she asked.

Vaen twitched and cast a glance over his shoulder, his eyes wide. "You heard me?"

"Of course. Heightened senses." She chuckled. "But vent away. I understand not wanting to do something yet being made to."

"It is insanity. Caah remains behind, we have females on the *Aroagni*, and yes, the mission is complete, but you are also the same species that killed the Senate." He growled. "This cannot end well."

"What happened to the Senate?" she asked, concern furrowing her brow.

"Did I not tell you about the dead humans in the Carne pods?" Nenn frowned. "I shall fill you in on our mission parameters and what dangers lie ahead. If any." He glowered at Vaen.

The door opened to Gusin and Ulvus. Nenn swallowed a curse. He didn't need Ulvus to lash out at Tiny with his negativity.

"Welcome," Gusin said, striding forward to clasp Tiny's hand.

She offered a tight smile.

"This is Zuphayr aac Gusin Taed." Nenn slid her hand from Gusin's and laced his fingers through hers.

She laughed. "Just give me his name, Nenn. I don't need his last name and rank."

He stiffened then chuckled. "You are correct. This is Gusin, Tiny."

"A pleasure to meet you." She shifted away from Nenn but didn't release him. "And who is this?" She stared in Ulvus's general direction.

"Ulvus." Nenn waited, and as usual, the male disappointed.

"She is blind?" Ulvus spat in Qaldreth. "She is weak and should be killed. This is not how we strengthen our lineage."

"Oh, he's a grumpy one," she said, inching back until she was at Nenn's side.

"Ignore Ulvus, Tiny," Gusin said, striding past her. "We do."

"This is unacceptable. Does Aehort know?" Ulvus demanded. "If he condones it, the new Senate will be most displeased."

Paying his doomsaying no mind, Nenn picked up Tiny's bag and led her from the bay. She followed, her trust breathtaking. Not once did her steps falter.

He stopped at her door. "This is your quarters," he said, tapping the panel to gain access.

"Okay," she said. "Want to describe it to me?"

"It is unadorned." He pulled her inside. "On the right is a hard bed. To the left is the indoor waterfall. A bin"—he took her hand and placed it on an indent—"is where you throw your dirty garments. We take turns to do that chore. Above it and around it are storage compartments."

He dragged her fingers to the left, guiding her to the water nozzle. "To activate, twist the dial to the left for hot, to the right for cold."

"Are there restrictions in place?"

He frowned, taken aback at her odd question. "In what way?"

"To limit the amount of water we use?"

"No, Ivoy is a planet with water in abundance. The tanks on the *Aroagni* contain thousands of liters and are often replenished when we pass a non-inhabited planet."

"Wonderful." She smiled. "Anything in the way? Like a step or a chair?" She angled her head to glance at him. This close, her scent tickled his nose, tempting him to bury his face in the curve of her neck.

"Nothing," he said, pulling his focus away.

"Oh, that's good." She tugged, and he released her. Around the room she moved, trailing her fingers along the walls, into the indents, until she met the air above her bed. "It's so clinical." She wrapped her arms around herself. "And cold."

He agreed, hating the chill that lingered in an unused room. "Whatever you need, I shall attempt to provide. The latter, immediately. The temperature can be set to your preference."

"Twenty-four, please."

He tapped a panel by the door, adjusting it as she requested. "How do you want your bed?"

"Pillows, linen, a mattress?" Both of her eyebrows rose. "Is that possible?"

He chuckled. "Of course. Let me fetch those for you now. I have placed your things to the right of the door." He bolted, sprinting down the passages to the storeroom in the bay. Upon passing Igar, he snagged the male's arm and dragged him along. "Need help carrying."

He was as giddy as the young child who'd gone foraging with his father so many years ago.

While Igar huffed under the ungainliness of the mattress, Nenn had a sheet, two blankets, and a pillow obscuring his vision. Tiny was playing with the water dial when he entered, drawing a gasp from her.

"My apologies for startling you. This is Igar," he said and gestured to the male to place the mattress. He did but ogled her, his mouth agape.

Nenn nudged him, snapping him out of his daze.

"A pleasure to meet you, Igar," she said, offering her hand.

Not knowing what to do with such a strange gesture, Igar clasped her forearm in greeting. "Is she not human?" he asked Nenn in Qaldreth. "Or is she part Awayar?" He gestured to Tiny's white eyes so like the Awayar tribe.

"She is blind," Nenn said. "I am hoping the Ivoyans will heal her."

"That's such a beautiful language." Her tone was sweet, but the lines around her mouth implied she didn't truly think so.

"Thank you for the aid, Igar." Nenn dropped his armload, caught the sheet, and fitted it in place. He folded the blankets at the foot end and left the pillow at the top of the bed. The door swished, marking Igar's departure.

Nenn waited for silence before facing her. "My apologies. Not all onboard speak human." He forced a chuckle at his deception. "All want to know who you are." *Like I did.*

She laughed. "Fair enough. I guess I shouldn't be so sensitive."

He grasped her hand and led her to the bed.

"You made it?" she asked, raising a wide-eyed gaze to him. "Thank you."

"I am next to you if you need me, Tiny." He hesitated, tapped his arm to summon the hologrammed commands, and aligned his room to hers. If she screamed, he'd hear her.

"Um, Nenn." She inched closer to him, her fingers extended. "How do I leave?"

He clasped her hand and drew her to the panel. "Place your palm here."

When she did, the door opened.

"I will ensure Gusin has programmed it for you and me. I have also set the sensitivity of the room to connect with me. If you need me, call my name."

With no more excuses to stay, he stepped through the door. "I will leave you to become familiar with your new home."

Her smile was tentative. She glanced behind her, then at him, before nodding. "Thanks, Nenn."

And just like that, he was alone in the passage and gazing at the door like Tugo had hit him with a rock.

Chapter Seventeen

Tiny blinked in the direction of the door. Just like that, she was alone on an alien spaceship heading to a planet no human had been to before.

She faced her temporary home. "Am I crazy?"

She'd fired off a quick message to Dad, skimming over the details. That she couldn't share her plans said it all. They'd have her committed for sure. She stifled a giggle at the idea of being in the same rehab center as Jamie. They'd have to put a guard at his door.

That thought destroyed her good humor.

Dealing with her anger, resentment, and unforgiveness wasn't on today's agenda, so she shoved them down. A time would come when she'd be forced to face how she felt about him. The maturer Tiny understood that her parents couldn't abandon him, no matter what he did. She also accepted that going off-world meant they'd once again focus on him since he was closer. Her relationship with her family...might never be her idea of normal.

She skimmed her hand over the wall to find her bag, then lugged it toward the hidden closets. This room was smaller than Celestial's but not as miniscule as on the *Mula Pesada*. And she had Nenn next door.

Her heartbeat scattered, fluttering butterflies in her chest, while it found its rhythm again. Everything had gone bat-shit crazy. From worrying about what to do to stave off boredom to people dying, healing prisoners, letting an alien man charm her, to 'moving in' with him.

"And you haven't even slept with him yet." She snorted at that. "Matter of time," she muttered. She almost rolled her eyes at that bit of nonsense. Having had zero sex since her kidnapping incident, she'd give her left kidney for a little action.

Farg. Just to be held, if she was being honest with herself. Humans needed affection. She craved that *and* sex. If Nenn cuddled afterward, she was keeping him.

It didn't take her long to pack away her meager belongings.

She stripped and tested out the shower, towel-dried herself, then climbed into bed. Exhaustion sapped her energy, and she sank into the mattress with a moan. But sleep didn't come. She lay there, her mind reeling. Alone. Blind. In space. She couldn't be more vulnerable than that.

The only people she could lean on were Nenn and Vic, who was a little preoccupied. So, just Nenn then. She sat up, and sniffed, the tears falling without warning. "Computer," she whispered, "Please play my beats." Silence met her request. She laughed amid sobs. "Play the audiobook?" This time, she succumbed and let the weight of sorrow bow her shoulders and her tears dribble off her chin.

Warm arms engulfed her. Without questioning the sensation, she curled into the embrace. She'd cried over the loss of her eyesight, prospects, and a career so many times but hadn't truly let herself grieve. She'd promised herself she'd do it tomorrow, or when she had a steady job, or found her place in the world... And when those moments had presented themselves, she hadn't taken the opportunity.

A hand stroked her bare back, another splayed at the base of her spine, sending tingles outward. The cologne was sunlight and hot rock. She stiffened mid-sniffle. Her cheeks exploded with heat. *Oh my word, I'm naked.*

"Nenn?" she asked, her voice hoarse. *Oh, Lord, let it not be a stranger.*

"Yes, *hirihadie*?" He tightened his arms, crushing her against him.

She exhaled in a sigh.

Velvet skin, as bare as hers, was under her fingertips. Her breath hitched. Desire unfurled in her belly, but she didn't pull away. Gathered against him allowed her to maintain her modesty, for now.

"Was I too loud?" she asked, clinging to his chest.

"I apologize. I could not bear your pain a moment longer." When he unraveled his arms and stepped back, she squeaked, yanking the sheet up to her chin.

"Why are you shirtless? Did..." She winced. He might have been readying for bed or in the shower... "Did I disturb you?"

"Never, Tiny," he said, his voice husky. "I am not naked. My symbiotes form an armor, even beneath my pants and boots."

She frowned, throwing out a hand and smacking his chest. For a moment, she met a wall of solid muscle before hot velvet registered. "I felt it... You said your armor fades." *Wow.* It coming and going had to be an awesome sight.

"At your touch, yes." He layered his hot hand over hers, trapping her.

"I need my sleepshirt," she said, nudging her chin at the hidden closet.

He released her and marched across, proving he wore boots. She hadn't heard him enter. Grimacing at what he'd walked in on, she massaged her temple. *Why do I insist on embarrassing myself?*

"What is a sleepshirt?" he asked.

"A garment that covers my top half." She smiled. "I don't have symbiotes."

The riffling stopped. His breathing turned ragged, then the closet panels popped open and shut. He returned to her and placed something on her lap.

She tested the texture of the fabric and grinned. "Please, turn around."

"Why?" he asked.

"So that you don't see me naked. Humans are fussy like that."

When he shuffled, she had to assume he'd granted her some modesty. She dropped the sheet, flicked out the shirt, and peeled it on. "Thanks," she said, tugging the hem beneath the sheet to cover her hips and ass. "Um, Nenn, would you mind if I read you?" She moved to the edge of the bed, angling toward him while praying he'd let her.

He caught her hand and rested it over a pec. "I do not understand." His chest rose and fell, a little fast. His heartbeat thumped against her palm.

"So I can visualize what you look like."

"If I can read you?" he asked.

She laughed. "Sure." She pushed herself onto her knees to give her a little height then peeled her hand out from under his. This close, heat poured off him. She slid her fingers up, his sternum guiding her to his collarbones, his strong neck to his sharp jawline. Fluttering over his face, she halted at the top, by his temple. Hair tickled her knuckles, so she dived in, stroking the silkiness of his...mohawk.

He shuddered. Though she didn't know what that meant.

She smiled. "Love the hairstyle."

He didn't respond. She shrugged and continued over winged brows, flickering eyelashes, and a long nose to soft lips, wide and full. He exhaled, blasting her fingers with warmth.

With a shiver she couldn't hide, she withdrew her hands. *He's gorgeous.* Her mouth dried, forcing her to lick her lips. It would be so easy to place a kiss on any part of him within reach.

"My turn," he growled.

He caressed her from temple to chin, his touch gentle but pulsing waves of goose bumps outward. A stroke along the shell of her ear and a thumb running the length of her jaw to her chin shot her breathing to hell. She pinched her thighs together and shifted nearer to him. He brushed his fingers over her lips, using a little force to part them.

With a groan, he pressed his mouth to hers.

She gasped in surprise. His lips were so supple. Her senses zinged. She gripped his torso and retreated to angle her head for a better taste, but he broke away, almost sending her toppling forward.

"Forgive me," he mumbled.

She frowned. "I—"

He cupped her face and kissed her again.

She glided her hands around his waist, leaning against him and trapping him. This time, she hurried to slip her tongue in, moaning when his taste tightened the knot of lust in her core. He stiffened, but she was beyond stopping, desperate to learn every crevice of his mouth. When she thought he'd pull back, he didn't. Instead, he splayed his hands between her shoulder blades and crushed her within his embrace.

Want, need, lust, desire…whatever the word, she didn't care. Kissing him was heavenly, more so when he ravaged her, owning her senses. Never had she been so overwhelmed and in such a good way.

He dusted his lips along her cheek to her temple, his breathing harsh. "This face-latching is called kissing, or so Drafe said. I never expected it to be this wonderful. With you, Tiny, I have no resistance."

Face what? He'd never kissed anyone? She blinked, her thoughts…wits scattered. "It's called many things," she managed. Her pulse skipped a beat at the realization she rattled him as much as he did her. She ran her fingers to his chin, then pressed her lips there. "Peck." Another on his cheek with a lip-smacking sound. "Smooch." And before her courage abandoned her, she whispered into his mouth, "This is French."

With him so attentive, she flicked the tip of her tongue along his bottom lip then dove in. He growled and glided his hands around to sink his fingers into her ass. Not once did she think his touch too intrusive. She relished ever caress and squeeze, like the long stroke when he'd carried her, going from the underside of her thighs, along her ass to her back. At the time, she'd assumed he'd done that to ensure she found her balance. But now, with his mouth on hers, perhaps he'd been more attracted to her than she'd picked up.

Panting, he broke the kiss but didn't release her. "No wonder humans greet each other like this."

"What?" She lifted her head from where she'd rested her temple on his sculpted pec, drawing in his scent with every ragged breath. "Only lovers," she hurried to say in case Qaldreths went around kissing diplomats.

He hummed, caught her chin, then angled her head for another kiss. "I could French kiss you forever," he rasped.

She was butter in his hands. Not the hard kind, but the gooey, melt-in-your-mouth kind. Her taut nipples throbbed, her sex thrummed, her stomach tightened, and she'd swear she'd developed a fever. What she wanted was for him to throw her down and plunder her.

Sanity prevailed. She'd met him today. And even though she'd done quite a few one-night-stands, this...had to be different. She was older, wiser, and would be stuck with Nenn for however long this trip took. There was no fucking-and-ducking for her. Not to mention, she'd promised herself she wouldn't seduce him. But she'd hadn't sworn to not hug or kiss him.

She looped her arms around his neck and tucked her face into the angle of his neck. Contentment settled in her chest, and she sighed, rubbing her cheek across his velvety skin. *Farg, it's so good to be held.*

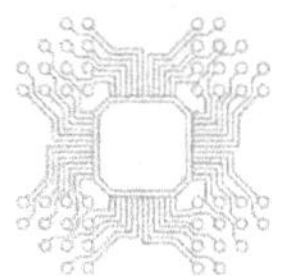

NENN REELED, LIKE HE'D fallen off a cliff and hit the ground, face first. His thoughts whirled, his instincts made demands, and his symbiotes were in a frenzy. His hard koq ached, pulsing pain outward. He was *that* aroused. Kissing Tiny had been more than he'd dreamed and nothing like he'd expected. Her taste, the agility of her tongue, her breasts against his chest, the way her fingers dug into his hair... She was shredding his control, tossing aside his ability to rationalize.

Just under his palms, thin fabric prevented him from reaching her skin. Only the fragile grip he had on his control prevented him from testing the pliancy of her bare backside.

When her sobbing had penetrated his room, he'd bolted. Her bare shoulders should've warned him, but he'd only sought to offer comfort. Osnir help him, she was so soft all over. That registered first. The way she curled into him had summoned a desperate urge to protect her and an overpowering need to mate her. It had taken everything in him not to lift her into his arms and sprawl her on the bed.

The temptation had yet to fade, now worsened by her flavor coating his tongue. The scent of her skin clung to his, and like he'd experienced before, she filled his arms to perfection.

"Hungry?" he asked.

If he could get her away from a bed, he might retain some of his sanity. Then again, he didn't know if humans mated at first sight. Being cautious might not be appreciated. The air in his lungs seized. He could have her this instant. Nothing stopped him. Except, he wanted her to come willingly without the haze of lust drowning her inhibitions.

'I want you, Nenn,' had to come out of that sexy mouth of hers.

"I could eat," she said, striding away to dig in the cube storage. The 'sleepshirt' rose dangerously high as she bent over.

When she'd said she didn't have his symbiotes, fire had blazed along his veins. If things went well, she would. But what had truly sent him spinning was the image of the armor encasing her breasts. It would do nothing to hide the shape or her taut nipples. His fingers twitched so he drew them into fists and clasped them behind his back.

"Turn around, please," she said, holding garments against her chest.

He coughed to hide a chuckle. The last time he'd done a full circle, having not expected her to drop the sheet and expose her body to him. He'd given her his back when he caught her explanation, but it was too late by then. Never had he seen a more beautiful creature: smooth, creamy skin, plump breasts, the curve of her stomach into flaring hips...

"Ready," she said, interlocking their fingers.

He glanced at her upturned face, her unseeing white gaze not diminishing how she affected him. "Do you have a food preference?" he asked and led her from the room.

"I can eat anything if it's human compatible."

As a maed, he should have considered this a possible issue. He frowned, not liking his lack of foresight. "Vic has not had a problem yet."

She laughed. "Vic's superhuman, I swear."

He scowled. "In what way?"

She shrugged. "I meant it jokingly. She's so strong and capable that she'll make any woman in a large radius self-conscious."

He studied Tiny's face, trying to understand what she meant. "Would she hurt them? You?"

"Oh, no, not like that. Just a kick to our self-esteem." Tiny flicked a hand at her eyes. "I can't compete."

Anger was swift to strike. His vision tinted red. With a growl, he halted, gripped her elbows and forced her to 'look' at him. "Why would you think that?"

She gaped, her brow furrowing. "I…"

"You are no less female than she is. You are incredible—a blind maed determined to conquer her disability. Foq." He released her to cup her face, leaning in so that she pressed against him. "I find you…breathtaking."

Her eyes widened. "I didn't say that to garner compliments. Vic's an inspiration, someone I wish I could emulate."

His thoughts spun. Couldn't she see herself as he saw her? "I do not wish that. You are perfect the way you are."

She scoffed. "Except for the blindness, right?"

He jerked back like Ulvus had managed to land a punch. "If that is true, then why am I hard for you now? Surely I would wait for you to be healed to get you beneath me?"

Her cheeks flushed. "You didn't just say that, Nenn."

"I am honest in my need for you, Tiny."

She exhaled, squared her shoulders, then lifted her hand, finding his jaw. Before he could guess her actions, she rose onto her toes and kissed him. "I want you, too." She smiled at him like she hadn't tilted his world on its axis. "Now feed me."

CHAPTER EIGHTEEN

Nenn settled Tiny at the table in the galley. His fingers trembled when he ran his hand along her shoulders. He could have her now.

'I want you,' rang in his ears and opened the gates to his emotions, which he struggled to control. He need not rush this when they had plenty of time before they reached Ivoy. They wouldn't be chasing pods this time.

"Greetings," Juunn said, striding into the room.

"Hello." Tiny faced him, her reaction a little delayed. Her gaze trailed his passing then rested on the bang he made when he put down his jar.

"Tiny, this is Juunn," Nenn said, wishing the male hadn't intruded.

Juunn stumbled, flicked a gaze between her and Nenn, then nudged him on the arm.

Nenn nudged him back and broke away to rest his hand on Tiny's shoulder. "Do you want hot or cold?"

"Hot, please. A warm belly might help me sleep."

"Do not make your tisane," Juunn muttered. "It smells like a dead animal."

Nenn bristled. "It is delicious—"

"So you say. Order Meorri tulsig." Juunn took his jar of fruit juice and left.

"I'll try both," she said, clasping her hands in front of her. She angled her head, her focus distant. "And whatever Juunn has. It smells like mango." She hummed, pursing her lips. "I can't remember when I last had fruit."

Her sweet smile had Nenn staring at her.

"Same," he said, offering her his back.

He gripped the edge of the counter. She shouldn't affect him this quickly or strongly. Truth. It had been a while since he'd last seen to his own pleasure. Mating a female back home only happened if she was a lonely widow or unmarried by choice. Either were rare, and being chosen was dependent on their preference. The symbiotes shared glimpses of matings. He grimaced. With a Qaldreth female, he'd flounder but find his way. With a human, he was at a loss. New respect for Drafe arose. The male must have honed his knowledge of human female anatomy enough to bring Vic to orgasm; he had to assume. Never would he ask Drafe anything so...intimate.

The replicate dinged, snapping him out of his thoughts. Perhaps he need only ask Tiny for guidance. He carried the plate of salt cakes to her and placed the tisane on the table. He took the time to guide her hand to each one before sinking onto the bench opposite her.

She stroked a cake, learning its shape as she circled it then testing its consistency by pressing the center. "Smells good," she said, scooped one up, and bit into it. "Oh."

Her moan shot heat to his already hard koq. Maybe feeding her had been rash on his part.

"Will you teach me to mate with you?" he asked.

She choked, coughed, then grabbed the tisane for a gulp. Her cheeks blazed a bright pink, and her eyes shimmered. "Nenn," she croaked. "This—"

"Please. I want to give you pleasure."

She placed her unfinished cake onto the plate, licked a fingertip, then held out her hand.

He didn't hesitate, grabbing it and lacing their fingers.

"If you show me how to please you."

Hot ice slid across his shoulders at her consideration. "Yes," he managed.

"Good." She smiled, withdrew her hand, and brought the jar to her mouth. "It smells like a rotting corpse but tastes like hot vanilla-lavender tea." She smacked her lips. "Aren't you hungry?"

No. He couldn't eat. His groin ached. A maed had to heal himself or ask another to do so. His breath caught. Before him sat Tiny, a maed, and the cure to this incessant agony.

"For you," he said, relishing her renewed blush. 'Attraction,' she'd said, triggered her changes in color. And intense emotion. Yes, like pure lust.

"I hope to get used to your honesty," she said before popping the last bit of a tulsig cake in her mouth. "I must admit, though, it's good to know where we stand. No guessing games." She tore a cake in two but paused with a piece halfway to her mouth. "I'd like some sex, but...you're my only ally in a new world. Vic's busy, so she doesn't count. If what we have is just sex...I can accept that, but promise me that I won't lose you in the process." Her brow furrowed as her expression turned pleading.

"Just sex?" He'd never mated, but an instinct or prediction warned him that once he lay with her, there'd be no turning back.

"As much as I crave some sort of affection, even transient, I couldn't bear to be alone in the unknown." She cleared her throat, dropped the uneaten tulsig, and drew the jar nearer.

Her concerns were valid.

"Then you must get to know the crew. Should anything happen to me, none of them, excluding Ulvus, would abandon you."

She flinched and lowered her gaze but too late. He'd caught the sadness tugging down her lips.

"What is it, Tiny?"

She sniffed. "Out of obligation like I'm a chore? I don't need pity." She raised her chin, revealing her stubbornness and pride. "I refuse to let my blindness dictate my life. Well, within my control."

"Fair enough," he said. "The only thing that would take me from your side is if Kreta herself climbed out of her hell to take me. In that case, you will return to Lunar Base."

He didn't have the authority to promise Tiny that, but he could talk to Aehort and the Q.C.C. His armor flickered on and off, making his skin itch. His symbiotes didn't like the idea of no future between them.

"I will not forsake you," he gritted out, willing his symbiotes to calm. "No matter what. I insisted you come with me. You are my responsibility: a cherished chore if you like."

"I...didn't have much of a choice. I could've traveled to Europa for who knows how long or remained on the *Mula Pesada* with its uncertain future. Neither is what I signed up for." She flashed a tentative smile. "You offered me an exciting alternative with the possibility of regaining my sight."

He frowned. She'd given his offer thought. Not that he'd been aware she'd had other options. "Why didn't you make Europa your new home?"

"It's a medical facility with loads of doctors. I'd be as useless there as everywhere else." Her top lip wobbled.

"You could be an anomaly in Ivoy," Vaen said, sitting beside Tiny. "You going to eat that?"

She slid her half-empty plate across to him. "Do you think they'd want to dissect me?"

"No, but they would study you. After all, your kind killed the Senate."

Nenn glared at Vaen, who met his glower without concern.

Tiny's chuckle wasn't joy-filled. "I suppose I could endure a few tests in the name of science."

Nenn stiffened, his armor forming in an instant. "No. I will not allow that."

Vaen snorted then said around a full mouth, "You against the full might of the Ivoyans and the Q.C.C.?"

"We will not reveal she is onboard." He grimaced. Deceiving anyone was dishonorable and a sure way to a harsher outcome.

"That would work if the entire crew had your back." Vaen pointed a greasy finger at Nenn.

"Ulvus," Nenn growled.

"Indeed," Vaen said.

"At least we have a plan of sorts," Tiny said with a smile that didn't reach her eyes. "Tell me, what do you do for entertainment?"

"Juunn plays the reed. Gusin likes to spar and tinkle, creating useless objects he calls inventions. Nenn climbs walls and idles away his time on teyor."

"I suppose I could learn to play a musical instrument. Do you think Juunn would teach me if I asked?" She flicked her thumb nail like a nervous tick.

"I cannot speak for the male." Vaen slapped the table and stood, his gaze on Nenn. "Oh, Gusin hurt himself. You are needed."

Nenn scowled. "And you tell me now?" He leaped to his feet, then paused beside Tiny.

"Go. I will stay." Vaen sank onto the bench. "Tell me, Tiny, what do you for entertainment?"

She faced him. "I dance, listen to audiobooks, and play chess."

Nenn frowned at having to miss out on the conversation, but duty called. By the time he found Gusin in the activities room, his symbiotes had begun to heel the gash across his upper arm. Nenn tutted and ran the med-dev over it. He knew better than to lecture Gusin on caution when using sharp weapons. But forced to clean up blood instead of chatting to Tiny, Nenn's temper was short.

"As Osnir is my witness, Gusin, take better care," he snapped, spraying the mat and Gusin's arm with disinfectant before wiping both with a towel. "What is this? The seventh time since we left Ivoy?" He huffed. "I shall teach you to use a med-dev."

"That would be wise." Gusin patted his arm where the wound had been. "My thanks, Nenn."

He marched to the galley, then hesitated at Tiny's laughter amid breathy whistles of a reed flute. "Juunn," she said. "I'm so bad at this."

"I have been playing since I was a child. Anything worth learning takes time," Juunn said.

"If I tried it, I would be as bad." Vaen chuckled.

No, Vaen without a scowl? Nenn inched closer to catch that miracle. His grin was broad, changing the usual taciturn into someone...charming. Tiny sat on the table, a reed pressed to her lips. She blew until her cheeks filled will air then blasted out, half making it into the instrument.

Juunn tutted. "You are trying too hard." He demonstrated by angling another reed so that just his top lip breeched the mouthpiece. "Remember, a gentle approach." He shifted her reed until it sat just right. "Now try."

She blew. A long mournful note penetrated the galley. She squealed, bouncing on the spot. Nenn leaned against the bulkhead, crossed his ankles, and gazed upon the sweet joy that she was.

"Good," Juunn said. "You need to hit each note with consistency."

She clutched the instrument to her chest and beamed. "I'll have something to do. I was so worried I'd die of boredom."

The room fell silent.

"That is possible?" Igar asked, a lump of cyan-colored moss he called patsil in hand. He sat behind her, cradling a plate laden with patsil and white jelly-like lumps of raslu.

She laughed, throwing back her head as she did so. "No. It's a saying."

Nenn's chest cinched in tight. With her throat exposed, vulnerable, delicate, he couldn't help but run his gaze to her flushed face. Why did she invoke such potent emotions within him?

"Did you say Nenn climbs?" Confusion merged with her good humor.

"Yes, cliff walls." Vaen stood to one side, cradling a jar of water. With his normal scowl in place, he met Nenn's gaze.

"He is teaching me," Juunn said, spinning his reed in one hand. "Would you like to learn?"

"Oh, no," she said, flicking her wrist. "It's bad enough navigating the horizontal world around me without adding vertical to the mix." She waved her arm. "Besides, I doubt I could support my weight." She lowered her hand to cover her mouth. "Sorry," she said with a tired smile. "It's time for bed. Can someone—"

Nenn pushed off the wall and weaved between his males. "I shall escort you."

"Oh, you're back. Is Gusin okay?"

"He is." Nenn grabbed her by the elbow and helped her step off the bench.

"Juunn, thank you." She thrust out the instrument.

"Keep it, Tiny," he said, sliding onto the bench beside Igar.

"For real?" she asked.

He grinned. "Of course. How else will you practice?"

"I won't let you down, Juunn. Good night, all of you," she called, letting Nenn lead her out of the galley and along the passage to their quarters. "Your crew are so kind," she whispered, dipping her head to do so. A lock of her hair brushed his shoulder in a tickling caress.

"They are good males," he said, clasping her hand. Even there, her skin was silky smooth against his. "Had enough to eat?"

"Yes, thank you." She flashed him a smile when he ushered her into her room.

A glance at her bed had him releasing her. "I...shall leave you."

"I'm not *that* tired," she said.

He chuckled at her lie. "Until tomorrow." Before he left, he stole a peck. Salt and a hint of usturo lingered on her lips. It took all his strength to leave.

"Is she your mate?" Igar demanded from where he leaned against Nenn's door.

"I do not know. Why do you ask?" He narrowed his eyes on the golden-eyed male.

"I wish to claim her."

Fury exploded like a volcanic eruption. Breathing didn't matter when Nenn fought to control his reaction. "No, she is mine."

"Fair enough." Igar pushed off the door to squeeze Nenn's shoulder. "I wish you Osnir's blessings."

Foq. Nenn glared at Igar's departing back then at Tiny's door. He tapped his forearm. "Gusin, ensure no one but Tiny and I have access to her room."

The male chuckled. "So it has started, then?"

Nenn stiffened. "What do you mean?" He did know, and the fear summoning his armor said it all.

"You brought a tribeless female onto the *Aroagni*. What did you expect would happen?" Gusin ended the comm.

Nenn threw out a hand to steady his weak knees. No way would he let a male take what was his. She'd said she wanted him, and he had to assume that meant him alone. *Foq*. He'd ask her tomorrow. One last glance had him contemplating sleeping on the floor outside her room. Just in case.

But he trusted Gusin to do as asked.

Or did he?

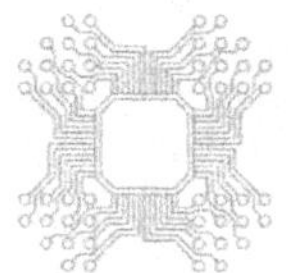

This time, when Nenn left Tiny alone, she didn't feel so lost. She smiled, placed the reed in a closet, and activated the shower. It was such a luxury to bath in actual water and more than once a day. The madness of it boggled her mind. On Earth, the diminishing levels of water had long ago started a war—the not-haves with the haves. Now, everything was powered by sol, and any remaining bodies of oceans or seas were desalinated for consumption. She couldn't imagine what the planet of Ivoy would look like. Excitement made her swing her hips to an unfamiliar rhythm.

Yes, deciding to accept Nenn's offer had been a good thing.

Nenn.

She hummed. Such honesty was almost beyond her ability to endure. After towel-drying, she pulled on a sleepshirt in case he intruded. Though, she did hesitate. Being naked for him might entice him to follow through with his intentions. Damn, she hoped it was soon. She yawned and climbed into bed. Tomorrow held promise. She could learn how to play a reed, and at some point, she could teach Nenn the game of chess. Vaen had said he wasted his time on something she hadn't caught the name of.

Her eyelashes fluttered, exhaustion forcing them to shut.
She succumbed on a breathless sigh. Yes, tomorrow.

153

Chapter Nineteen

Nenn couldn't recall a time he'd slept this badly. He tossed and turned, awoke to listen in on her room, confirming she wasn't disturbed, only to kick off his blankets and eventually rise. His constant arousal didn't help matters. He sat at the table in the galley, the silence of the ship soothing his frazzled symbiotes.

"What has you up so early?" Vaen said, striding past to order from the replicate.

"She is not mine yet."

"Ah." Vaen sipped his water. "I must admit I thought you mad, but I can see the appeal." He brought his jar and sat opposite Nenn. "Is she soft all over?"

"I hope to find out soon," Nenn said, cupping his lukewarm russmar tisane. "I can share that face-latching or kissing is magnificent."

"Oh?" Vaen arched a brow.

"Tiny says it is reserved for lovers."

Vaen hummed. "Good to know." He twirled the jar. "I believe her blindness might save her."

"Why?" Nenn frowned, focusing on Vaen's pensive expression.

"To the Ivoyans, healing her might be more tempting than studying her."

Nenn sucked in a sharp breath. "Let us pray Osnir lights the way for her."

"Vic finding who caused the explosion might help your cause."

"Indeed," Nenn said, offering Vaen a smile. To save Tiny, he'd need all the advice he could get.

Vaen twisted to rest his back against the wall and his legs along the bench. "Perhaps I should get my own human." He grinned.

Nenn blinked at it. Twice in one day? "It would mean returning for Caah." Nenn shrugged. "He might have a female by then."

"True. If we were not cautious with our fuel reserves, we would travel faster than a lunar month." With a wince, Vaen swept his gaze across the galley. "I do not enjoy long voyages."

Nenn chuckled. "Bored?"

Smirking, Vaen rested his head back. "Indeed." He slapped the table. "Now, head to bed or cover the bridge so I can sleep. Your choice."

Nenn nudged his chin in the direction of the quarters. "Go. I will monitor the ship." He rose, emptied his tisane into the waste disposal, then paused beside Vaen. "Thank you for your guidance."

Alone, on the bridge, Nenn scanned the black forevids splattered with stars. The lights on the console remained red. White would be a concern, but none were that color. The silence engulfed him, and he lost himself to the space flickering past.

When they reached Ivoy, he needed to have his defense in place. Hiding Tiny on the ship was a start, but he couldn't do so for long. The udaps would ask why if he disappeared for extended periods of time. He had to report to duty and pretend all was well. Not to mention that sneaking a female into the Med-Tech barracks unseen would be impossible. And it wouldn't be fair on Tiny to keep her imprisoned. No, the truth had to come out. But he didn't know how to phrase it to ensure she wasn't harmed.

"Your concern bothers me, Maed," Aehort said, gliding to stand beside him.

Nenn stiffened at the intrusion then slumped. The Ivoyan was far too perceptive. "My apologies, Aehort Uz," he said.

"You care for this female?" he asked.

"I am starting to," Nenn said. There was no point in lying to an Ivoyan. As skilled empaths, they perceived far more about himself than even he knew.

"You have taken on a burden because you are trained to offer healing. No, the Senate will not heal your Tiny. I have foreseen it." Aehort patted Nenn's shoulder with his elongated orange fingers.

His hope shattered, dampening his vision until darkness circled it. If no healing, that meant... "Will we be able to return her to Lunar Base?"

Aehort remained quiet. "This has not been revealed to me." He focused his all-seeing gaze on Nenn. "Do not worry over this when it is beyond your control. All things will be resolved." He left a bowed Nenn resting his chin on his chest.

He'd promised Tiny.

How could he tell her this was all for nothing?

"She will understand," Aehort called from the passage. "Have faith, young Qaldreth."

Nenn squared his shoulders. Aehort was right. He had to trust Osnir wouldn't abandon him. As he wouldn't forsake Tiny. Despite the awful news, peace consumed him. If he hadn't promised Vaen, he'd head to bed.

He glanced at the dial on the wall. A half-dark, half-light ball spun as time passed, marking the end and start of the next 'day.' Soon, he would awaken Tiny, perhaps with a kiss. Like Vaen had said, the journey to Ivoy would take a lunar month. Plenty of opportunities to get to know Tiny better. Perhaps together, they could learn how to play a reed. It wasn't a skill that had interested him, but to spend time with her, he'd do it.

He swept his gaze across the console and the forevids, then at the ball, watching time inch by. And repeat until his neck ached. He'd start with a shower, then collect her for a meal.

A squeal woke him. He must have dozed off. A glance at everything showed all was well, and the day imminent. Then, what had—

His eyes widened, and he bolted for Tiny's room.

"Grunt, you sly dog, I love you," she sang.

Nenn faltered, slowing as he reached her door.

"Play audiobook," she said.

A faint monotone voice responded.

"'What the frack? Those were synths?'"

"It shouldn't surprise us. After all, they're the product." Naomi snuggled her backside deeper into her chair and leaned back. "The Zetas are impressive as an introduction to their deluxe range."

"I couldn't tell they weren't human," Gibs grumbled. "State of the art and certainly not anything they currently sell."

"How would you know?" She popped an eye open while her ruby lips curled in a sensual smirk.

"Research, rookie, especially considering Thomas Walker's infatuation. And before you assume the worst, I didn't fuck any of them."

She arched a knowing brow. "Just checking, partner."

Silence filled the chaser, and he pinched his lips. His mother's nasal voice reprimanded him, and he found himself blurting out an apology. Without alcohol having passed his lips, too.

"Sorry for the blow-job remark. Just not used to...partners."

"Women." She kept her eyes closed as if the day had tested her, too.

"Huh?" He allowed his gaze to travel along the arch of her throat, the stubborn tilt to her jaw, and the ruby softness of her lips.

"You're not used to women."'

Tiny chuckled. "Yup, you summed that up quite nicely, girl."

The spray of water drowned out the odd voice.

With his heart pounding against the cavity of his ribs, Nenn slumped against the wall beside her door. She was fine. He nodded at Juunn striding toward the bridge but didn't say anything. What to feed her settled on Nenn's mind. She couldn't exist on tulsig cakes, and he wasn't sure she'd take to any of their strange foods or whether it was safe for her.

Swiveling on a heel, he headed to Gusin's quarters and tapped the panel, alerting the male that Nenn waited outside. The door opened.

"What is it?" Gusin asked, rubbing his face.

"As our taed, would it be possible to add human foods to the replicate?" Nenn splayed his fingers on the bulkhead near the top of the door.

"No. Without a sample, the replicate cannot dissolve, analyze, and reform the item." Gusin arched both brows when Nenn hesitated. "Will that be all?"

"Thanks," Nenn said and returned to Tiny's door.

Unless she'd hidden something edible in her bag, there was nothing he could do but let her try what the tribes ate. He shuddered at the idea of ordering slimy malugu from Awayar, and he doubted her teeth could penetrate the carapace of os-ayys.

He let her know he was outside while he sifted through the options available. Perhaps he should introduce foods by tribe? She'd started with Meorri, liking the tulsig cakes. It was the oily, gooey, saltiness of them that made his tongue sing.

"Morning, Nenn," she said, a bright smile in place. Wearing odd-flowered leggings and a baggy sleepshirt in blinding yellow, her hair still damp, she glowed with life and beauty.

"Ready to journey through each tribe's preferred meals?" He caught her hand and ushered her toward him. Because he couldn't resist, he gave her mouth a peck. The taste of her alone tempted him to deepen the kiss to French. A sharp flavor that wasn't unappealing coated her breath.

"All at once?" she asked, splaying her fingers across his chest.

He laughed. "One at each meal."

"Phew." She slid her hand across his forearm to loop her arm through his.

"What has you so happy?" he asked, not wanting to reveal she'd woken him this morning with her antics.

"Grunt left me a tablet." She sighed. "I love him. I do. Such a sweet gesture."

Nenn kept a smile in place by sheer will. "Love him for that?"

"I'm just so grateful," she said, pressing her cheek to Nenn's upper arm. "Now I have my beats and audiobooks. Is there a way I can connect the sound to a speaker? I like my music loud."

"Music?" He twisted to glance at her.

"Yes, what did you think I meant by beats?"

"Tribal drums?" he said, grinning at her.

"Oh, yes, there's that, but wait until you hear it all, Nenn." She jiggled on the spot.

He dipped his gaze lower and lingered on her breasts. In Giniiri, no female danced around the bonfire. Not even during mating season when males offered gifts in the hopes of snaring a mate. All applicants had to demonstrate their flexibility, physique, and stamina before the females chose. Kimgi hadn't averted her gaze from Tugo the entire evening.

Her open admiration had made Nenn's heart ache.

He wanted a female to gaze upon him with such devotion. Cupping Tiny's face, he ran his thumb over her lips. "I look forward to you sharing this with me," he said.

She clasped his wrist and beamed. "I want to teach you chess, too."

He laughed. "And we can learn to play the reed together."

Her cheeks pinkened. She parted her lips to speak.

"Morning," Drafe said, a plate of tulsig in hand.

She angled her head, lines marring her brow.

"Drafe, would Vic have any human food?" Nenn asked, revealing who stood before Tiny.

"No." The male frowned. "A good idea, though." He glanced at the plate. "If we send a ship for Caah, we shall task them to expand the replicate's offerings."

"My thanks," Nenn said and ushered Tiny to the galley.

"Human food?" she asked, sinking onto the bench he led her to.

"Yes, in case none of our choices suit your palette."

"Aw, Nenn, that's so thoughtful. I like tulsig and your tisane so far." She rested her elbows on the table and her chin on her palm.

"We shall continue with Meorri this morning," he said and turned away. The tisane was the quickest, which he placed before her while the replicate worked on her breakfast. At the ding, he grabbed the plate and sat beside her. "I have not tried all that the Meorri have to offer. We shall taste them together."

What followed was a memory he'd cherish forever: her squeals of delight, her gags, the smacking of her lips to the licking of her fingers. She hummed when something pleased her, and she sampled all the food between sips of russmar tisane.

"I cannot believe you shared your vile-smelling tisane," Gusin said, sliding onto the bench with his gaze on the almost empty plate.

"It's yummy," Tiny said, flushing a smile. "Smells awful, though. Have you tried it?"

Gusin jerked back. "No."

"Then no complaining until you do." She wagged a finger in an odd gesture. "Otherwise, you have no leg to stand on."

Gusin laughed. "I have two legs."

"No one likes a smart ass," she snapped. "It's a human saying that means if you don't have experience, your opinion doesn't matter."

"Fair enough," Gusin said, snatching Nenn's half-drunk jar. After a taste, he stilled, his mouth gaping. "It *is*...yummy. My apologies, Nenn. Now, do I have a leg, Tiny?"

She giggled, her shoulders shaking. "You have two."

Chapter Twenty

BETWEEN CHESS, REED-BLOWING, AND listening to her audiobook, Tiny's days filled with many happy experiences. Nenn was attentive, but his presence *and* kisses rattled her. She wanted to drag him to bed. It sucked not being able to read his expressions or the damn room. She yearned to come out and say, 'Do me already.'

Instead, she shivered at his touch, tingled at his kisses, and sighed when he left her alone and horny. And knowing he listened in stopped her from rubbing one out. Which then left her on edge and doubting the attraction. Had she said something to change his mind? She couldn't have been clearer than 'I want you, Nenn.'

Pfft. Men. Even alien men.

"Play audiobook," she said, sprawling on her bed.

She pressed her body against his, bringing with her a sweet rose scent, nothing too cloying and no stench of old sex. With nimble fingers, she had his uniform open, grazing her nails across his bare skin. A shiver pebbled his nipples.

"Candy," she said, rubbing her parted mouth across his chest hairs.

He gripped her shoulders, reminded of doing this earlier to Naomi, and almost shook the woman. "Your real name."

"Sophia." Her dark eyes mesmerized him. Chocolate swirled in their depths.

Spinning her, he yanked her against him and grabbed her breasts, filling his palms. He pressed a kiss to the pulse beating at her neck. "Do you have time for me?"

"As long as you need." Her husky voice shot straight to his groin as he glided a flattened palm over the soft curves of her belly.

"An hour, no more." He dipped his fingers lower, drawing a gasp from her. As beautiful as she was, perhaps a little missionary wouldn't hurt.

"Pause," Tiny snapped, then pummeled the bed with her fists. Even Gibs was getting it on.

A chime had her leaping off the bed like she'd been caught red-handed. She opened the door and smiled, greeted by Nenn's hot-rock cologne.

"Thought you went to bed," she said, stepping aside to let him in.

"I did until your tale took an interesting turn..." He cleared his throat.

"Oh," she said, dipping her head to hide her blush.

"I want to hear more of this audiobook," he said, catching her hand and tugging her to the bed. "Come, let us listen together."

Unsure what he meant, she sat on the foot end.

"Lie with me, *hirihadie*," he said.

She pinched her lips, then lay on the bed, inching back until her ass hit the wall.

Bringing his glorious heat with him, he joined her on the bed. He shifted her like a doll until she splayed across him, her head on his chest and his arm around her.

"Play audiobook," she said into his pec and snuggled against him.

Chapter Fifteen.

Nova City was like a pie cut into five sectors. They called the blue sector where the rich middle class lived, Holies. That wasn't saying much. The white sector was a squalid cesspool known as the Dump where the poorest of the poor lived, but even they had standards. None ventured into the Deadzone since it was where the Kicks tossed bodies and killed snitches. There would be no need for Gibs to visit the Dump anytime soon. Rarely, did he venture into the green sector, the Kicks, but he'd been there twice in the last week. Memorable experiences both times. Thanks to Sophia, he was himself again and in control. He hadn't sampled the full bouquet the Kicks offered, and his tastes were tame in comparison to most men his age or younger. Or older, he grimaced, thinking of Lawrence.

Having someone to sleep with added a comfort Tiny hadn't known she missed. Her one-night-stands hadn't included this as part of the evening's offerings. Which explained why, despite having Nenn where she wanted him, she dozed off to the steady thump of his heart and the heat pouring off him like a thermal blanket.

She jerked awake to Gibs yelling.

"Davis," he growled into his holo-wrist.

It took an agonizing second before Davis answered. "What?"

"Naomi's been poisoned. Search her home for the chocolates someone sent her on my behalf. Test them. We need to know what we're dealing with."

"Frack, Gibs. How is she? Where are you?" Davis's nose bumped his wrist and sent his holographic striations spinning.

What patience Gibs had evaporated, tainting his vision red. "Davis, find the poison." His roar drew cries of alarm from the medical personnel and patients around him. He didn't care.

Davis jerked back. "Right. On it."

She frowned, having missed so much. Beside her, Nenn's breathing was even but not deep. "You're still awake?" she asked, pushing up to glance at him.

"I like this story," he whispered.

"So do I," she said. "Can't you sleep?"

"No," he said, cupping her face with his rough palms.

"If I had my injection gun, I could give you something for it."

His husky chuckle grazed across her senses. "Indeed."

"That is if your physiology can handle our pathetic medicine." She twirled a pattern on his chest, loving the velvety texture of his skin.

He caught her fingers and trapped them against him. "My tisane usually calms me."

"You don't mind if I sleep?" She covered a yawn by pressing her temple to his knuckles.

"Of course not," he said and curled his arm, bringing her tighter into the curve of his body.

"Okay," she mumbled with her cheek once more on his chest. "Play audiobook."

Gibs collapsed into the closest chair, dropping his face into his hands. This made no sense. Why target Naomi? Why spur a romance when there was none? Well, none from her side. Was it a side effect of the toxins scouring her system? Shame hit him hard, burning his cheeks anew. He'd wanted her, relished the feel and taste of her, yet she suffered, drugged with who knew what. Had he been on his game, he'd have noticed sooner, reacted quicker.

If she died, it was on him.

Tiny heard no more.

Someone rolled her onto her left side, then pulled her snug against hard loins. Heat engulfed her back. She smiled. Nenn had stayed with her. Instincts said it was morning, but she was loathe to move. She got to 'cuddle' without sex; the second choice in her book.

He rubbed his hand over her hip then inched her shirt up, sighing when he reached her waist. There, he splayed his fingers, digging them into her then releasing without causing pain. Only a desperation remained. She wiggled, trying to ease the growing ache between her thighs. That man had no right to affect her like he did. Either that or she needed sex more than she'd thought.

The kiss at her neck made her shiver. He was so gentle and sweet, nuzzling her hair out of the way to press his cheek to hers. "Tiny," he rasped. "Please teach me."

She twisted to catch his mouth with hers while she snagged his hand and brought it to her breast. A groan passed from her to him when he flicked a thumb across her nipple. She pinched her thighs, longing burning at her core. He deepened the kiss and snatched her thoughts, urging her to kiss him back. Her neck muscles twanged, but she had every intention of ignoring the discomfort.

When he teased both breasts, she grabbed his hand and slid it lower, whimpering when he cupped her sex. Through her leggings, his stroking had her breathless. She wanted to strip so that nothing hindered him.

"Please," she begged.

"What do you need?" His voice was husky, summoning another shiver.

Her thoughts were hard to grab onto. "Inside," she managed, yanking up the hem of her shirt to take his hand past her waistband. His palm across her bare stomach shot fire through her. But that couldn't compare to his fingers feathering across her clit. She cried out, arching into his touch.

"Am I hurting you?"

"Oh, no, don't stop," she said between ragged gasps.

"You are so soft and slick."

"Ah-ha," she mumbled when he rubbed her back and forth. "There," she said when he circled her clit.

"You like this?"

She was past listening to him or talking while he continued to tease her. Need burned. The cliff drew near. She climbed, desperate and afraid he'd stop. Every flick made her whimper. The sensations shuddering her body were so exquisite. He kissed her, thrusting his tongue into her mouth but fumbled his fingers. The change in the rhythm was so unexpected, it threw her into an abyss of sweet pleasure. She screamed, riding an orgasm like no other. Heat, ice, tingles, and waves of bliss bombarded her until she trembled against him.

She cupped his hand, trapping it between her thighs. "So good," she whispered, letting the lingering ecstasy bring her back to reality. "Your turn."

"What?" he asked, pulling free.

"No, stay," she said, rolling over. After stroking his waistband in search of some way to open his pants, she huffed. "Nenn, I need access to your cock."

He chuckled then yanked. Something tore free, like magnets or Velcro. He shuffled, and three thumps followed. She had to assume that meant two boots and a pair of pants. Then velvet skin engulfed her. He wrapped his arms around her while pressing his body against hers.

"Want me naked, too?" she asked, kissing his neck.

His breath hitched.

She laughed, shoved him back, then wiggled until she could whip off her shirt. Silence met her when she tossed off her bra. A thousand ant bites skittered along her skin at him being disappointed in her appearance, but then he ran his hand from her back to her ass.

"Beautiful," he mumbled, dusting kisses over her bare shoulder.

She swallowed at the awe in his voice. He truly believed it. "Nenn," she rasped, "lie back."

He paused, his breath hot against her skin. His warmth was gone when he did as she commanded. She threw out her hands and met his hip and stomach, indented with abs.

'Wow,' she mouthed. Her implants sent her nothing, no doubt unable to process alien physiology. She was truly blind, but she didn't mind, choosing to pretend she wore a blindfold.

Skimming her fingers up took her to familiar territory—his pecs, broad shoulders, angular jawline, and pliant lips. Down was a different experience, his sharp hips and an Adonis belt leading to an impressive hard-on.

She started at the rings around the base of his cock, up along the ridges, to further ridges just under the head of his cock. He was hot, hard, yet velvety to the touch. His breathing became ragged, but he didn't stop her from exploring. Flicking her thumb over the tip caught drops of pre-cum. He hissed. His body stiffened beside her. That she could draw such a reaction from a man this wonderful made her chest swell. Sparkles exploded in her belly, and her clit throbbed in anticipation. She ran her tongue along the length of his cock, tasting the cotton-candy sweetness of his pre-cum.

A strange gurgle came from him.

She straightened, tossing him a glance out of instinct. "Did I hurt you?"

"Osnir," he moaned. "Please...do not cease this torment."

She grinned and took him into her mouth.

A drawn-out groan inspired her to take as much of him as she could, making sure that with every dip of her head, he hit the back of her throat.

He clutched her hip, his grip almost bruising. With every flick of her tongue or slow suck, he dug in his fingers, whimpers and growls escaping him. She'd missed this: intimacy, bringing another person to ecstasy, having him at her mercy. Between sucks, she stroked him.

"Tiny," he roared as liquid sweetness bathed her mouth and slid down her throat. She didn't stop until he twitched, his breaths coming in huffs.

"You taste amazing," she said, lying beside him.

He drew her against him, almost crushing her in his embrace. "*Hirihadie*, that... Whatever that was, I have never experienced such joy..."

She snuggled, feathering kisses along his collarbone and any part of him she could reach. Darkness formed a ball in her soul while she waited for him to get out of bed and leave her. Time passed. He didn't move, nor did he stop rubbing her back. Tears burned her eyes that he hadn't abandoned or used her.

She snoozed, too comfortable to resist the lure of a nap, especially post-endorphin-rush.

"Next time, we shall remove your pants," he said, his voice low when he dusted a kiss across her lips.

She hummed in agreement and let sleep claim her.

Chapter Twenty-One

With Tiny filling his arms, Nenn just lay there, his mind reeling, his body pinging with residual joy while his symbiotes vibrated through him. Since he'd met her, he'd wanted to learn everything about her. So far, he hadn't regretted a moment spent with her.

He caught fleeting expressions where sadness lingered, but before he could ask her about it, she'd laugh, and the opportunity was lost.

As a maed, he understood that everything needed balance. When stability was threatened, chaos ensued. She couldn't be cheerful all the time. There had to be darkness for light to shine. And if she kept that side of her hidden, it was sure to come out when he revealed the Ivoyans wouldn't heal her or that he wasn't certain she could go home. Like he'd promised.

He refused to give up, though.

Drawing her closer, he pressed his lips against her temple. Her scent surrounded him. They had just this journey together before she would leave him. His breathing shuddered when pain crushed his heart. As much as he wanted to keep her with him, she had a right to choose.

He extracted himself then tucked a blanket around her semi-naked body. Unable to resist, he stroked her upper arm, relishing her softness. "*Mhi' hirihadie,*" he whispered and kissed her cheek.

He slipped out and into his room, aiming for his waterfall. Not that he wanted to wash the scent of her off his body, but the day had started. While he stood under the scorching spray, he ran his hand over his chest and stomach, to his koq. Her mouth... He groaned. So hot, silky, wet...

With one hand splayed on the back wall, he dipped his head under the water, reliving what she'd made him feel. The way she'd made his body sing still lingered in his soul.

After allowing the heat from the room to dry him, he pulled on his boots and clean pants. A listen told him she still slept, so he headed to the activities room. Upon seeing Ulvus, Nenn almost turned around. Instead, he drew in a deep breath, squared his shoulders, and approached his wall.

"Morning," he said.

"Since you are not looking after your weak female, I demand a rematch." Ulvus spun a sword, his agility mesmerizing.

"Why?" Nenn flicked a glance at him, ignoring the insult to Tiny. If Ulvus couldn't see her core of inner strength, then the male was a fool.

"This time with weapons." Ulvus smirked. "I shall let you choose."

"How magnanimous of you," Nenn said. "I am trained to take a warrior down to heal him. No matter what weapon you hold, Ulvus, you will find yourself on the floor." Nenn faced him. "You are a sava, skilled with every weapon. A taed can work and fix anything. I cannot be a sava, a taed, or an arrak."

Ulvus glowered. "By that thinking, I should only challenge savas."

"Or arraks." Nenn shrugged and raised his gaze to the climbing wall, considering this conversation over.

He hit the mat hard, jarring his shoulder. Pain exploded outward, numbing his fingers. He should have expected Ulvus's attack, something he admonished himself for.

"Ulvus," he snapped, wincing when each move to free himself hurt.

The male smirked, his face too near. Without hesitation, Nenn slammed his forehead into Ulvus's nose, sending the roaring male stumbling back, clear blood pouring to his chin. At least, it had wiped away his smugness.

Gripping his upper arm, Nenn rolled onto his knees then bent a leg to stand. "Was that necessary? What did that gain you?" He leaped aside when Ulvus staggered forward. "I am in no mood to entertain this nonsense. We both need healing."

"The idiot cannot understand that," Vaen said, his ferocious scowl in place when he strode into the activities room. "Attack anyone again and you will have all of us to deal with." He dug inside Nenn's pocket and pulled out his med-dev. "In fact, I shall report your behavior to the udaps. Let them decide your fate."

"No, it is not necessary," Nenn muttered while scanning his shoulder.

The pain eased, and feeling returned to his fingertips. He swung his arm to test his shoulder's mobility then approached Ulvus to heal his nose.

"Stand still," Nenn said when the male inched back as if he expected retaliation.

Vaen huffed but didn't walk off, choosing instead to remain at Nenn's back.

"Why wait until now, Ulvus? It has been days since our sparring," Nenn asked.

"You have been playing with your pet," Ulvus gritted out, disgust coiling his upper lip. "She is always by your side."

"Sounds like envy to me," Vaen said, snapping Ulvus's glower to him.

"Mate with such a species, the very ones who killed the Senate?" Ulvus settled his amber gaze on Nenn. "They cannot all be love mates. Vatia sahaars are rare."

Nenn froze, his hand in mid-scan. "What did you say?" The flames of an active volcano poured down his back. He gaped. "Why do you think this?"

He'd heard of love mates but never met such a fated pair.

"I have seen such behavior before. Drafe has found his vatia sahaar, the son of Kreta," Ulvus spat. "Like that male can never do wrong and is favored by the gods. Even mine."

"I know you can hear me, Nenn. I'm starving. Are you fetching me or what?" Tiny's voice added fuel to the fire lambasting his body even as her voice penetrated the room via his forearm.

"Go, I shall take care of him," Vaen said. "Maybe smack some sense into him."

Nenn hesitated, cast a glance at Ulvus, then handed over his med-dev to Vaen. He marched out the activities room without looking back. His mind circled, settled, then spun again. Could Tiny be his mate? He almost snorted at that silly hope. Despite their rarity, he could believe Vic was Drafe's.

"Morning," Nenn said when he opened the door to Tiny's room. "Let us start by getting a language nodule inserted into your neck."

"Really? Just like that?" She gripped her hip. "Not, Tiny, would you mind if I put a foreign object into your body?"

He winced, aware she was wary of augmentation. "Please. It would mean safety, interpretation, and the ability to talk to me directly."

"Fine." She huffed. "I suppose it makes sense with me going to strange worlds. Does that mean I'll be able to understand Ivoyan?"

"Yes, and Qaldreth."

She smiled. "I'd allow it for that reason alone." She patted the air.

He stepped into her reach, almost sighing when she splayed her fingers across his chest.

"Where do you want me?" she asked, looping her arm through his.

"My med bay."

"Oh, at last." She chuckled. "I finally get to see where you work."

He gazed upon her upturned face. "Did you sleep well?"

"Lovely," she said. "But I wasn't lying. I'm famished."

"Food or implant first?" he offered because he didn't like her being hungry, not for a moment.

"Implant. Get it over and done with."

He grinned. Yes, core of strength. He led her to his med bay tucked between the docking bay and the galley. The bed had to be flipped down in the tight space. He did so, then hoisted her onto it. She swung her feet like a child, her gaze unseeing. As he gathered the tools and nodule he'd need, he snuck glances at her, admiring the shape of her cheek, her breasts rising and falling in yet another loose bold-pink tunic over black-and-yellow horizontal-striped pants, to her nibbling on her bottom lip with her white teeth.

"Tell me, Tiny, if you can, how were you blinded?"

She sucked in a sharp breath and straightened. "You want to know?"

"Please."

"It all has to do with my brother, Jamie." Anger and resentment saturated her voice, yet behind the emotion was the haunting note of betrayal. "I was about to graduate from med school…"

As she told her story, he listened, watched, and learned. The darkness she hid lay in her unforgiveness. Had he been able to heal her, she could've set this aside. He swabbed her neck, numbing the area, then set to installing the nodule. It didn't leave a hole but flattened the muscle fibers beneath it. He wiped away the blood before it stained her tunic.

"I know, I shouldn't hold grudges, but he ruined my life, Nenn. I'm so angry with him that I want to hit him." She waved a small fist in the air.

"This may sound selfish, but if you had not lost your eyesight, you would not have been on the *Mula Pesada*, and I would not have met you."

She stilled, her eyes widening. "All true. And as sad as that thought makes me at the thought of not knowing you, I could've saved so many lives. I've been useless for years."

"How would you feel if you never saw your family again?" Erasril was his home, but he had no father waiting for him. Sure, he'd love to visit with Tugo, but he wouldn't return to live there. Not if he didn't have to.

"Dad would be sad," was all she said, bowing her head. In doing so, she revealed how it would devastate her not to see her father again.

Nenn gritted his teeth. To keep his promise, he'd steal a ship if he had to. "When we return to Lunar Base, would you introduce me to him?"

She whipped up her head, her eyes glistening. "Of course."

"I look forward to it," he said, lifting her off the bed.

"Are we done?" she asked, cupping her neck, finding the small metal circle, then running her fingers over it. "I didn't feel a thing."

"But now you can hear only me," he said, tapping his device.

She squeaked. "I can."

He chuckled. "Time for food. Which tribe this morning?"

"Yours," she said, lacing her fingers through his.

Between tasting strips of calpli, vibuy, and banaari, she sipped a steaming jar of russmar tisane. He left the onis for last, not sure she'd like such a potent flavor.

"Licorice?" she squealed and scooped in another mouthful of the purple moss, staining her lips and tongue.

He laughed. "Not my favorite."

"Why?" she mumbled, a piece on the way to her mouth.

"It overpowers, I suppose," he said, having not analyzed his dislike of the moss before.

"I guess," she said, cradling her jar. "I have to be in the mood to enjoy it." She leaned back on a sigh. "That was delicious, Nenn."

He grinned. "Have any preferences yet?"

She tapped her nose—whatever that meant. "Too soon to tell."

Ulvus harumphed when he stomped into the galley. "Feeding your pet?"

Her eyes widened then narrowed. "Well, that smacks of jealousy."

Ulvus gaped.

She gasped. "Am I speaking—" She faced Nenn. "Qaldreth?"

"Of course," he said, adoring her expressive features.

"I said Ulvus was jealous, too." Vaen chuckled, weaving around Ulvus to reach the replicate.

Into the silence, Ulvus snapped, "You gave her a language implant? This will not go down well with—"

"The udaps and the Ivoyans," Vaen said. "We have heard your opinion on welcoming the killers onto our ship."

"Each race has good and bad people." She flashed a smile when Nenn took the empty jar of tisane from her. "Hell, in my family, I can, without a doubt, state that's true. I wouldn't say my brother is pure evil, but he has no consideration for others." Her gaze was distant with sadness lingering in the white depths of her eyes.

Vaen arched a brow at Nenn, who gave him a subtle headshake.

"Another tisane?" Nenn offered, inching closer to Tiny.

"I thought I was done until *he* walked in. Now I'm staying put. So, yes, please." She folded her arms across her chest.

"Prior to Nenn kidnapping you, what did you have for your morning meal, Tiny?" Vaen asked, settling opposite them. He cradled his jar of water.

"Mm, on the *Mula Pesada*, bacon, eggs, toast, coffee." She closed her eyes and hummed. When she gazed in Nenn's direction, her eyes sparkled. "Bacon are thin strips of meat fried in sunflower oil. Eggs are from chickens. So versatile. Scrambled, boiled, fried, poached. Some people eat them raw." She scrunched up her nose. "Toast is a slice of bread roasted on both sides, and you slather butter all over it. Then coffee. Oh my word, do I miss that. Nothing compares." She bowed her shoulders. "On Lunar Base, I lived off protein bars or ramen. Back home with my parents, more protein bars, other reconstituted meals, and my mom's lasagna with fake meat, pasta, dairy. I don't know it any other way."

"Morning," Juunn said, striding into the galley. He didn't glance over his shoulder while he ordered his meal.

"Juunn," Nenn whispered in her ear.

"Morning," she said, with a weak smile. "I've been practicing, I promise."

Juunn laughed. "I am here to eat, not to check up on your progress."

"Phew," she said, running her hand across her temple. When she relaxed, she bumped her jar, spilling her leftover tisane over her tunic. She scrambled back, almost tumbling off the bench. "I'm so sorry. Is it a big mess?"

"Do not worry, Tiny." Vaen ordered the rinse which flooded the floor with an inch of water before draining. He wiped the table with a pointed look between Tiny's wet tunic clinging to her breasts and Nenn.

Nenn captured her hand and helped her to her feet. "Let me escort you to your room...to clean up."

She nodded and squeezed his forearm. At her door, she faced him. "Just going to hop into the shower. Will let you know when I'm done."

He shifted back, let her pass, then stared at nothing before striding to the bridge, aware he was acting like an idiot. Lost in the view out the forevids, he didn't greet Igar. He leaned against the bulkhead, content to let his thoughts whizz past while he analyzed what she invoked in him. Vatia sahaar circled. Ulvus couldn't be right. The male wasn't known to be insightful. But Nenn couldn't shake the hope.

A squeal snapped him from his daze. He bolted along passages to burst into Tiny's room. Only to skid to a halt at the sight of a naked, dripping female with her arms thrown out. Presented with her full beauty, his breathing seized his chest. She muttered curses while she patted the air. Every step made her breasts jiggle, her taut nipples drawing his focus. The dip of her waist to the flare of her hips to plump thighs with some muscular definition tempted him to run his hand along her shape.

"Why does the tap have to be so damn sensitive?" She switched off the shower, then, shivering, found the towel and began to rub herself all over.

She bent, twisted, and rose, flashing him parts of her body between swipes of the towel.

A flood of heat hardened his koq. His fingers twitched to touch her, but his boots were riveted to the floor. When she raised her arms to dry her hair, he froze, mesmerized by her.

She sniffed then gazed at the door. "Nenn?"

"My apologies, Tiny... You screamed," he managed, his voice hoarse.

She squeaked and clutched the towel in front of her. "You've been standing there the entire time?"

"You are beautiful," he said, drawing closer.

She gasped, pink flushing her body. "Please tell me you're alone?"

"I am."

"Phew." She grinned, releasing the towel to loop it around her. "Didn't mean to scare you. I nudged the nozzle with my hip, changing the water from lovely to ice cold. When I leaped out of the way, I lost my bearings."

He crossed to her, switching his gaze from the knot between her breasts to her flushed face. When he cupped her cheek, she stilled.

"Tiny," he rasped.

She layered a hand over his. "What's the matter?"

He succumbed and kissed her, willing his symbiotes to fade so her skin would be against his. The scent of her teased him. He broke away to draw in a deep breath, expanding his chest. She blinked at him, her lips swollen. Slipping his hands down her back, he yanked her against him then frowned at his uniform separating them.

"Do not move," he said and stripped, tossing his boots and pants aside.

"Nenn?" she asked, a brow arched, but a twinkle in her eyes preceded a smile. "You can't be thinking of taking advantage of little ol' me?"

He chuckled and crossed to her, his stiff koq aching. This time, her silkiness pressed against him like the softest of moss. She sighed and scraped her nails over his torso, summoning a shudder. He ran his hands to her backside where he dug his fingers into her cheeks. When he hoisted her up, she squeaked. He groaned, his koq rubbing against her sex.

"Well, you did 'buy' me dinner," she whispered, looping her arms around his neck.

She peered at him then kissed him, plucking at his lips with hers before thrusting her tongue in. His breath caught. Emotions stung his eyes with unshed tears.

She made him happy, which he hadn't experienced for so long. Not since before his mother's disappearance, if he was honest with himself.

He lowered Tiny onto her bed then stepped back to admire her sprawled before him. Running his palm from her toes, along her shin, over a knee, up her thigh and hip, a twirl around her belly button to tweak a nipple, had her trembling. Minute bumps formed across her skin. Her nipples tightened. That peach color he loved flushed her body in a path he wanted to trail with his tongue.

He pressed a knee to the mattress, then climbed onto the bed, nudging her legs apart with his. Settling between her thighs, nestling in place, fluttered warmth through him. The sensation was odd yet familiar, like he'd found the fabled Pools of Abstyn—guaranteed to grant the drinker eternal peace.

She stroked from his shoulders to his elbows, her unseeing gaze just to the left of his face.

"What do you want, *hirihadie*?" he asked. Osnir knew what he craved, but he had to make sure she desired him, too.

"You," she said, without hesitation. Her cheeks pinkened, and she glanced away, trying to hide her expressions from him.

He grinned, not doubting that she shared the same affection. With his fingers in her hair, he held her still as he sipped from her lips, flicked his tongue across the plumper bottom one, all while listening to their thumping hearts merging into a primal rhythm that his body recognized.

"You will need to guide me," he said, plucking curls off her temple and brushing them aside.

"Oh," she gasped. "Roll over."

"Why?" he asked, frowning.

"Nenn... Please."

He flipped them, wrapping his arm around her to keep her close. She wiggled, her hands feathering across his body as she spread her thighs and exposed her sex to his wide gaze. Dark pink folds glistened like the petals of an exotic flower. She shifted back, rubbing herself over his koq.

He hissed, squeezed his eyes shut, then jerked, forcing them open to not miss a moment. With her breasts bouncing, she circled her hips until the head of his koq hit the hottest part of her sex. She moaned but didn't stop.

Incredible heat engulfed his length. Inch by inch, she impaled herself, her face revealing the bliss burning through him. Never had he experienced anything like this. She'd sparked an explosion of joy when she took him into her mouth and swallowed his seed. But this... It was like her mouth but tighter, hotter, smoother.

She leaned back and speared him with pleasure.

He gripped her hips, ogling her breasts and the curve of her waist.

"You're inside me," she said, her eyes shut, her teeth dimpling her bottom lip while she gyrated. Each swirl summoned a teasing flash of heat. "You can take control again. Pull out and thrust in."

Yes. That urge was there, driving him to sit up, curl an arm around her waist, and press her back to the bed. He did so, making sure his koq stayed in place. With her beneath him, her smile sweet, he withdrew and plunged in, both summoning a fission of electric ecstasy.

The head of his koq rubbed against something that had her writhing and panting, her nails digging in. Pleasure rippled over him, stroking the length of him when she cried out, arching into him. He knew that expression, that position, her reaction. A flood of wet heat exploded, pushing him toward a pinnacle he'd climbed just yesterday. He couldn't stop his hips from pistoning in and out of her, driven by a primitive need he didn't know the name of.

Every move she made, each sound spilling from her lips, the texture of her skin and hair, all imprinted on him. His overactive symbiotes bolstered every ounce of happiness she inspired. Blinding white ecstasy burned away all shadows in his soul. As he soared, he didn't know what words he spoke or what he did. He locked himself in her, between her thighs, at the most vulnerable part of her, and vowed never to leave.

She was his.

At last.

CHAPTER TWENTY-TWO

TINY STROKED HER NECK, finding the cool metal disk a little disturbing. Still, it had made sense to get one. At least it wasn't a full-on augmentation, and she doubted the Ivoyans got complaints from the users. She flicked her thumb off her index finger, content to fidget while sitting in silence in the activities room. After a mind-blowing orgasm from a man who claimed he needed guidance, Nenn had drifted off to sleep. She'd snuck out, needing a little distance to rein in her thoughts and emotions.

Asking to meet her dad had been sweet, but she couldn't reveal to Nenn how much she longed to introduce him. Although, she wasn't sure her parents would react well to an alien in their apartment. She giggled, imagining Mom carrying out a lasagna then wondering if Nenn could eat human food. His questions had made her realize how much she loved and missed them, and how irresponsible it had been of her to not fill them in on everything she'd been doing. Their only daughter lost in space would devastate them.

Heat fluttered in her core. She pressed her hand to her chest and smiled despite the tears slipping free. At the first opportunity, she'd message them. It was time to face her anger, fear, resentment and put it all behind her.

Someone sat beside her, the fragrances of sun and baked sand settling on her.

"Why are you so miserable, Ulvus?" she asked, hazarding a guess. Her first guess had been Drafe, but she doubted he'd leave Vic for a little chat.

"Why are you?" Ulvus snapped.

She tutted. "I'm blind; what's your excuse?"

"I lost my arm."

Shit. My bad. "Oh." Not willing to back down, she faced him and continued, "Were you this unhappy before that?"

"Yes," he said. "I had yet to find my place in the tribe. I had no purpose and saw no future where my path would be revealed. You were right. I have been this...jealous. At the time, it was Drafe I envied. No matter what I did, who my family were, it made no difference to how the tribe saw me."

"So you carry the hatred through to this new life instead of tossing it aside? When it hasn't helped you once?" She frowned, recognizing the same within her. "Sure, I get that Carne sent out corpse bombs, but justice has been served."

"Even in this doomed-to-fail mission, he succeeded."

"You could have played a pivotal role. And remember, the crew isn't just Drafe. *Your* name's on the manifest." She tried to convey the concept of 'one for all and all for one,' but somehow, her brain short-circuited and left her scrambling.

"I do not know how to gain honor," he all but whispered.

Ahh. Now that made sense. "I suppose it's like bravery. It's in the moments when you are faced with a choice between honor and inaction." She shrugged. "Look at me, Ulvus, lost in an unknown world." Another tear slipped free, but she chose to believe if she couldn't 'see' it then no one else could. "Sometimes death feels preferable to this existence. I used to be so independent with the belief that I could conquer the worlds despite not mattering to my parents. Now, I'm reliant on strangers...like a child. My purpose...the impact I so desperately wanted to make...was gone. Taken from me." She curled her fingers into fists as if she could rage against the circumstances. *Been there. Done that.* "Want to know what's worse?" She laughed through the tears. "My brother did this." She flicked her hand, indicating her eyes. "Someone I trusted... And I doubt he's remorseful."

"Would it matter if he was?" Ulvus asked.

She stilled, imagining Jamie groveling for forgiveness. The idea didn't bring her pleasure. "Nothing he could say would undo what happened."

"You need to let it go... Move on." Ulvus snorted. "Harder to do than to speak it."

She wiped her cheeks. "True." Tossing a smile at him, she said, "Look at us fools stuck in the past. If you figure out a way to forgive and forget, let me know."

"Habits are difficult to break."

Wise of him to say. "Also true," she said. "You count to ten before you react. That will give you a chance to choose honor."

"You rise to your feet. Standing is a step toward action."

"I can do that," she said with her legs akimbo. "Now help me up Nenn's wall."

Ulvus laughed. "How do I do that when your arms are too weak?"

She slumped. "I was afraid you'd say that."

"May I?" he asked and took her hand. What followed was a physio-like examination of her arm. "You have the muscles but are too soft."

She winced. "That's bad?" she asked, knowing full well it was.

He chuckled. "For climbing, yes. To lure a male, no."

She scoffed. "If only. I don't know what I look like anymore. Just memories of my appearance pre-blindness."

"Qaldreth do not choose mates based on a shifting parameter."

"Shifting?" She tried not to let her mind run away with that image. They were aliens after all, and who knew if their faces changed on a whim?

"The passing of time alters one's features. Personality is the true attraction. And had you asked me prior to our talk, I would have said the symbiotes have some impact. I am learning they do not influence one's hearts. Drafe and Vic prove that though I do not condone their union because of the unknowns."

She remained silent while she mulled over his words. "As long as they are happy—"

"That too is fleeting." Ulvus ground his teeth. "Everything he touches—"

"Ah, so out of principle you will protest?" She was starting to understand what made Ulvus tick.

"Yes. It is childish to not think of the possible consequences. I have learned this the hard way. If something bad happens, I can say I warned them, but they did not listen. If nothing goes wrong, then all is well."

"Covering your bets. I get it." The need to say, 'I told you so' crossed species and galaxies. "They won't understand or thank you for it."

"I do not need their gratitude."

Of that, she had no doubt. It sounded like he did nothing without thinking it through first. "When I go back to Earth, will you come with?"

"You...would like me to?"

Why is he surprised? She smiled. "Sure. Maybe you can find ways to be honorable."

"This is true. I do wish to become an arrak."

Ambition she understood. "If you have a goal and work hard toward it, then realizing it is a question of time."

"You believe this?"

"As long as I can remember, I have wanted to be a doctor. Everything I did was with this in mind." All those hours...wasted.

"Being blind did not stop you?"

"It did for a while. It took me months to leave my bed. Nothing mattered. I had to learn who I was without the goal driving me. It had defined me for so long." She folded her arms around her waist, wishing Nenn was close enough for a hug. "My friends fell away, leaving me alone with my parents who had, for most of my life, shown me less affection than my brother." She sniffed while flicking aside a fresh outpouring of tears.

"I miss my mother," Ulvus said, breaking the silence and reminding her that she wasn't alone, not even on a spaceship heading far from all she'd known.

"I miss my dad." She smiled. "We make quite the pair."

"We are not mates," Ulvus snapped.

"Of course not. It means we share a commonality." She harrumphed, wanting to say, 'Well, not with that attitude.' But she didn't want him to think she was hoping for a dalliance when she had something wonderful starting with Nenn.

Her heart skipped a beat. It had been so long since she last experienced the excitement of the chase. She almost huffed at that thought. Chase? The man had good and proper claimed her in her bed just an hour ago.

"Tiny, Aehort wants to speak with you," Vaen said, his grouchy tone a clear tell.

She swallowed. Why would Aehort want to see her?

"Stand. Rise. Take one step," Ulvus said.

She touched air then his hand he must have thrown out to help her. "Thank you," she said and pushed to her feet.

Veering toward Vaen's voice, she pictured in her mind's eye that he waited at the doorway to the wide passage leading to the bridge—left with the galley to the right. She trailed his breathing and stopped when his footsteps did. Cold bands wrapped around her wrist and drew her into a room charged with static and filled with muted beeps.

"Thank you, Tinika, for coming. Riermus aac Vaen Arrak, you may leave."

"As you command, Aehort Uz."

She waited until Vaen's heavy tread faded while she relived every moment with the Qaldreths to recall revealing her name, ever. "You know my real name." She offered a smile to hide her nervousness then sighed when she realized her fingers twitched—grabbing and releasing the hem of her shirt.

"I do." Aehort's voice warmed. "I anticipate a little...interest when we arrive in Certorth."

"Where's that?" She peered in his direction, making out a tall, fuzzy shape.

"Ivoy's mother city, the home to the Senate. Come." He clasped her hand, lacing his cold fingers through hers. "Humans are limited by their reliance on the physical. I have been in Vic's mind. With you, I would like to try something, if I may?"

"Of course," Tiny said despite a slight throbbing behind her left eye. *Try what? Physical?* She scowled, winced when her heartbeat pounded her temple, then forced herself to relax.

A burn brushed across her forehead. She would've thought Aehort touched her, but the sensation was hot and tingly.

"Close your eyes. What do you smell, hear...sense?"

She did as asked, more out of curiosity than a fear of the man everyone on this ship revered. "Electricity in the air. Many machines whirring and humming." She angled her head to better listen. "You make no sound. No breathing or movement that I can track. The smells are quite clinical—not chemical but cleansed. There's a hint of burnt steak which I'm told is normal."

"And your peripherals?"

She concentrated, sensing nothing but Aehort looming over her. "I'm not standing near anything except you."

"Good." He tapped her temple.

Light flashed, scorching then cool. In a nano second, images flooded her mind. She stood at the center of them. Before her was her face, familiar yet older than she remembered with faint lines around her eyes and mouth. The white of her eyes was as startling as her unkempt purple hair. And what was she wearing? Pink Zebra-printed leggings with a neon-blue baggy shirt? Mom had promised her that all her clothes were in interchangeable grays and blacks. She froze. *No, this is what I've been wearing all this time?* Her cheeks burned, embarrassment striking when it was too late to do anything about it.

She was thinner than she'd expected. So, that was a plus.

The room came into view. Above a central table, 3D holographic images of space were projected and spinning.

She glanced at the bright-orange elongated fingers touching her temple. "What is this, Aehort? What did you do?" she asked, awe hoarsening her voice.

"You are seeing through my eyes."

She gasped then gaped at her wide-eyed white eyes, drawing his attention to them. Gone were her green irises she'd once thought her prettiest feature. "How is this possible?"

"Ivoyans have many abilities. This is one of them."

Sadness hit her hard. From sight to blind to sight but with supernatural assistance was like offering a man dying of thirst a mirage with not a drop of water... "I suppose, once you stop touching me, I'll be back to normal?"

"For now." Aehort shifted back, and darkness descended.

"Thank you," she managed through the tears, wishing she'd thought to call Nenn. To 'see' him would be a gift from the heavens. Still, her face... She hadn't seen herself in so long. On instinct, she wrapped her arms around Aehort's mid-section.

"Nenn is searching for you." He patted her shoulder, his tone fatherly.

"Tiny?" Nenn's voice came through her neck thingy a second later, proving Aehort's abilities went beyond his demonstration.

She broke away to cup her neck. "I'm with Aehort. We're done, right?" She angled her head in his direction.

"Indeed," he said.

"Please fetch me, Nenn." She swept her hand at the table she could no longer see. "All this?" she asked Aehort.

"The command room. This is how we located Earth."

She chewed on her lip, then blurted out what had been niggling her. "Do you think the Ivoyans will blame me for the bombs?"

"Some might. I do not." Warmth saturated his voice. "You have one ally."

"She has many," Nenn said from the doorway. When he placed his hand at her lower back, she shivered.

"Aehort showed me a vision." She flashed a smile at her orange friend. "Thank you, again."

"My pleasure, Tinika."

She let Nenn usher her away.

When they were alone, he paused, drawing her to a halt. "Tinika?"

She liked how he said it: Tin-ikka instead of Tineeka. "That is my name."

"It rolls off the tongue like birdsong."

She dipped her chin, hoping to hide her flaming cheeks.

"Hungry?"

She grinned. "I could nibble. Tulsig cakes and russmar tisane?"

"If you like," he said and led her to the table in the galley. "Vaen says he found you with Ulvus. Was that male bothering you?"

"Not at all. He isn't as bad as I used to think," she said before biting into the hot cake Nenn placed into her hand. The salt hit her tongue like an explosion of fireworks. She shut her eyes on a hum and chewed in utter bliss.

Nenn growled, "I do not trust him."

"Why?" she asked around a mouthful of glorious gooeyness.

"He attacked Vic and challenges me often when there is no cause for either."

"I'm sure he has his reasons." Sniffing, she followed her nose to the glass of tisane to her left and took a sip. "If not a little misguided."

She licked her lips, searching for every drop of saltiness.

The air charged, rippling awareness down the nape of her neck.

She shuffled on her ass, unable to shake the sensation of being stared at. "Nenn?" she whispered, angling her head. "Are we alone?"

"Yes," he said, his voice gravelly.

"Oh." She squared her shoulders and ignored the sensation. "Thought someone was watching me."

"I am." A plate scraped closer, the aroma alone confirming more tulsig cakes were before her. But his words had her frozen.

"Why? Is it my face?" She wiped her temple, unsure whether Aehort's touch had scarred her.

"No, there is nothing wrong with you." He caught her hand and held onto it. "I find you breathtaking."

With her aged appearance revealed by Aehort still fresh in her mind and Ulvus's words on what attracts Qaldreth warriors, she scoffed. "My face will shift." She let go of her tisane in search of another cake.

"Yes, as will mine, but who you are shines through."

Again, she wanted to scoff or roll her eyes though she doubted Nenn would understand either. "Bitter, unforgiving, scared, and lost me? Shining?" She bit into the cake to do something instead of sitting there listening to Nenn wax poetic nonsense.

"Joyful, brilliant, charming, determined, strong, and fearless."

Is that what he thinks of me? She blinked to hold back tears as if she hadn't emptied her ducts during her chat with Ulvus. "I'm human," she said, her voice cracking. "There has to be some bad."

"For Qaldreth, too."

"Well, you're perfect, or you've been hiding all your awful qualities." She forced a smile. Knowing her luck, he could turn out to be some alien version of a psychopath. Her gut churned, and everything in her rebelled against that thought.

"I lack ambition, can be single-minded," he cleared his throat, "and a coward."

She tightened her fingers in his, squeezing his hand. "Now, *that* I don't believe."

"I wanted my father to die when I was away so that I did not have to deal with his death."

Her heart melted, and a tear slipped free. "You are just scared of losing someone you love. We all are."

"My mother…" His warm breath on her knuckles preceded the softness of his lips when he placed a kiss there.

"You are *not* a coward," she said, dropping her half-eaten cake to reach for him.

"It does not matter, *hirihadie*. It was his dying wish that I train with the Ivoyans. Without his sacrifice, I would still be on Qaldreth."

"No," she gasped, cupping their clasped hands. Her mind spun while a strange weight crushed her chest, affecting her heartbeat. "How soon?"

"Between his death and the Ivoyans collecting me?" He released a shuddering gasp. "Hours."

"Oh my word, Nenn, I'm so sorry. Grieving and leaving your home are two of the worst stressors. How did you cope?"

"I threw myself into my studies. I refused to bring dishonor upon my tribe and nullify my father's sacrifice."

She inched closer to him. "Do you have siblings?"

"None."

She frowned, her heart cracking for the man she'd grown so fond of. Despite Jamie being an ass, she had a brother. And both her parents lived. As much as she bemoaned their neglect, their deaths would destroy her.

"I'll be your family," she said, flashing Nenn a smile. "Then you won't be alone."

Silence met her offer, for so long that she wondered whether she'd said the wrong thing.

"I should not desire my sister," he said.

Every muscle in her body tightened, cramped, forcing her to lean back and pull her hands away. The air charged again, ramping the tension between them.

"No, you shouldn't," she rasped, her heartbeat pounding in her ears.

His touch at her jaw tilted her head back, then soft lips brushed across hers. Her breath caught a second before he kissed her.

When he thrust in his tongue, he wrapped his fingers around her throat, warming her as he dominated her. Heat coiled in her belly. Her nipples tingled as they hardened. He devoured her, taking his sweet time to plunder her mouth, toy with her tongue, and control every one of her reactions.

"You cannot be my sister," he whispered, his breath fanning her lips.

She swallowed around the lump of her throat. "No, I rescind my offer."

He chuckled. "Good."

Chapter Twenty-Three

ALONE IN HER ROOM, Tiny sucked in a deep breath, her thoughts circling Ulvus's advice. She couldn't carry her anger forever. While Nenn was climbing his wall, she wanted this done. And who knew when next she'd be alone to do so.

She said to her tablet, "Open email. Compose to Henry and Maria Bryant. Speech to text."

Dear Mom and Dad,

I'm sorry for my silence. I've been kidnapped with my consent by an alien race offering me a possible healing. I'm loving the trip, and I've met someone too.

I just wanted to get something off my chest, once and for all.

Why was Jamie loved more than me? Why did you neglect me? Was I a bad daughter? Did I do something to make you love me less?

I don't think you'll get this message, considering I'm isolated, one of two human women onboard. That's a good thing when I'm writing this fueled by anger and resentment. I'm sorry this is out of the blue, but it's been a long time coming.

All my love from a daughter who does *matter,*

Tiny.

"Send." She slumped, drained, and yet somehow, that shadow that had clouded her thoughts was gone as if a weight had been stripped from her. "New message. Compose to Jamie Bryant."

Dear sweet baby brother,

To say I hate you would be wrong, because I don't. I should for what you put me through. I'm blind, you asshat, thanks to your drug dealing and general disregard for everyone else in your life. I'd call you selfish, but that would mean nothing to you.

So, here goes. I forgive you for always stealing Mom and Dad's attention and affection and for ruining my life and career. And, I guess, for making my existence pointless.

Maybe one day, I can look back at this and feel nothing.

I will find my new purpose, and I hope you find yours.

Tiny.

"Send," she said and sniffed. Why was she crying? Enough was enough. Ulvus was right; she had to move on, to forget. She leaped to her feet. Okay, she was standing. Now what? She wiggled her butt, longing to lose herself to music. But how? The speakers on the tablet wouldn't do it for her. She headed for the door, not wanting to bother Nenn during his climb. When the door swished shut behind her, she paused. Right was the bridge. Someone there might be able to help her. Seventeen steps brought her closer to the quiet hum, purr, whizz of the bridge.

"Um, hello?" She paused in the doorway and sniffed, trying to guess who was on duty. Molten metal met her sensitive nose. She grinned. "Igar?"

"Yes, Tiny? Is there anything you need?"

She crossed to him. "I want to play music. Is there a way to connect it to the speakers in my room?"

"Music?" His smell became stronger with his heavy tread.

"Just for me, not to be broadcast across the ship." She waved her tablet. "My playlists are on here." Silence met her words. She frowned. "I can show you. Tablet, play my favorite beats." She raised the tablet between them when a song played.

"Oh," Igar gasped, taking the tablet out of her hand. "This is...fascinating." He walked away, something squeaked like a chair, then boom went her music as it filled the room.

She laughed, relishing the vibrations coursing through her. "Yes, like that," she yelled just at the music cut off.

"Very well," Igar said, catching her hand to slide the tablet onto her palm. "It is set up as you requested."

She clasped the tablet to her chest and beamed. "Thank you so much."

"What was that?" Vaen demanded from behind her.

She squeaked and stepped aside, then winced when she bumped into something hard. Now wasn't the time to rub her hip, no doubt bruised.

"Tiny's...playlist." Igar sounded both confident and hesitant.

She nodded, switching her gaze between the two shadows that seemed not as blurry as she was used to.

"A cultural thing?" Someone else joined the conversation. She'd hazard a guess it was Gusin. He didn't speak much, and she hadn't had that much interaction with him to memorize his voice and scent.

"Sort of," she said. "I used to dance at a nightclub."

Chaos ensued while the men argued over and around her. They spoke too fast for her to follow along, but when silence reigned, Vaen touched her forearm.

"Will you share what you have?" he asked.

"Oh," she gasped, shoving out her tablet. "I didn't know you'd be interested."

"Some tribes have these...sounds." Gusin drew closer, bringing his charged-air smell like electricity coursed through his body. "Ours does, to an extent, with the thrum and boom of thunder."

"Mine, too," Nenn said, his tread approaching her. He threw an arm around her and pulled her against his warmth. "Though it is only reserved for mating ceremonies."

"What's going on?" Vic called, her dainty tread crossing to Tiny. "What did you do, babe?"

"Just wanted to listen to my music loud," she said, raising her chin in defiance. No way would she act as if she'd done something wrong.

"You have tunes?" Vic's surprise had Tiny shuffling on her feet.

"Club music, maybe a few ballades."

"The most music I got to listen to was my arena intro and exit. And always the same damn song. Along with the other Carne gladiators, of course. Trust me, they got pretty tired fast." Vic leaned in to whisper, "Thought we could chat. You free?"

"Um, sure," Tiny said, patting Nenn's stomach.

He released her. "I will fetch you from the galley."

"Get my tablet when they're done, please," she said and let Vic pull her off the bridge.

They headed to the kitchen in silence while the men flicked through her playlists, blasting two-second snippets, one after the other.

"Well, I see you're doing well," Vic said, ushering Tiny onto a bench.

"Causing havoc, you mean," she said, tossing the woman a smile.

The replicate dinged. Vic shoved a cold glass into Tiny's hand.

She raised it for a sniff, then sighed. "Mango?"

Vic chuckled. "Something like that." A slight shift of air confirmed her sitting opposite Tiny at the table. "Thought I'd check in on you. How are things going?"

"Well, Nenn's made this transition...um, journey, smoother, better. I am worried about the Ivoyans imprisoning me and poking me with their orange fingers. Aehort said as much."

"Did he now?" Vic smacked her lips.

Reminded of her juice, Tiny sipped the sweet nectar and hummed at the tartness coating her tongue.

"Whatever happens, I'll fight to protect you, Tiny." Vic cupped Tiny's hand. "Drafe, too."

"I know, and I'm grateful. Just don't get hurt or die, okay?" Tiny peered at the shadowy outline that was Vic. "They'd have to study me to maybe heal me. I've accepted a little prodding's in my future."

"I don't know, Tiny-babe. I'm a tad bit worried since I convinced you to come with, then abandoned you to..."

"Have sex?" Tiny grinned. "No judgment from me. I've got Nenn, you see."

"As in *got*—"

"Yes," Tiny blurted. Heat exploded across her cheeks.

"Oh, thank God." Vic squeezed Tiny's hand and released her. "I'm glad you're not alone. Are you his vatia sahaar?"

Tiny frowned. "His what?"

Vic cursed under her breath. "If you don't know, then you're not. He'll tell you if you are."

"Tell me what?" Tiny snapped.

"That you're his love mate. It's rare for Qaldreths, apparently, and yet, Drafe's mine." Vic stood. "I see you got an implant. Call me if you want girly companionship."

Puzzled by Vic's words, Tiny didn't listen for her fading footsteps. "Um, will do," she muttered and cradled her juice.

Oh, what she'd give to stay with Nenn as his mate. Yet, rare meant the chance was slim. She sighed, drained the juice, and rose. Not sure where to put the glass, she took it and inched in the direction Nenn always went. A counter was within her touch, so she left it on the smooth surface.

No Nenn met her on the way to her room. She entered without hindrance, and the closing of the door weighed heavily on her heart. Being alone didn't used to bother her, probably because her parents had always been reachable...physically. That wasn't true anymore.

And even though she was heading toward an unknown galaxy, it was good to know she had Vic in her corner. Though how much an augmented human could do against a superior, orange species... Well, she'd find out soon enough.

She sat on the bed and slid the reed from on top of her pillow. Already, the notes Juunn had taught her didn't warble as much, and she could hold them for longer. As a doctor, she likened the playing of such an instrument to breathing exercises. She drew in a long inhale to prove she'd improved her lung capacity, then ruined it by giggling at her silliness.

A buzz made her jump, and she fumbled the reed. It clattered across the floor and rolled away from her.

"Shit," she muttered before commanding the door to open. While it did so, she crawled in the direction the instrument rolled. Wincing at the hard floor, she patted around her, inched forward, and repeated.

"What are you doing?" Nenn asked, bringing his amazing cologne with him.

"Dropped the reed."

"I will get it." And up she went with a barely muffled squeak. He dumped her on the bed and marched off.

When he sat beside her, his thigh warming hers, she twisted to smile at him. He placed the reed in her hand, then clasped it shut but didn't release her. "What did Aehort want?"

"Oh," she gasped and bounced on the spot. "Nenn, he touched my temple, and I could see through his eyes. It was amazing. I wish you'd been there." She raised her free hand to fluff her hair, then lowered her chin to her chest. And he called her beautiful? She sniffed, tears pressing behind her eyes. What a sweet man.

"Did he say anything about the Ivoyans healing your vision?" Was there concern in his voice?

"The Ivoyans helping me was always a gamble. If they can't, that's okay." Of course, she'd be devastated, but while there was a chance, she wouldn't worry about it.

The silence stretched. She raised her face as if she could read his expressions. "What's wrong?"

His mouth across hers made her squeak. She threw out her hands to hold onto his biceps, needing him to stop her from toppling over. His ardor and skilled lips took over, seducing her and melting her insides.

He broke away, his breathing ragged. "I love kissing you, Tiny."

She forced a smile while her heart lost its rhythm. "What, don't like calling it face-latching?"

He laughed. "I love face-latching with you, Tiny."

"How much longer before we reach Certorth?" She ran a fingertip along his smooth jawline.

"Three weeks," he said though his tone had curiosity.

Then her life would change again. "Well, we have all that time to face-latch as much as you want."

"Oh, I intend to every chance I get," he said, drawing her closer.

CHAPTER TWENTY-FOUR

Three Weeks Later
Approaching Certorth, Ivoy
Onboard the Aroagni.

NENN KEPT TINY BUSY, whether in bed, learning to dance, playing chess, or sitting through the audiobook, and she couldn't recall a happier time. Despite the impending arrival and what she suspected would be a showdown, she cherished every moment with him. Within an hour, they'd land. After that, she could die, have her sight restored, or say goodbye to Nenn forever.

With fake smiles and laughter, she hid her worry. Not to mention that for some strange reason, she could see more. His outline had detail. The darkness of his skin against his bright red hair, for one thing. The exact shape and color of his eyes—no, that wasn't clear. Not yet.

How this was possible was a mystery. The doctors had assured her that she wouldn't heal over time. So praying for a miracle was stupid. She was the idiot for hoping. Soon, she'd find out if she'd taken a leap of faith off the wrong cliff.

"Are you ready?" Nenn asked, grabbing her hand where she rested it on the galley's table.

She pulled the anbru closer, needing the chill from the condensation to ground her. "I don't know. We're hiding here?"

"You are. I must be in the Q.C.C. chambers as a member of the crew."

She squeaked, squeezed his hand, then shuffled to the side. "I'll be alone?" Hiding her horror was a struggle, so she buried her face in her glass, taking a long gulp.

"For a little while."

She set the juice on the table and clasped her hands on her lap. Being on her own wasn't new, but on an alien planet?

"You may stay, Giniiri aac Nenn Maed." Aehort glided past.

Hope exploded like fireworks inside her chest, filling her with heat and relief.

"He is right, Nenn. It is better you guard Tiny," Drafe said, his tone matter of fact.

Nenn threw his arm across her shoulders and tucked her against his body. "As you command."

The silence that fell after the mass exodus threatened to crush her spirit. She patted Nenn's knee, loving the muscle beneath her fingers even as their time together was ending.

"Whatever happens, Nenn, know that I'm so grateful to you." She dipped her head, hoping the tears burning her eyes wouldn't slip free.

"Tiny, I—" He leaped to his feet and bolted out of the galley. "What is the meaning of this?" he demanded.

She angled her head to listen, picking up the gentle cadence of Ivoyan steps.

"It is procedure to clear a ship post-journey," a man said.

She inched to the doorway, many tall orange blurs coming into view.

"Including taking the human." A man stepped forward, acting very much like the leader of this group.

"No," Nenn growled. "She stays with me."

"You have no authority here, Maed," the man snapped.

Tiny narrowed on the Ivoyans, willing her eyes to pick up details. Pain pinged in her temple at her futile efforts, forcing her to duck behind Nenn. One moment, he was before her, the next his shadow and warmth was gone. She gasped when something heavy rested on her foot.

"Nenn," she cried out, dropping beside him on the floor.

She ran her hands over his body as familiar as her own. He didn't respond to her nudges and pleas, but his breathing was regular like he slept. No part of him was wet or sticky, so no wounds needed immediate attention, but unconsciousness could hide a life-threatening injury.

"What did you do?" she screamed at the leader. "Give me a med-thingy." She wiggled her fingers, praying the idiot listened.

"He is well, death dealer," he spat.

Death dealer? She stilled, ice sliding over her and sending a shiver across her body. Aehort had said there might be some resistance. He'd also said she had allies. But with him not on the ship and Nenn knocked out, she was alone. She stroked his face and pressed a kiss to his slack jaw. He'd tried to shield her, the sweet man. Tears slipped free. *Whatever happens, right?*

"I love you," she whispered, resting her temple on his right pec.

With a deep breath, she pushed to her feet, locking them in place when her knees trembled. 'Just stand,' Ulvus had said.

"Come with me," the leader said.

She snorted. "When I can't see?"

"Your species is weak," he snapped.

She wanted to remind the asshat that one human corpse killed his people, but self-preservation prevailed. So, she stood there, unmoving. Maybe if he grew impatient, he'd abandon her and Nenn. With a bruising grip on her upper arm, he dragged her across Nenn's sprawled body, forcing her to jump. She stumbled then caught her balance. He didn't release her, making her jog behind him—his stride too long and fast for her.

Bright light made her flinch, but being in their sunlight was short-lived. He escorted her onto a smaller ship, then shoved her into a seat.

"What do you want with her?" Ulvus demanded.

She slumped. His presence brought her some relief though why he was there had her frowning.

"She is not of your concern," the Ivoyan man said.

"If your intention is to harm her, then yes, I will concern myself."

"You would die for this...shit?" The man lowered his voice, now filled with malice.

Ulvus's silence summoned a fresh wave of tears. She wanted to rail at him to find honor in the moment, but the lump in her throat burned so much, she struggled to speak.

The door shut, and the ship took off, slamming her back.

Ulvus clasped her hand and gave it a squeeze. Her breath hitched. *What does that mean? He's sorry? Not to worry?* She stared at his hand warming hers and swallowed a gasp. His skin was orange, his veins raised. She could *see* them. *Am I hallucinating? Have I finally lost my mind?* She swallowed hard and focused on their companions. Tall, long-limbed, and long-fingered aliens held odd-looking weapons. They wore blue overalls, and some sort of a visor hid their eyes.

"Aehort?" she whispered, hoping his influence lingered in her mind. That would explain her 'restored' eyesight.

"He is not here, Tiny," Ulvus said. "He cannot help you."

She shook her head, unable to accept that her sight was back when it made no sense. To do so would set her up for heartbreak when this was fleeting, at best. She nibbled her lip and scanned the ship, marking where everyone stood. Two men at the door, another near the pilot, and the leader, pacing from the front console to the rear of the compartment. They thought her blind. That gave her some advantage. But even if she managed to steal a gun, she didn't know how to use it. Never mind that it went against everything she stood for to not harm a living soul.

She gaped at the scene through the windscreen, or whatever it was called: lilac-gray skies, pale sunlight, and deep green mists hiding the ground below high mush-room-shaped towers. Tiny ships flowed between buildings. It was surreal, slamming it home where she was.

She rubbed her eyes, blinked them open, then narrowed on the farthest Ivoyan, testing her limits. *Holy farg.* Excitement and sheer joy exploded through her, bouncing her on the seat. She snuck a glance at the scowling leader and stilled.

"Ulvus?" She smiled at him, admiring his amber-colored eyes against his obsidian skin. He was handsome, too, with his wide forehead, sharp cheekbones, and pointed chin.

"Yes?" He gazed at her.

"Do not let them know...but I can see." She smothered a laugh.

His brow furrowed. "I do not understand."

She flicked a dismissive hand at him. "Think they plan to kill me?" On a gulp, she twisted in the seat to face him. "What are you doing here?"

He bowed his head. "I am viewed as a failure when all I did was force Vic to show the Q.C.C. her skills. It is true; my reports do smack of resentment." Sadness darkened his expression. "I did as you suggested: chose honor..." He leaned back and stared at the door. "I also revealed where Nenn was and with whom, believing the udaps needed to know all to make informed decisions. I am sorry if you being here is my fault."

His logic was sound; she'd give him that. "They said they were clearing the ship as procedure." Though, why she wanted to ease his guilt, she didn't know. They'd known she was onboard, and maybe that was because of him. She couldn't say for sure. "Any ideas on how to escape?"

His jaw dropped. "No," he rasped.

"If I steal a gun, can you use it?"

His eyes bulged. "Tiny, what are you saying? This is madness."

"Ulvus, I'm standing." And she did, drawing everyone's attention to her. "I need to pee," she said, staring ahead. "I don't want to wet the floor like an untrained pet."

The leader recoiled. "Escort her to the waste closet," he said to another man.

She held out a hand and waited.

"I will take her," Ulvus said, clasping her elbow.

"No." The leader shoved Ulvus into his seat, then yanked her forward.

She scowled. "Quit pushing me around. I have legs."

That got her almost dragged across the floor to a narrow door. She stepped inside and tried to seal herself in.

"You do not need privacy," the new man said, his tone bored.

"I refuse to pee with you watching," she gritted out.

He nudged her in and hit a button. Three beams swept over her, making her skin tingle. And out she was pulled. "Now sit."

She ran her hand along the wall to settle beside Ulvus. *Well, that was pointless.* "That got us nowhere," she whispered.

"What did you think would happen?"

"Really? Do I have to spell it out? I was to be a distraction." She folded her arms across her chest. "I assume you watched me instead of stealing a gun?"

"And do what with a weapon, Tiny?" He chuckled. "Even as a sava, I cannot take on three Ivoyans with phasers."

"Of course you can if you have the element of surprise."

He scoffed. "I could take one, maybe two, but by then, we would be dead."

Hope fizzled like a dying flame. "If you steal a gun and so do I? Maybe then?"

"Where is Nenn?"

She bit her lip, tucked her chin against her chest, and said, "They knocked him out somehow."

"Ah, the phasers are set to stun. This is good. He will awaken and beg the udaps for help." Ulvus patted her hand. "Your salvation is near. Mine is not."

Nenn would rescue her, that she knew. "What will they do with you?"

"Return me to Qaldreth in disgrace."

She grabbed Ulvus's hand. "Did you explain why you—"

"The udaps would not listen. I have proven my hatred for Drafe taints my actions. Anything else would be deception to them."

"Farg," she muttered. "We escape, steal a ship, and fly back to Earth. You can live free there."

He laughed, but it was cold and mirthless. "There or on Qaldreth, an exile is still without honor."

The ship touched down, jolting her out of her thoughts. Alien fingers wrapped around her upper arm and dragged her toward the opening door. Before her was a platform without a safety railing. The wind whipped her hair across her face, plastered the T-shirt to her body, and threatened to sweep her into the clouds below. A narrow bridge led to tall doors built into a pretty building with high arches carved into its sides.

She clung to the alien's arm, praying she could hold on if she stumbled off the side. Only when they paused at the door did she release a pent-up breath.

"This is the human?" someone spat, drawing her gaze. "Bring her in, and the traitor, too."

She allowed her shoulders to slump an inch in relief. At least with Ulvus along, she had some sort of company. A massive hall held gray-stoned statues and beams of lilac light shining on a gold-inlaid floor. Those milling about paused to stare at their passing.

"Her kind killed my Daiwan?" Despite her ability to see, dodging the slap was beyond her.

Fire blazed across the side of her head, making her cry out. She cupped her cheek while tears flowed.

"Your hospitality leaves much to be desired," she gritted out then winced. Staying quiet would've been wiser.

The Ivoyan screamed and lunged at her.

I'm about to die. She stepped back from the swinging claws and hit her escort's wiry frame. He did nothing to protect her, but instead, shoved her forward into her attacker's range. She hissed when nails dragged across her forearms, summoning a scorching sting.

"Assaulting a prisoner says much about your culture," she said, then pinched her lips shut.

"Give me a phaser. I will kill this...thing."

She frowned. Why did Qaldreths serve a dishonorable race? She shook her head. These must be outliers. Nenn wouldn't have stayed on Ivoy otherwise.

"She is to be examined and documented, Oban. You know the instructions as well as I do," the leader said. "I am not pleased, but the good of Ivoy far outweighs our need for revenge."

"Nothing was said about injuring her." Oban stole the leader's phaser and aimed it at her.

Ice coated her skin, rippling over her.

Ulvus gasped when Oban fired.

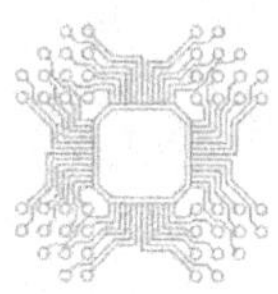

Nenn stormed into the Q.C.C. chamber, uncaring whether he violated protocol. Sheer, blinding fear narrowed his focus on finding Tiny when nothing else mattered. Most of the warriors milled about while Drafe and Vic spoke with the udaps.

He barged across to Drafe. "They have taken my Tiny."

"Do you know where?" Vic asked, gazing at Drafe.

"Your what?" Giniiri aac Marl Udap demanded.

All those near stilled.

"Tiny is a blind human female who joined us on the return voyage," Drafe said, drawing Vic close to him. "I thought her blindness would be intriguing to the Ivoyans."

Vaen nudged between Drafe and Nenn. "She is a friend of Vic's, and under the circumstances, we could not leave her unprotected on the ice hauler."

"And she is Nenn's vatia sahaar," Vaen said, squaring his shoulders.

"Is this true, Maed?" Marl Udap asked, peering into Nenn's eyes.

"It is, My Udaps." He smothered a wince at the hope tightening a knot in the pit of his stomach. "I did not know this when I offered her healing and refuge."

"So who has taken her?" Meorri aac Kish Udap asked, summoning warriors to gather around them.

"Ivoyan los and uzes said it was protocol to clear the ship after a long journey. Their focus on Tiny told me they deceived. When I refused to let them take her, they stunned me. I awoke to her gone." He squeezed his eyes shut for a moment, reliving the silence of the ship along with the certainty that he was alone. "She is helpless, at their mercy…"

"We ride at once," Marl Udap called out.

"Can we track her?" Vic asked, tapping the nodule in her neck.

"Yes." Nenn offered a tight smile. "She was heading to the Great Library."

"Warriors, to me," Kish Udap ordered. "Those with access to velorxes, mount up. Others, file into every available shuttle."

"I shall reach out to the acting Senate," Ward Udap said, waving his hand for them to hurry.

Leaving en mass gave Nenn the strength to push through his fear. Tiny didn't believe him to be a coward, and at that moment, he wasn't. He'd lay down his life for her. Over the last week, he'd wanted to tell her what she meant to him, but his tongue had tied, or he'd been interrupted. In that, he'd lacked courage. But here, now, she needed him.

He scrambled onto a velorx, fired it up, and propelled it south to the oldest spire in Certorth. It had miles and miles of cellars holding scrolls, tomes, and tablets of ancient knowledge. The many rooms housing los meant finding her would be that much harder. He stroked his nodule, thanking Osnir that he'd insisted she get one. Tapping his wrist activated the flashing locator. When the stun wore off, tracking her had been the first thing he'd done.

Not that he dared talk to her in case she wasn't alone. He gazed to the right and left of him at the many Qaldreths heading into battle for him. His chest swelled. What this would do to their standing, he couldn't say. Perhaps Ward Udap would garner understanding and forgiveness with the Senate. He'd known this was a possible outcome, but he'd hoped his respect and reverence for the Ivoyans wasn't misplaced. Heal Tiny. Send her home. Those were his promises.

He crushed the sadness in his heart. Vic could protect herself. Tiny… No, he'd done this, put her in danger by bringing her here, by promising her healing he couldn't deliver. He scowled. There was still time to rescue her. But he'd doomed her to a life tied to his by claiming she was his vatia sahaar even if he wished it was true.

Drafe whizzed past, Vic clinging to his back. Her expression said there would be hell to pay for anyone harming her friend. Nenn trailed them then pushed forward until they were side by side. They dipped as one, aiming for the occupied platform. He parked the velorx on the balcony that circled the doors of wisdom and insight, both carved from the oldest tree on Ivoy, or so the legend went.

He curled his fingers into fists. The way he felt, he'd set them on fire to find Tiny.

Thankfully, they opened, allowing them entry.

"What is the meaning of this?" a lo demanded, coming forward to meet them.

"Release the human." Kish Udap strode across to glare at the Ivoyan.

Marl Udap joined him. Drafe and Vic took up their rear. Nenn did the same. He peered around the hall, searching for a sign of Tiny. The dot said she was here, near. But with so many Ivoyans blocking his line of sight, he couldn't spot her. He tapped his wrist and followed the flashing signal. Vaen ran before him, clearing the way.

"Tiny?" Nenn called.

"Nenn?" she cried out.

Hot relief had him bolting forward and tossing Ivoyans back in his haste to reach her. He drew to a halt when he found her kneeling on the floor, leaning over an unconscious Ulvus. Nenn dug his med-dev out of his pocket and settled beside her to run it over the male.

"He leaped in front of a shot meant for me," she sobbed. "Please heal him."

Ulvus saved her? "Are you well?" he asked as the med-dev beeped. Ulvus's symbiotes had formed his armor, which meant the male was only stunned like Nenn had been. "He is well, *hirihadie*."

"Oh," she gasped, then glanced at Nenn.

He jerked back, his jaw dropping. Green eyes met his. And across her skin, she shimmered as if she wore armor.

She threw herself at him, wrapping her arms around him when she buried her face in the curve of his neck. Her tears warmed his skin where they fell.

"I'll kill you where you stand if you don't get the farg out of my way," Vic growled then bent over Tiny, rubbing her shoulder. "You okay, babe?"

"I am," she said, sniffing. "If it wasn't for Ulvus, though, I'd be dead."

Nenn doubted that. He swallowed a smile. His symbiotes had spread to her as they'd done with Drafe and Vic. He'd thought her nanites played a role, but now he knew, humans were susceptible to the transfer without the Jakar's intervention.

Vic pulled away, joining the argument between the los, udaps, and warriors.

Tiny leaned back. She smiled at Nenn, cupping his cheeks with her soft hands. "You're gorgeous," she whispered, trailing a fingertip from his earlobe, along his jawline, to his chin.

"You can see?" He brushed a curl aside.

"Yes, for now. Don't know why or how..." She shrugged. "At least I get to look at you before I leave."

He grimaced. Her departure was still an unknown. But he was damn sure he didn't want her to go. He ran his thumb over her bruised cheek. "Who did this to you?"

"Oban," she said, then showed Nenn her forearms. "These, too. The man was so angry—"

"I will kill him." Nenn leaped to his feet, fury propelling him up. He took Tiny with him but tucked her against him. "Which Ivoyan?"

"It doesn't matter. Use your device and fix me." She held out her arms.

The urge to do this Oban some harm couldn't compare to the compulsion to see to her needs. He succumbed and ran the med-dev over her, taking his time to ensure he caught every scratch and bruise.

"This is the blind human?" Marl Udap asked, snapping Nenn's focus.

"She was," Aehort said, parting the crowd. "Tinika Bryant, I must apologize on behalf of the Ivoyan Senate for your mistreatment. I expected the temptation to seek revenge would draw out the outlawed faction, Kandaya. I did not mean for you to be harmed." He glanced at a moaning Ulvus then at Tiny. "You did well."

Nenn glared at Aehort. "You purposely endangered her—"

"It was needed," Aehort said, his tone level. "The final step to her healing required your symbiotes to act. Only placing her in harm's way would do that."

Nenn's anger deflated.

"I will take care of Ulvus." Aehort glanced at the great doors. "You and Tinika have much to discuss...on the *Aroagni*."

Chapter Twenty-Five

Tiny clung to Nenn's hand, hesitating when he climbed onto one of those hover bikes. He arched a brow at her, forcing her to slide onto the seat behind him. When he shot off, she pressed her cheek to his back and wrapped her arms around his waist. The scenery whizzed past—not a chance would she miss every beautiful inch of it.

"Wait until I tell my parents," she whispered.

Shielded by his body, she didn't suffer from the chilly winds, but when he landed beside what she assumed was the *Aroagni* and slipped off the bike, she shivered. He held out his hand. She stared at it, at the wide palm and strong fingers that knew her intimately.

Her cheeks burned. She slipped her hand into his and let him lead her onto the ship. He didn't stop until they reached her room. When the door shut behind them, he settled her on the bed then paced.

For a minute or five, she ogled him, relishing his strong thighs, that tight ass that had filled her palms many a time, and those broad shoulders she'd held onto in the throes of ecstasy. "What's wrong, Nenn?"

He faced her for a second then turned away. "What if you cannot go home?"

She stiffened. "What aren't you telling me?"

He crossed to her and wrapped his arms around her, bringing his scent with him. "I do not know if the Ivoyans will send you to your Earth."

She jerked back, breaking contact. "What do you mean? As in never?" Never hear Dad's voice or have her mom's lasagna again? "Where will I go?" She was lost, homeless, heading into a future without prospects. Overwhelming panic fuzzed her thoughts and drowned her hearing with a dull hum.

"You stay with me," he said with decisiveness.

Sure, they were lovers, but that couldn't mean anything permanent when it had only been a month. She loved the man, but still, she couldn't expect him to feel the same. Not so soon.

"I don't want to be an obligation or force you to take care of me." She grimaced. "Besides, do you have a house on Ivoy?"

"No, I live in the Med-Tech barracks with other Qaldreth maeds."

She'd be staying with him in cramped 'dorm' rooms. This wasn't fair on him or her, but she *had* taken him up on his offer based on hope.

"Life's not full of guarantees," she said through the lump in her throat. A lesson she'd learned the hard way.

She'd gotten her eyesight but had lost her family in the process. Her heart twanged as the urge to cry scratched her throat. What she wanted to do was pace, yell, demand they fire up this ship and return her to some semblance of normality. But what if Nenn loved her? Dare she give up on a chance with him because fear had its icy grip on her gumption?

'Stand,' Ulvus had said.

She squared her shoulders and reached for Nenn. He embraced her, giving her his all. She rested her temple on his shoulder and hugged him back.

"They could very well say yes, especially after this Kandaya incident. Let's not build the worst scenario in our minds." She nestled into his embrace, burying her face in the curve of his neck. Hours could pass and she'd happily stay like this.

"Agreed." His tone was too solemn for her liking. "I...lied to my udaps."

"Oh?" she asked, rubbing her cheek over his shoulder.

He leaned back to meet her gaze. "And trapped you to me."

That didn't sound bad. She tried not to smile in the face of his seriousness. "Okay, for how long?"

He closed his beautiful red eyes then opened them to meet her gaze. "Forever."

She barked a laugh. "Right."

Shock contorted his features. "You do not believe me."

She ran her thumbs over his red eyebrows, loving the chance to read his expressions. This handsome man had brought her to ecstasy too many times to count, had kept her company, showed her his culture, taught her to face her past and deal with it, not to mention rallied his men to rescue her.

If he wanted forever, she was all for it. Except, he was delusional to believe it even existed. "As a doctor, I know there's no such thing. We have longer lifespans thanks to our medical technol—"

"With symbiotes, you will be known for an eternity. If we return to Qaldreth soil, my tribe's symbiotes will record who you are. Generations to come will know your name and deeds."

"The same symbiotes that healed me?" She hadn't once considered they'd affect her as much as they had Vic. Maybe she should have, but being with Nenn was all that had mattered. Now, she had him to thank for her healing. And Aehort had known all along. "In your sperm?"

Nenn's breath hitched, and his eyes darkened to a crimson when he ran his gaze over her. An all-too-familiar fluttering uncoiled heat in her core. If he kept looking at her like that, they'd have to postpone this conversation.

"All right, Nenn, start from the beginning."

He clasped her elbows, his touch hot and so addictive. "In front of the Q.C.C., I claimed you are my vatia sahaar, my love mate. I had to convince them to save you..."

Ice coated her heart, and a crushing pain squeezed until she thought her ribs would crack. "An eternity with me is horrific to you?" She tried to wiggle out of his grip, but he didn't budge.

Feathering his touch from her arms to her cheeks, he drew her closer. "It will be a torment for you if you do not love me. For I have sentenced you to a sad life."

As fond as she was of him, she couldn't endure an arranged marriage when he didn't love her and never would. She froze, sucked in a shuddering gasp while willing her tears not to fall. "A sad life for you, too?"

He chuckled, his joy stark against the sorrow coating her soul in shadow. "Never, for I shall have you beside me. A Qaldreth can ask Osnir for nothing more than to have you as his female."

She blinked at his sincerity. "You're happy about this?"

"Yes." He dipped his head to rest his temple against hers. "I am aware I should not be when I would rather die than bring you unhappiness. I do not want you to leave me, Tiny, and perhaps this selfishness is what drove me to claim you before my elders and fellow warriors. By claiming you as my vatia sahaar, the symbiotes will honor my decision. There will be no other female for me."

Time slowed. Each second crawled past while she gaped at him. Pure delight warred with her shock. *He loves me?* Happiness bubbled inside her and filled her chest to snapping point. She cupped his face to peer into his eyes. "I love you, too, you idiot."

His eyes bulged. "You do?"

She kissed him but didn't shut him out. Losing herself in his glorious eyes would forever be a gift. He crushed her to him, his groan firing darts of need through her. "Tiny, *mhi' vatia.*"

"Nenn, my love."

He shuddered then crushed her against him. "I do adore you," he whispered, his breath warm across her ear.

She threw back her head and laughed, happier than she'd ever been. "Strip. I want to *see* every inch of you."

He smirked, his fingers digging into her hips. "As you command."

About the Author

Sevannah Storm is a fiction writer who immerses herself in fantastical worlds both magical and science fiction. She has a flair for the creative having studied art and interior architecture and spends her time drawing, oil painting, and writing. An avid reader from an early age, Sevannah finds her inspiration from various sources: games, novels, music, and the land of make-believe. The unique versus the practical has brought on numerous debates.

In her spare time, she does Krav Maga, CrossFit, and rereads novels that snatch her breath away. Having embraced the social media world, you can find her on most platforms.

Her home is a land south of Wakanda, where animals roam free. Born in Zimbabwe, she grew up in South Africa. The crisp blue skies with cotton-candy sunsets expand her heart and soul, encapsulating a sense of freedom.

Words she lives by: "Know your pothole and dodge it. Don't work in a pencil factory if you're a vampire."

Sevannah loves to hear from her readers. You can find and connect with her at the links below.

Website/Newsletter:

https://www.sevannahstorm.com/

Facebook:

https://www.facebook.com/sevannah.storm

Instagram:

https://www.instagram.com/sevannah.storm/

Twitter:

https://twitter.com/sevannah_storm

TikTok:

https://www.tiktok.com/@sevannah.storm

https://sevannahstorm.com

Thank you for taking the time to read *Dark Survivor*. If you enjoyed the story, please tell your friends and leave a review. Reviews support authors and ensure they continue to bring readers books to love and enjoy.

Sol Survivor

The Qaldreth Warriors #1

Vic's dream was to expand the solar farm her mother left her. Instead, she must survive as an arena gladiator for Carne Corp. to pay off her father's gambling debts. Now her dream is ultimate freedom which is granted to the arena champion. At last, the future she planned for is within her grasp, but when Carne conspires against her and augments her against her will, she flees into outer space, hoping to disappear. A chance encounter with an unknown alien species awakens her sexuality. Plans go awry, and there is much she must defeat before she can truly be free.

Meorri aac Drafe is on a mission to find who assassinated the Ivoyan Ot he was tasked to protect. As a Qaldreth warrior, his tribe's honor rests on finding the killer. Forming an unheard-of union with a servant Ivoy, the other witness to the crime, they locate the killer's homeworld. There, Drafe encounters a female like no other.

To regain his honor, he will need to ask for her aid, go against his protective instincts, and endanger her.

Hunted by Carne, Vic must trust her heart, life, and newfound freedom to a Qaldreth warrior she cannot resist.

Read it here:

https://books2read.com/u/3Jq7xv

SOUL FORGED

THE GIFTING SERIES #1

Know-it-all Oriana agreed to travel with aliens who need women. But she didn't agree to abduction, life/death battles, and escaping with a bossy, arrogant man. She was sabotaged, attacked, and kidnapped, but she is far from beaten. Forced to participate in an alien battle arena with no promise of freedom, she has to forget the loss of her family and focus on surviving.

Enyl has given up hope. His people are dying due to a genetic modification gone awry. Darkness is consuming his warriors, and his world, as he knows it, will end. His father, the king, has rolled out a plan to save them all. But Enyl doubts a solution will be found in time.

And when a compatible female is found…and lost, he must rescue her, a human female capable of surviving despite all odds. However, freeing Oriana serves to anger the aliens holding her captive. Ensuring she is cared for—as per Etterian protocol—he is stunned by the strong connection between the two of them. Such a bond was only experienced between Etterian mates.

Is she his salvation or is that wishful thinking on his part?

Read it here:

https://books2read.com/u/m2qJLk

THE SHIKARI

Space Hunter Chronicles #1

Unlike her brilliant xeno-zoologist father, Mikaela can't keep an alien creature alive. During her futile attempts, an alien rat bite triggers superhuman mutations, changing her into who knows what, and it might be killing her. Desperate to keep her late father's ship running, she accepts a lucrative contract to tag and bag a dragon-like creature. She teams up with her childhood crush, Kiros, and his merry band of mercenaries.

En route to the faraway Cetus constellation, while fending off attractive Kiros, downright erotic dreams of a yellow-eyed man named Tieren torment her. When Kiros steals her prize and lures her into danger, she must rely on the real and gorgeous Tieren to stop Kiros. The xeno fauna injuring Kiros and Tieren forces her to choose who to save, her lying friend or her new flame who's stolen her heart across parsecs.

Read it here:

https://books2read.com/u/49d28k

www.ingramcontent.com/pod-product-compliance
Lightning Source LLC
Chambersburg PA
CBHW070606120726
47909CB00007B/2458